Mystery and Horror, LLC

Tarpon Springs, FL

HISTORY AND MYSTERY, OH MY!

Copyright 2015 Mystery and Horror, LLC
Edited by Sarah E. Glenn

ISBN: 978-0-9915825-6-3

Library of Congress Control Number: 2015900920

Published in USA by Mystery and Horror, LLC
Tarpon Springs, FL

TABLE OF CONTENTS

DEDICATION

This book is dedicated to our many Sisters and Misters in Crime, for their contribution to our understanding of mysteries and how they should be written. Our heartfelt thanks to all of you.

The Cape

By Patricia Abbott

"You make me a *cappa*? Si?"

This whispered request came mostly in Italian. The man at the counter had entered the shop surreptitiously and the proprietor, Joseph Valentino, wondered if the bell usually triggered by the opening door was broken. Then he saw the gray gloved hand holding it. Joseph knew enough Italian to realize that *cappa* meant cape—he was just surprised to hear a man inquiring about one. Perhaps it was for the gentleman's wife, for this was certainly a gentleman.

The fellow continued to talk about the cape, making it clear through his gestures that it was for him. He looked familiar, but the tailor couldn't place him. He spoke with a heavy accent when he managed to get the occasional word out in English. It was an accent that Joseph's Neapolitan wife, Valentina's family shared. But no relative of his wife dressed like this man, who was so elegant in his checked, single-breasted waistcoat with a prominent watch chain, wing-collared shirt, and bow tie. The color palette was dove gray and soft black. Joseph quivered just looking at his potential customer.

It was a scorching hot day, and Joseph suffered in his light cotton shirt and summer trousers. How did this man survive the temperature in his extravagant dress? The man also wore a homburg on his rather large head. It was rare that a man dressed like this one entered his shop. Not merely rare, unheard of.

Although the tailor had made capes for women on rare occasions, he'd never made one for a man. And especially not for a man clearly used to the finest tailoring available in a city that offered the best couture outside of Europe. Mulberry Street would be slumming for his kind. All of these thoughts passed through Joseph's mind with lightning speed as the businessman in him finally answered.

"An opera cape, sir?"

It had to be that. Joseph's mind flew to his pattern books for men's clothing. Did he even have a book with a cape in it? Perhaps he could alter a cape meant for a woman—change the cut, the shoulders, and the collar a bit. A job like this could bring in money. He'd have to be very sharp to impress this man. But why was he here in the first place? How was it possible that his shop—or Joseph Valentino, for that matter—had made itself known to this gent?

Shaking his head, the man told him the cape would be for outdoors. Moving his fingers in demonstration, the man wiped his brow with a large white handkerchief. "*Andare.*"

"You want a cape to walk outside?"

"*Si.* Fur *cappa. Per inverno* in da zoo. *No vorrei prendersi un raffreddore.*" Catch a cold, Joseph translated silently. He doesn't want to catch a cold when he walks in the zoo. How odd. Was he a zoo administrator of some sort? Or perhaps a wealthy patron of the uptown institution?

The customer waved his fingers like the Pope or a king might, looking at Joseph as if the reason for such concern was blatantly obvious. Joseph smiled and nodded as though it were. Perhaps the man was suffering from consumption, although he looked very well-fed for a disease that left most of its victims looking— well—consumptive.

Joseph watched as the man walked to the door and stepped outside, pulling a tiny case from his breast pocket and putting a lozenge in his mouth. The humidity from Tina's laundry business in the back of the shop took some getting

2

used to. Even now, after years of proximity, Joseph could still smell the noxious laundry powder and bleach. But the scent of a hot iron on a heavy cotton shirt held its own delights, which was what he smelled this morning. The Irish girl who assisted his wife was singing, "Let Me Call You Sweetheart" in a lilting soprano. Joseph usually found this habit a pleasant diversion from his work. His customer, however, seemed unimpressed, even annoyed, as he re-entered the shop. He made a face that demanded action.

"Theresa, we have a customer," Joseph sang out. He didn't like to hurt her feelings, but the customer came first in his establishment.

The singing ended abruptly and something clattered to the floor. The two men looked at each other for a moment, sizing the other up in some indefinable way, and then Joseph reached for his drawing pad and began sketching. After a few minutes, he turned the pad around and slid it across the counter.

"Something like this perhaps?" He could have drawn a better cape if he hadn't been shaking with anxiety. Or if he had seen a man wearing a fur cape just once in his life. His fingertip added a bit of shading to highlight how the cape would catch the breeze.

The man looked at it carefully and nodded with a small smile. "And da fur? *Che categoria?*"

That such an elegant man would ask for his opinion on this important question was inconceivable. Perhaps it was a test. And one he might fail. Closing his eyes, he sped through a virtual furrier's display. Better to suggest the easiest pelts to obtain, the most familiar. He had done some stoles in mink.

"Mink, I think. And dark red lining would be elegant."

He could almost picture it now. People would laugh at him if only behind their hands. The zookeeper, on his morning stroll, might think a bear had escaped and tackle him to the ground.

The man smiled. "Red. Is not — *come si dice?* — garnish?"

Joseph nearly laughed. As if a fur cape on a man could be anything but garish. "Not garish at all," he said, subtly correcting his customer's mistake. "*Moto elegante.*"

"*Si. Uno minuto,*" the man said, turning the pad back so it faced Joseph. "*Necessita un taglios per mie mani.*" He drew a finger along the sides of the sketched cape. "*Qui penso.*"

A slit for his hands! "Normally a cape ties at the neck, sir, allowing complete mobility for your hands. You won't need a — slit."

The man shook his head, looking Joseph in the eyes for the first time. "*Cucire un taglio?*" He mimicked the action.

There was no arguing with a customer. "Certainly. A slit would satisfy that requirement."

The man fairly hummed with pleasure. He was probably imagining himself in this fine fur cape already.

"A black lining, yes. As long as I can acquire the proper materials, it shouldn't take more than a few weeks."

In truth, Joseph was a novice with fur. He used no regular furrier. Nor did he really know what working with this amount of mink would entail. Or cost. He'd suggested it because it was the fur he saw most often when he went uptown to look in shop windows. The one used for a stole or two he'd made. Perhaps his machine would need a special needle for this job — even a particular needle foot. Could he get such a thing on short notice? But he'd learn quickly, get what was needed at once, because the price of this assignment would keep his family in coal for the winter and put a piece or two of red meat on the table.

Perhaps there'd be money enough to purchase Mr. Hoover's new machine for Tina's precious carpets. She had been swept off her feet, so to say, by a demonstration of its efficiency at a local fair. And if this cape suited his customer, perhaps his rich friends would make their way downtown. Or, even better, perhaps Joseph would make his way uptown.

"You'll never guess, Tina," he told her that night. "An elegant man came into my shop today and asked me to make him a fur cape. Me," he repeated, putting his thumbs under his arms. "He seemed to know my work." Was this true or had his head puffed up like his mother always warned him it would?

"Oh, Joseph, that is fine news. And where did this gentleman hear about you?" she asked, echoing his first thought and calling into question his last.

Joseph was quiet. "I never asked him," he admitted.

"What is his name?"

"I never asked him that either."

"Oh, Joseph."

The excitement had apparently wiped questions like these from his head. But the gentleman, at his own suggestion, had left him with a generous down payment, so he was not too concerned.

He could see the wheels turning in Tina's head.

"I wonder if he saw that forest green dress you made for Mrs. Walton. Remember the fur trim you added around the hem and neck."

He'd forgotten that gown. Mrs. Walton had worn it to her son's marriage to a society girl in Connecticut last winter. Perhaps that was where this customer saw it. Up in Hartford, he thought. Of course, he'd hand-stitched that fur onto the neckline and hem. His stitches were so tiny that Mrs. Walton asked for a magnifying glass to see them. This gentleman must have attended the wedding too. It was settled in his mind.

The next morning Joseph began his hunt for the proper materials. A furrier on Mercer Street had several nice pelts and was able to provide him with advice and the proper needle foot.

"For a man, you say," Mr. Gross asked him.

Joseph paused, wondering if it was a good idea to admit it given the gentleman's surreptitious visit. "For his wife, I imagine. A surprise, I think."

"She must be a large woman." Mr. Gross looked with

interest at the measurements. "Enormous shoulders, hasn't she?"

The job went more quickly than he expected despite the handwork needed. The cape was ready in less than a month. Tina stood over him every night, offering her opinions on the alterations in the pattern he'd made. She'd found the perfect binding for the slits, in fact. It was a black braid with a faint gold thread running through it. Sturdy, yet elegant.

"Is it really for a man, Joseph?" She asked him this every night.

"Yes, yes. And one I have seen before if I could just remember where."

"This cape will make you famous." She ran her hands through the fur again. "But why these silly slits?" She poked her fingers through the openings and wiggled them.

Joseph shrugged. "Rich people. Who can understand them?

"He will stick out indeed," Tina said, wriggling her fingers through the slits again.

Enrico Caruso walked into the zoo in Central Park in November, 1906. Over the summer, he'd taken his exercise at the Bronx Zoo uptown, but the recent commotion over Benga, a pygmy who slept in a hammock in the monkey house, brought him down here. John Verner's exotic African find had brought riff-raff into the quiet of the monkey house. Benga, famous for shooting arrows into the bull's-eye of a target set up amidst the primates, also marauded about the zoo on a hot day. He had a talent for finding a person who would find his attention repellent rather than amusing. On one distressful occasion, Benga followed the tenor himself, pretending to steal his cotton candy to please the crowd. Caruso would have no more of that attention. He did not go to the zoo to be part of the attraction. He would save that talent for the stage.

The zoo in Central Park was far less impressive but would do for Caruso's purposes and save him the time spent on the longer carriage ride.

The cape was more glorious than he'd even anticipated. He felt embraced by the soft fur: warm and elegant. He strolled toward the monkey house, taking in the chill air. Once inside, adjusting his eyes to the darkness, he spotted his quarry. He preferred blondes, and this woman was ideal for his game in her thin winter coat. She stood in front of the orangutan cage, watching a female nurse her baby. Her intense interest in this activity gave him an advantage.

Caruso looked around. Although his fur cape allowed him to blend into the dark enclosure, he had to be sure that pesky guard had not spotted him. Only a few weeks earlier, the man had tapped him on the shoulder with his nightstick, warning him about standing too close to the women. He couldn't identify himself in such circumstances, so he was forced to accept such treatment. With a bowed head, he moved away. Of course, the fur cape was still too warm to wear in October. Now it freed his hands to roam less conspicuously.

In a flash, Caruso stood right behind the blonde, his knees pressed against her thighs. His fingers darted through the slits, grabbing a handful of the woman's bottom. Just as quickly, he stepped away. Her scream echoed through the empty monkey house.

"Sir!" she said, spotting him in the dark. "How dare you."

He looked around to suggest perhaps that another person might be guilty of the crime. It was then that the same guard stepped out from behind a pillar fashioned with plaster of Paris to look like a palm tree. He gestured to the tenor. Within minutes, the cop had handcuffed him and led him away. Luckily, his cape made the cuffs nearly invisible.

"Joseph, Joseph," Tina cried, waking him the next morning. "You will never believe who commissioned that fur cape."

Joseph was more asleep than awake.

"What?" he asked, throwing the blanket aside. His bare feet hit the chill floor in a rush.

"Your cape, your cape. The fur one. The man who paid you in bills."

In a flash, Tina was standing at the kitchen table with the New York Post spread open. Drowsily, Joseph made his way across the room. Had his cape turned up on the society page?

Joseph saw the face first—the face that had haunted him.

"It was Enrico Caruso," his wife said, before he could read the caption. "He's been arrested for fondling a woman in the monkey house in Central Park." She giggled and then covered her mouth. "He told the zoo guard a monkey did it. A monkey named Knocko."

"Well, with a name like Knocko, I suppose it is possible," Joseph said. He had stood too close to the cages himself on more than one occasion. The creatures were always looking for food. Always trying to grab a loose scarf or hat.

"They are looking for the woman he...touched. Her name is Hannah Graham."

"I can read it myself, Tina."

"The police want to know where he acquired a fur coat with slits for his wandering hands," Tina continued despite his comment. "They think the tailor was in cahoots with Mr. Caruso. That's you, Joseph," she added unnecessarily.

Joseph's heart sunk. Was he now to be part of a criminal case? Would he be ruined by conspiring with a masher? Was he to be known for crafting those slits? Such an intention had never occurred to him.

"He's going to have to go to court." Tina told him, apparently unwilling to let him read a single word of the story himself. "But they're allowing him to meet his obligations at the Met."

"The Met's patrons run City Hall."

This was a subject they often discussed. The City was run for the rich. Only the crumbs from their table fell on the Lower East Side. Blah, blah, blah. When would it ever change?

"Why would a man with good looks, money, and a voice like that need to find his fun in the monkey house?" Tina asked. "I can't believe you didn't recognize him, Joseph. He's in the newspaper every day."

Joseph shrugged. "It's a game probably. A rich man's game." Although then he remembered reading that Caruso had been born in the slums.

"They're talking about closing it down," Tina read. "There's a petition by a women's group."

"The Met?" Joseph said, scanning the article for further mention of his cape.

"No, Joseph, the monkey house. You silly man." She paused, and then giggled. "Where will he ever find another place so dark?"

"The subway is finished, let him go there." Joseph said. "It's dark on those platforms. Darker than a monkey house."

He was angry for some reason. His beautiful cape had been merely a means to a reprehensible act. He was glad Mr. Caruso had paid him the rest of what he owed in cash the day he picked up the cape. It would be difficult to extract it from him now.

"What upper-class gentleman would use the subway?" his wife asked him.

"What society gentleman would pinch a woman's bottom in a monkey house?"

The coming days were tense in the Valentino household. Every time the bell rang, Joseph expected to see a uniformed policeman enter his shop.

But such a thing never happened. Mr. Caruso paid a small fine and continued to charm opera lovers across the globe. The fate of the cape is unknown.

Patti Abbott is the author of more than 100 stories, published in print and online. She is the author of two ebooks, Monkey Justice *and* Home Invasion *(Snubnose Press). Two print books are coming out in 2015 through Polis Books:* Concrete Angel *and* Shot in Detroit. *She won a Derringer Award for her story* "My Hero" *and is co-editor of the ebook anthology,* Discount Noir. *You can find her blog, with links to some of her online stories at* http://pattinase.blogspot.com

More stories appear in Murder At The Beach, *(the Boucbercon anthology),* The Kannibals Cookbook, *and several other online and print venues.*

A Questionable Death

Edith Maxwell

Helen and I sat on a cloth under a maple tree by the banks of Lake Gardner, the tree's wide leaf-lined branches providing welcome respite from the July midday heat. I loosened the collar of my shirtwaist and fanned myself with my book, one of A.M. Barnard's scandalous tales, which I had only recently learned were actually penned by Miss Alcott herself.

"Bertie should be along soon with our picnic," I said.

Helen lay back on the cloth, one arm across her eyes, her pregnant belly pushing her dress up.

"Another dizzy spell?" I asked my client, who was also becoming a friend.

"Yes. They plague me. And my head aches, as well."

"Thy pregnancy is going along normally, though," I reassured her. "And thy baby's heartbeat is strong."

"I suppose you should know, being my midwife." She leaned her head toward me and gave me a faint smile. "Will this all pass once the baby is born?"

"I hope so. Thee has two months to go." In truth, I wasn't certain if her symptoms would go away. I wanted my friend David Dodge to examine Helen, but her ill-tempered husband Rupert would not agree.

"Tell me again why you use that old-fashioned manner of speech, with your thees and thys," Helen said.

I laughed. "In earlier times people used 'thee' for

familiars, and 'you' to address those of a higher rank. Quakers honor the testimony of equality and made a point to address all in the same way. Now, though, the use of 'thee' in the common parlance has given way to 'you', yet the Society of Friends maintains the old way."

I heard a clop-clop-clop on the pavement behind us and turned to see Bertie Winslow ride up on her horse. She was postmistress of our town of Amesbury, and as unconventional a spirit as I'd ever met.

"Whoa up, Grover," she called, pulling on the reins. She carried a basket on her lap.

Only Bertie would name a horse "Grover." I always smiled to hear her refer to a large animal by the name of our country's president. It was delightfully subversive. And only Bertie had the nerve to ride astride instead of sidesaddle. She slid a leg clad in a long bloomer over Grover's back and hopped off the animal. As she tied him to the tree, the hem of her skirt fell down over her pants. The bloomers, made from a cloth that matched the skirt, always showed when she rode. Bertie didn't care what people thought.

"I bring sustenance," she announced, and plopped down on the cloth with us. "How is my favorite Quaker midwife? And the bearer of the new human?"

"I am well," I said. "But Helen is ailing a bit, I'm afraid."

Bertie frowned. "Come and eat, then. My picnics can cure anything." She set to drawing paper-wrapped packets and two bottles out of the basket. "See here? Cold meat pies, dilly beans, berry tarts, even a bottle of ale." She glanced at me. "And lemonade for our teetotaler Rose."

Helen hoisted herself up onto her elbows and then to sitting, her knees to one side. "My stomach is unsettled, as well."

"Did thee eat this morning?" I asked.

"Oh, yes." Helen smiled. "Rupert always fixes my breakfast. But I'll take a little ale to settle myself."

Bertie poured a metal cup of ale for Helen and herself, and handed me a portion of tangy lemonade. "I saw your husband in the post office this morning," she said to Helen, raising her perfectly arched eyebrows as she unpinned her hat and threw it on the cloth.

When Helen reached for her cup, her loose sleeve fell back, revealing a dark patch on her forearm. She pulled her sleeve down and her smile turned nervous. "Rupert told me he had a parcel to send. I don't know what it was."

Bertie pressed her lips together and didn't comment. I bit into a meat pie, thinking that patch on Helen's arm looked a lot like a bruise.

"Mmm, perfect crust, delicious filling," I said once I swallowed. "Thank thee, Bertie."

We ate and chatted for most of an hour, although Helen nibbled more than ate. A family picnicked a little ways down and we watched as the children splashed in the water. A song sparrow entertained us from a nearby bush while a breeze brought a semblance of water-scented coolness off the lake, which was really just the Powow River backed up behind the Salisbury Mills dam.

Bertie rose with a sigh. "Back to work with me. My employees always come up with some trouble for me to solve when I'm away for too long."

After I tidied the food and repacked Bertie's basket, I handed it up to her on Grover and waved farewell.

"And we have your antenatal appointment, Helen." I tied my bonnet back on, then gave Helen a hand up to standing. We strolled the few blocks to my office, located in the front parlor of the house I share with my brother-in-law and his five children. I still suffer a pang of longing every time I approach the house, despite my pride in seeing the shingle announcing *Rose Carroll, Midwife* hanging out front. The pain of missing my late sister has not lessened in the two years since her death.

I made Helen comfortable on my examination chaise,

then brought each of us a glass of water. We went through the arrangements for when her time came.

"Who will thee have to help thee at home?"

"My mother will come for as long as I need her. My family is in Newbury, so it's not far."

"Excellent. Next time I'll come and see thee at home to make sure all will be ready, in case the child decides to come early." After I took her pulse, I said, "I'll need to palpate the baby today, Helen. Is thee ready?"

She nodded. She lifted her skirts, holding them up under her armpits, and pulled her drawers down below her belly. Her ribs on one side bore a yellowing bruise. I touched it gently.

"What happened here?"

She didn't meet my eyes as she said, "I was clumsy. I ran into the corner of the bureau."

"Is that what happened to your arm, as well?" I pulled her sleeve back.

This time she looked straight at me. "Yes." Her voice was defiant but she blinked away a tear.

I busied myself with measuring the length from her pubic bone to the top of the womb. With the listening tube pressed against her belly, I tracked the baby's heartbeat. Manipulating gently with my hands, I felt the baby's head and bottom to assess his size. I checked Helen's ankles. While not overly swollen, they showed a yellow cast to the skin.

"Thee can restore thy coverings now," I said, turning to my desk to jot down my findings. I faced her again. "Thee can feel safe with me, Helen. Is thy husband beating thee?" If he was, there was nothing I could do except hope to keep her and her baby safe. Our local police took the position that what happened in a marriage was the business of the man and his wife, not the authorities.

She gazed at me with dark eyes. "Sometimes he gets carried away. But he loves me. He tells me so. And he watches out for me, truly. I told you he makes me breakfast every day."

I sighed inwardly. How many times had I heard that? Once it was from a client who ended up dead at the hands of the man whom she declared loved her.

"Has he always made the morning meal?"

"No, just for the last month." Helen squeezed her eyes shut and grimaced.

As she did, I noticed that her face also bore a faint yellowish tint. "Thee is having another headache."

She nodded. "I think I'd better go see your doctor, after all. What was his name?"

"Good. His name is David Dodge. Let us go across the river." I checked the mantel clock that had been my grandmother's, which read two-thirty. "David holds office hours at the new Anna Jaques Hospital in Newburyport all afternoon. I'll have thee home in time to make supper. Put thy hat on and come along." I was glad I was free to accompany her. She was my only antenatal appointment for the afternoon, the children were spending the summer on my parents' farm in Lawrence, and my brother-in-law had told me he was dining with friends that evening.

I bustled us both out of the house and we went looking for a conveyance for hire on High Street.

"I'll need a small lock of your hair," David told Helen when he was finished examining her. It had taken us twenty minutes to find a hack, we'd had to wait a bit to see David, and he had taken care with his examination, so it was now getting on for five o'clock.

"Why?" Helen asked, taken aback.

"Just to aid in assessing your health," David said, slipping me a look behind Helen's back. He handed her a small pair of scissors.

Helen shrugged, but handed the scissors to me. I clipped off a small bit from near her neckline and handed the deep brown lock to David, along with the scissors.

"Thank you for coming in," he said. "I'll have an answer for you within a day's time. And Rose, thanks for bringing her. I'll summon my carriage and driver to take you both back to Amesbury."

"That's very kind of thee," I said.

"I'll need to use the outhouse before we leave." Helen blushed a little.

"Oh, we have the new chain-pull toilets," David said with a note of pride in his voice. "The lavatory is just down the hall to the right. It's labeled 'Ladies'." He pointed the way.

After the door closed behind Helen, I gave him a quizzical glance.

"My teacher in medical school would call it gastric fever." He gazed at me. "I suspect poison."

"Poison?" I whispered, moving to his side.

"Arsenic. I'll tell you for certain after I've analyzed the hair." His brows knit, he went on: "Don't let on to her. Yet."

After David's driver dropped Helen at her home, I had him leave me at Bertie's house. She would be closing up at the post office about now, and I wanted to talk this business through with her. We'd been friends for several years. She was ten years older than I, but although she was nearing forty, her energy for both fun and justice never flagged. We were neither of us married and she felt like a kindred spirit. Some in town muttered about her being in a so-called 'Boston Marriage' with her friend Sophie, with whom she shared the cheerful cottage I now stood in front of. I knew she had strong feelings for Sophie, who traveled so much for her work that Bertie and I had time for our friendship. That was their business, not mine.

I wandered through the riot of color that was her front garden, a tangle of flowers and greenery in a controlled chaos of all hues and shapes. I found a full watering can and gave a drink to several pots of pansies that had wilted from the heat.

Sure enough, up Bertie clattered on Grover not five

minutes later. She jumped down. "What, blessed with another Rosetta visit so soon? Come with me while I put this man in his quarters."

I followed her back to the shed that doubled as stable. I lounged on a bench under an enormous elm tree to watch as she wiped Grover down and gave him fresh water along with his portion of oats. Her small back garden was shady and welcoming, and smelled deliciously of the sweet peas gracefully clinging to strings trained up the shed wall. When she was done, Bertie sank onto the bench next to me.

"I fear for Helen's life," I said. I told her of the bruises, and of David's guess as to the cause of her symptoms. "She acknowledged her husband gets a little carried away, as she put it, but says he loves her. But if he is adding a small dose of arsenic to her breakfast each day, he's killing her. Likely her child, as well. What kind of monster would do that?"

"A bigot and a philanderer, that's who," Bertie exclaimed. "Rupert Stillwell is rotten through and through. He mailed a package this morning, all right. The box was from Adelia's fine clothing and it was addressed to a Miss Chartreuse Lévesque."

I whistled. "I'd guess she's not his little sister."

"I'd agree. Yet you should see the looks he gives me. I hear him sniggering to his friends about Sophie and me. You know I don't care what people say, but for a miserable rat like him to think he's better than we are, that gets my goat."

"Rat." I stared at her. "Rat poison contains arsenic. What shall we do to make him stop?"

Bertie sighed. "What we should do is tell Amesbury's finest. This is a job for the police, not for us."

"Thee knows they don't care if men beat their wives. And they'd have to prove he is giving Helen poison."

"Unlikely to happen." She shook her head. "I think it's going to be up to you and me, Miss Carroll."

I was called to a birth the next morning. It was

blessedly uncomplicated, being the third baby born to a well-nourished mother who lived in a house with clean running water. As I arrived home, the afternoon post brought a note from David. His tests confirmed his hypothesis. I freshened up and headed for the post office. It was time to put the plan Bertie and I had hatched into motion.

Detective Kevin Donovan knocked at my door the next morning at nine o'clock exactly. I greeted him and invited him into the parlor.

"Miss Carroll, I understand that Helen Stillwell was under your care." The robust police officer stood with hat in his hands.

"She still is, Kevin." I cocked my head. "Won't thee sit down?"

He cringed a little at my use of his first name. We'd had prior contact, however, and he knew that Friends did not believe in using titles for anyone, not even for the authorities.

"No, I'll stay on my feet, thank you."

"I examined her only two days ago," I went on. "Her baby is due in approximately two months."

"Was she despondent? Anxious, perhaps?"

"A bit, but at that stage most first-time mothers are. The act of giving birth is dangerous for mothers and babies alike. She was having some other health problems, though. Headaches, dizzy spells, some stomach distress."

He waved that off. "You don't think she would harm herself?"

"Why does thee ask?" I folded my hands in my lap.

"She left her husband a note. Said she couldn't stand it any more, and was going for a swim in the lake. Forever, as she put it."

I gasped and put a hand to my mouth. "Does thee mean she drowned herself?"

"I'm afraid so. She is nowhere to be found, and we located her hat and handkerchief near the bluff overlooking the lake. There is the note, too."

"I heard the emergency bell tolling last evening." I shook my head in sorrow.

"Yes, Rupert Stillwell came to us just after dark with the note. He's distraught, as you can imagine."

"If only I had detected the signs." I shook my head. "Will thee be dragging the lake?"

"Likely not. It looks to be a pretty clear case. And bodies usually surface in a few days, unless they are weighted down," Kevin said. "Such a pity, a young thing like that, and their baby dead, too."

"Is there a possibility that the note is a forgery? Perhaps someone, even her husband, wanted Helen dead."

"What an imagination you have, Rose Carroll," he scoffed. "You think a pregnant woman was murdered? In Amesbury?"

I shrugged. "One wishes it not to be so, but people are murdered. Thee knows that better than I."

"This is no murder." He placed his hat on his head. "I'll be going now."

"I shall stop by and see if I can be of assistance to Rupert," I called as Kevin made his way down the front steps.

An hour later I knocked on Rupert's door. The apartment occupied the upper floor of a house down by Clark's Pond. He flung it open with a hopeful look on his face, which fell immediately upon seeing me.

"Rupert," I said, taking his hand in both of mine. "I am so sorry to hear about poor Helen's disappearance. What a sorrow for thee."

He stared. "You're the midwife," he finally said. His hair was neatly combed back and he wore a clean collar, but his tie was askew and his shirt misbuttoned.

I nodded. "I am Rose Carroll. May I come in?"

"Of course." He hesitated for a moment, then stood back and let me pass.

The door opened onto a kitchen in great disarray. The sink overflowed with dirty dishes. On the table the open newspaper vied with a plate of dried eggs, a tipped-over salt shaker, and a cup holding coffee mixed with flecks of curdled cream. Crumbs filled the cracks in the wide pine floor. No wonder he gave pause to letting me enter.

"I was just about to go out," he said. "Those police say they ain't going to drag Lake Gardner for my Helen. They have to!" He wrung his hands.

"May I offer to help thee? I can at least clean up the kitchen here, while thee is out."

"Oh, would you, Miss Carroll? Helen wasn't the best of housekeepers, and I'm hopeless, myself." Rupert jammed his hat on his head. "How can I hold a funeral without her body?" He walked through the still open doorway and clattered down the stairs.

I shut the door and got to work.

By the time the noon whistle pierced the air, Rupert had a spotless kitchen and I was walking into CL & JW Allen's Hardware on Market Square. JW himself greeted me.

"Friend Carroll, what can we do for you today?" He beamed from behind the counter.

I drew the slip of paper I'd found in Helen's apartment out of my bag. "My client Helen Stillwell bought this rat poison from thee in May. I was thinking of getting some of the same brand, in case rats come around our place."

He peered at the receipt through his reading glasses. "Oh, no," he said, looking at me over the top of the spectacles. "That was Rupert himself who purchased the arsenic. Said his wife told him they had quite the infestation."

"I see. Arsenic is pretty toxic, isn't it?"

"Yes, indeed. You'll want to be very careful with it."

I pursed my lips. "I think I'll wait, then, since we're not having a rodent problem at present. Wouldn't want the children getting into a poison."

He nodded gravely.

"I thank thee," I said, retrieving the receipt, and walked back into the busy square. Carriages and drays vied with the people of the town walking up Friend Street, down Main Street, coming in from Elm, heading out on Market, running for the train on Water. I made my way carefully up Main to the police station.

Inside, I asked for the detective and perched on a waiting bench, my toe tapping the marble floor. Kevin emerged into the lobby and stood with legs splayed, arms crossed. He didn't look happy.

"Miss Carroll, what is it now?"

I stood. "Kevin, I request a moment of thy time. I have evidence to show that not only was Rupert Stillwell beating his wife, he was also slowly killing her with poison. Thee must arrest him."

His eyes bugged open. "But his wife is dead by her own hands. And her mother showed up here wailing and nearly rending her garments."

"I don't believe that Helen killed herself. Must I show thee what I have here in the lobby for all to see?" In fact, a gentleman looking down on his luck watched us with great interest from the facing bench.

Grumbling, the detective led the way into his office. Unbidden, I sat in the only chair not burdened with books or papers. Kevin leaned against his desk. I drew several items out of my bag and began.

"First, at my last examination of Helen Stillwell on Monday, I noticed bruises on her arm and her ribs. She admitted that her husband beats her."

Kevin rolled his eyes. "Haven't we been through the legal status on this? My hands are tied."

"Second, she was complaining of physical symptoms not related to pregnancy. Doctor David Dodge of Newburyport gave her a thorough examination, also on Monday. He sampled her hair. The results were positive for arsenic poisoning in the last month." I waved the note from David as he opened his mouth. "It's here in writing. Third, she told me her husband has been making her breakfast every day for a month."

"Isn't that nice of him?"

I'd never heard Kevin so sarcastic. "Fourth, J.W. Allen himself examined this receipt and said that Rupert bought this rat poison – arsenic – in May." I laid the receipt on the desk. "Fifth, Rupert was seen mailing a package from a ladies' fine clothing store to a woman not his wife. And finally, thee will find in this packet the remains of cooked eggs and other breakfast foods from the Stillwell kitchen. I fully expect that they contain a portion of arsenic. Thee must find Rupert Stillwell and arrest him. I am convinced he wanted to get rid of his pregnant wife so he could marry his mistress."

He gave a grudging nod. "You seem to have a case. But what about the matter of the missing Helen? If he was poisoning her, why should she kill herself?" He rubbed his forehead. "Her body has not come to the surface of the lake. Should be appearing soon, maybe tomorrow."

"Rupert could have drowned her, and weighted her down. Or perhaps she didn't drown at all. She could have just wanted to get away, especially since he was hitting her. Maybe she went to a friend."

"It's true, without a body, we have no proof of her death. Either way, I will have the food tested, and Mr. Allen's story confirmed. I guess I should thank you for doing my work for me." He smiled. "Now get on with you and leave me to it."

The last post the next afternoon brought the news I awaited. I walked through Bertie's front gate at close to six o'clock, just as she rode up. I waited while she tied the horse to an iron ring in the hitching post. As we entered the kitchen, Helen glanced up from the bread she was kneading. Flour dusted the apron she wore loosely tied around her girth and a white smudge decorated her forehead.

"Any news?" she asked with a hopeful look.

I glanced at Bertie. "Yes," I said, smiling. "Rupert has been arrested for poisoning. The detective found the arsenic in the remains of thy breakfast and in the salt shaker. Thee is safe now, Helen, both from the poison and from his abuse."

"And his philandering, don't forget. I'm so grateful to you both," Helen said with a sigh. "And I already feel much better, going a couple of days without it."

"Good. Ale to celebrate?" Bertie asked as she flopped down in a chair.

"Thank you, but I should probably be getting home," Helen said. "My mother must be worried sick."

"What will thee tell the townsfolk?" I removed my bonnet and wiped sweat from my brow. The heat had not relented.

"That I needed to get away for a bit. That I was only kidding him in that note." She rolled the lump of dough under the heels of her hands and then slapped the top of it. "I am grateful to you both for rescuing me when you did. Even though I framed him, of course."

Bertie and I exchanged a glance. "What do you mean, frame him?" Bertie asked.

"I arranged for the arsenic to go in my own breakfast. Told Rupert it was a special pregnancy salt he had to shake onto my eggs. Didn't touch the shaker, myself, once I'd filled it and wiped it clean. I couldn't think of any other way to get clear of him, with his mistresses and his beating me. Don't worry, I'd read up on the dose. I was never going to kill myself." She removed the apron, dusted off her hands, and grabbed her hat from the tree. "Thank you again. I'll see you around town."

The door closed behind her. Bertie and I stared at each other in horror. Helen poisoning herself was one thing. Putting a near-term baby at risk was quite another.

"I'm heading directly to the police station," I said,

anger making my voice shake. "And thee?"

"I'll take you on Grover." Bertie's eyes flashed as she strode out the door. "Nobody dupes Bertie Winslow."

Edith Maxwell writes the Lauren Rousseau mysteries under the pseudonym Tace Baker, in which Quaker linguistics professor Lauren Rousseau solves small-town murders (Barking Rain Press). The second book in the series, Bluffing is Murder, *was released in November 2014. Edith holds a doctorate in linguistics and is a long-time member of Amesbury Friends Meeting.*

'Til Dirt Do Us Part *is the latest in Maxwell's Local Foods Mysteries series (Kensington Publishing, 2014). Her new Country Store Mysteries, written as Maddie Day (also from Kensington), will debut with* Flipped for Murder *in fall, 2015.*

Maxwell's Carriagetown Mysteries series features Quaker midwife Rose Carroll solving mysteries in 1888 with John Greenleaf Whittier's help, as portrayed in "A Questionable Death." The first book in the series will release from Midnight Ink in 2016.

Her most recent short story of murderous revenge, "A Fire in Carriagetown," also features characters from the Carriagetown Mysteries and is available as an e-book.

A former tech writer and doula, Maxwell lives in an antique house north of Boston with her beau and three cats. She blogs every weekday with other Wicked Cozy Authors (wickedcozyauthors.com), and you can find her at www.edithmaxwell.com, @edithmaxwell, on Pinterest, and at www.facebook.com/EdithMaxwellAuthor .

Amor Vincit Omnia

By Clint Wastling

There was no warning. The young man fell through the colours of the sunset, illuminated by the windows in the dome of Santa Maria del Popolo. The wings attached to his back failed to enable flight and his legs and neck snapped as his body broke on the floor. The wings delicately draped his naked form.

Merisi ran toward his former model. He felt the smooth warm skin and heard the last word of his former student. "Why?"

Merisi looked up into the decorated dome of the church and fought back the tears. Even in this emotional state, he was certain he'd seen a man move from the gallery into the inner machinations of the church.

"Why indeed Merisi? Why indeed?" The repeated question was accusatory. The Cardinal sat, his gloved hands poised for supplication, his thin face and lips naked beneath his bald head. "I pay you to create images of saints and you repay me with paintings of sinners."

"I can only paint as God instructs."

"But you go too far!" The Cardinal raised his voice then remembered the servants lurking in the shadows. "You paint too much reality."

"That was why you hired me, *Monseigneur*." Merisi bowed. He wanted to leave, but his voice rose as though there was much left unsaid. He spoke with conviction: "I paint real people as God intended. I am possessed by the way light catches faces and renders the background obscure—a deep shade where crimes might be committed."

The Cardinal clicked his fingers. A servant poured a little red wine into a glass. Merisi was captivated by the way light refracted through the transparent surfaces and the cruel angular face was momentarily transformed.

"Michelangelo Merisi da Caravaggio, step forward. There is only so much I will tolerate." As the artist moved closer, the Cardinal swiped him with the back of his hand. The rings broke the skin and cracked open the painter's lip.

The taste of blood fed Merisi's anger, "It wasn't me on the gallery of the dome. It wasn't me who pushed my Cecco to his death. I was the witness who helped a young man on his journey to God."

"So who pushed him?"

"A jealous rival?" It was weak but it was Merisi's only defence. The Cardinal waved the man away and guards dragged him into the vestibule, closing the great oak doors behind him. Merisi picked himself up and waited. The guards returned to their positions. He took a single step towards freedom, then, unhindered, another and another until he reached the portico overlooking the Tiber. The stench of stagnation and summer assaulted his nostrils. Merisi held his breath and made for the nearest tavern.

"He has been like that for three days, Your Eminence." Il Sordo clasped his hands behind his back.

The Cardinal moved forward and stepped over the unconscious artist. He examined the picture.

"It is immoral, isn't it?" Il Sordo pointed at the nude image.

"Amoral," the Cardinal replied. The back of his silk glove swept over Cupid's body, "and yet this is the only remnant of Merisi's beloved Cecco. Could any man destroy that?"

"Any man with a conscience could." Il Sordo turned away from the image of Cupid striding from his bed and trampling the accoutrements of modern life: music, science, art, government.

"*Amor Vincit Omnia.*"

Il Sordo moved closer, lifting his black cassock over the sleeping artist. "It is immoral," he repeated, "the crumpled sheets, the way the feather brushes the youth's leg and that look!" He raised a pomander to disguise the smell emanating from the artist.

"Yes," said the Cardinal, "but he's captured the moment, he's said more in this one picture than many say in a lifetime: Love conquers all, but we all yield to love."

The Cardinal lifted his own pomander. "Guards, sober Merisi up. Clean him up. I want him ready to paint once more!" The cardinal studied the picture whilst he thought no one was looking. "It is not the answer you wanted, is it, Il Sordo?"

"It is not, Your Eminence. Perhaps the answer lies by my own hand."

The Cardinal smiled, knowing that Il Sordo was not an artist to assault the senses. The guards dragged Merisi to a chair, stripped and restrained him. Water was brought and thrown over the artist until he shivered and shook with rage, but was powerless to move.

"When you're clean and sober we will talk, Merisi. In the meantime, I will take the picture as evidence."

Cupid's body was hidden under a veil of silk and taken out of the room. Merisi rubbed the skin of his wrist and ankles raw. The pain fuelled his anger, then finally assuaged it. He slumped, exhausted, in the heavy chair. The guards were merciless in the pursuit of their orders.

Under the dome of Santa Maria del Popolo, Merisi stood and remembered the final moments of Cecco's life. He removed a grey feather from his pocket and let the tip brush the contours of his face. Finally, he entered the tower and took the cold dark corridors upward to the balustrade of the dome. The arch emerged at a thin ledge. Below was the marble floor. There was nothing to restrain a man, and no warning of the drop. Merisi felt disoriented by the height and clutched the stonework. He knelt and looked over the edge from this safer vantage. Above, the fresco reigned supreme, and below the acolytes were preparing for communion. Merisi shook his head. It felt odd being sober, as though a veil had been lifted and his inner energy had returned. He had painted with enthusiasm since Cecco's death, each brush stroke a hymn to his pupil, each move from light to shade a foreshadowing of life moving towards death. A priest stood on the very place Cecco had breathed his last. Merisi shed another tear, then turned to go downstairs. That's when he noticed the black thread caught on the rough stone and the small piece of cloth, also black. He held it to the light. There was no denying its weave and colour. Merisi folded the evidence into his notebook.

The work Merisi was commissioned to create left him again in the church of Santa Maria: it was the conversion of Saul on the road to Damascus. The model who posed was rendered vulnerable and lower than the horse from which he had fallen. It was an image of a wretched man at a moment of epiphany. He had spent hours creating the scene and settling the horse when the summons came from Cardinal del Monte. He could find no excuse to refuse the order.

Del Monte stood in front of a large window equidistant between two veiled pictures. Il Sordo stood by a table nervously thumbing the pages of a book.

"Merisi, you are welcome. It has been a long time."

"That was not of my doing, *Monseigneur*."

"No, we are busy men and you are creating an image for our church in--?"

"Piazza del Popolo."

Il Sordo raised a half smile. He was still dressed in black, yet Merisi noticed he wore a large ruby ring.

"A new patron?" Caravaggio enquired.

Il Sordo grinned, "I've created a work for the Cardinal which will eclipse yours."

Merisi tilted his head and took more notice of the two canvasses still obscured by silk.

"At least my picture hasn't been bought by a banker at a much reduced rate!"

The Cardinal lifted a finger and wagged it. He stood between the two images and unveiled them.

Amor Vincit Omnia -- he recognised his own work immediately and felt his heart quicken. He swallowed hard on seeing Cecco almost alive in his portrait. Finally, he turned his attention to the second painting. Merisi placed his hands on his hips and laughed. "You've captured my image well as a devil!"

Il Sordo went bright red. He became speechless with anger. Merisi walked over to the painting. The Devil and Cupid were being forcibly separated by an angel.

"It has a certain humour," Merisi commented. "The images are well rendered, Il Sordo, I'll give you that -- but in four hundred years' time, whose painting will be the better known?"

"I hope, for the sake of humanity, not yours," the other artist said.

"Gentlemen, this is unseemly. You both enjoy my protection and patronage. Yet I hope Il Sordo is right. Your painting, though beautiful, might make a man feel love really does conquer all. Your angel is swaggering, Il Sordo's is vengeful, separating the two before the laws of nature are cast asunder."

"Love," Merisi whispered, "can never be against the laws of nature. Lust can, but never love." The artist bowed. "Who has bought my picture?"

"A banker. I gave two stipulations: it is not altered or destroyed, but it must be forever veiled, so people are not offended by its content." The Cardinal raised his hand and the guards came to attention.

Merisi sighed and his shoulders sagged. "How you kill me with your kindness."

The Cardinal enjoyed the triumph. "Wasn't it ever like that? I have to tame your daemons or I will lose you to the devil, as Il Sordo shows."

Merisi looked on Cecco's likeness. He moved forward and kissed the Cardinal's ring, then turned and did the same to Il Sordo. The Cardinal applauded this magnanimity, but as he bowed a second time, Merisi saw the pull and tear in the hem of Il Sordo's cassock. When he stood upright, he stared into the artist's eyes and saw realisation become a moment of fear.

Merisi crossed the Tiber at Ponte San Angelo, heading northeast toward his latest painting. Like Saul, he had received a moment of revelation. Now he had proof that his rival Il Sordo had murdered Cecco. What could that innocent student have done? Merisi banged his fist against the walls of the church until he drew blood. He wanted a drink. He desperately needed a drink, but that would render him incapable.

Instead, he picked up his paints and took over from his assistant. He painted furiously, creating a face full of fear in the apostle. His black mood was matched by the encroaching shadows, and then it lifted as he saw a figure move around the edges of the crossing and make for the stairs.

Merisi smiled and wiped his hands on his jacket. Smears of colour took hold. He followed the winding stairs. It was only at the very top that Merisi caught up with the man. He was on his hands and knees searching for something.

"Are you looking for this?" Merisi held out a gray feather.

The startled man turned and shoved his back to the

wall. "You frightened me," Il Sordo said, his voice tight with fear.

"Or were you looking for this?" Merisi held out the small piece of cloth and its thread.

"Thank you," Il Sordo stood and was about to push past.

Merisi grabbed hold of his throat and lifted him off the ground. "Tell me you didn't do it, and I'll let you go."

"I didn't kill your Cecco."

"No, falling from here did that! Why?"

"He looked like an angel, a beautiful angel, but his mind was filled with filth and the reality of Rome, your Rome, Michelangelo Merisi."

"My Cecco! My Rome! It seems you have already excluded yourself from life here." Merisi lowered the man; he smiled, then pushed with all his might. The artist was taken by surprise and staggered backwards, stumbling over the edge. His cassock billowed and the man fell from light into the deepest shadows until he landed on his back with arms outstretched like Christ crucified.

Merisi took the stairs and went to his side. He shouted for help. A small crowd gathered. They looked up into the dome and saw nothing. The guards were called and the body was carried away.

"If I ever suspected you..." Del Monte said, the hollows of his cheeks deep with shadow and his head lit like a nimbus by the setting sun.

"It is natural justice. Il Sordo was wracked by guilt and returned to the scene of Cecco's death. He too lost his footing and fell. The dome of Santa Maria is beautiful, but quite lethal."

"A second accident. It must have been a second accident, you're right." The Cardinal cracked open a walnut and chewed it slowly. Merisi was reminded of Cecco's brain loosened from its cavity.

"I have a favour, *Monseigneur*. Il Sordo's body. He lay stretched out like Christ on the church floor. I'd like to use his body to model The Deposition. Reality and light will combine to create a marvelous scene which will restore the faith and heal the soul."

Del Monte smiled, his shoulders rippled and he laughed, "A fitting end, my friend; one dead artist the subject of the living."

Merisi bowed and kissed the ring presented. He turned to leave, but stopped on hearing the Cardinal's voice.

"Take care to avoid that love which conquers all: *amor vincit omnia*. It is not meant for mortal flesh."

Merisi looked back and saw Cecco for the final time. He bowed to acknowledge his patron's words, knowing full well he would never be able to keep that vow.

Clint Wastling is a writer based in the East Riding of Yorkshire. He's had stories published in "The Weekly News" and online at Every Day Fiction. You can find links via his website at www.clintwastling.webs.com

His stories have appeared in anthologies in the UK and USA recently: Pressed by Unseen Feet *and* Still Life with Wine & Cheese. *His short story, "Calico Blue" charting one man's life through the 20th century is available for Kindle.*

The Geology of Desire, *Clint's first novel will be published by Stairwell Books in November 2014. Further information at: www.stairwellbooks.co.uk/html/clint_wastling.html*

The Decoy

By Christina L. Wilkinson

Missing in Action. Stamped in red, the words looked like a sinister gash bleeding across the face of the tattered envelope. Dorothy Nicholson held it in her hand and read the words again. "Oh, where have you been?" she whispered, knowing the answer before she asked the question. War and back, that's where.

At the college library, where Dorothy worked, the afternoon mail had just been delivered. On her desk were several letters from her soldiers – her boys, as she called them – but the one in her hand was different. It was her letter. One she had written to Corporal Warren Bailey, and it had never reached its destination.

Dorothy sank into her chair. In the year she had been writing to Warren, he had asked just one thing of her, but she had hesitated. No, procrastinated. Now the military had lost him. Dead, captured or simply misplaced? Those three little words – missing in action – told her everything and nothing.

She glanced hopefully at the big round clock on the wall. Three-thirty. It was time to go home. Dorothy gathered up her letters, stuffed them in her purse and quietly slipped away from her desk without saying goodbye to her colleagues. Head down, she negotiated three flights of stairs, crossed the lobby and burst out onto Euclid Avenue.

It was April 1943 and the mood in Cleveland was as gray as the sky over Lake Erie. Rationing was in full swing and everyone was feeling the pain. Why, in February they had started rationing shoes. Shoes! But leather was needed for boots, so few complained. It could be worse, they figured. At least bombs weren't falling on Public Square.

At the streetcar stop, conversation ranged from Eisenhower's appointment as Supreme Allied Commander in Europe to the planting of Victory Gardens. Those with newspapers reported that in North Africa, British and American forces were engaged in hand-to-hand combat against German troops in an all-out effort to gain Bizerte, a harbor town on the Mediterranean Sea. Dorothy felt a wave of sadness. Warren Bailey had been in North Africa.

Standing on the fringe of the group, she was trying to absorb all the discussions around her when a sudden gust of wind removed the hat of the woman next to her. Dorothy – small and athletic – caught the bright blue beret in mid-air.

"Gosh, thanks!" said the pretty redheaded owner, who introduced herself as Edith. "Last new thing I'll have for a long time, I fear. I would have hated losing it."

The streetcar arrived at that moment and Edith settled on the seat next to Dorothy. "Just got a letter from my husband," she remarked. "Have you anyone in the service?"

"My brother, Roy. He'll be heading for Europe soon, or so he says."

"Where is he now?"

Dorothy had to smile at that. "I can't be sure. They keep moving him around. The last I knew he was at Fort Benning." And then, because it seemed impolite not to ask, "Where's your husband stationed?"

Edith grimaced. "Somewhere in Louisiana. More training and all that." Tears came to her eyes, but she blinked them back. "We were married last year. I miss him dreadfully."

"I'm sure you do." Dorothy cast about for a more

optimistic topic. She studied Edith, who looked very businesslike in her smart tweed jacket. "Do you work?" she asked.

Edith nodded. "As soon as Harold left – that's my husband, Harold – I moved back home with my parents. Got bored to tears right away. Now I'm working in an office. Guy did my job got drafted and my mother knew someone there so I got in. Pretty lucky, really. How about you?"

"I'm a librarian at the college." How proud Dorothy was to say that. "The war has left job openings everywhere," she added.

"It's true, isn't it? And women are filling them," Edith grinned. "Doing a good job of it, if I'm any judge."

Dorothy agreed. "It's how I got my job, too. Replaced a guy who signed up."

"Guess he did you a favor." Edith shrugged. "Well, this is my stop. Be seeing you!"

Dorothy caught one last glimpse of her new friend pushing through the crowd with one hand placed firmly on the blue beret. Glad for the solitude, Dorothy leaned back against the seat and thought about Edith's words. Did me a favor? Dorothy had never thought of it that way before, but she supposed it was true.

She had been so determined to go to college, but struggled to find work after graduation. Then Pearl Harbor was bombed and everything changed. Patriotism ran high, and men enlisted in droves. When the assistant reference librarian joined the Navy, Dorothy was hired to replace him. Shortly thereafter, someone approached her about the letter writing campaign.

It was simple enough. On the library's bulletin board were small white cards bearing names and addresses of soldiers, former students who put education on hold to fight for their country. No one had to convince Dorothy that this was a great way to support the war effort. She embraced the idea immediately.

At first, they were just names. Names like Warren Bailey. Dorothy didn't know any of them, but it didn't really matter. All the boys were looking for was a connection to their hometowns and people they once knew. Dorothy tried to provide that, while keeping her letters lighthearted and amusing.

Then, three weeks ago, she received a heavily censored letter from Warren. It contained a simple request: Would Dorothy please – if it wasn't too far – stop by to check on his mother? His father was in the military and Mrs. Bailey was all alone. Warren was worried because he hadn't heard from her for weeks.

It wasn't much to ask. And he was doing so much in return. Alone and afraid and far from home. Him and all the boys like him. Like Roy. And Mrs. Bailey only lived a few miles away. But Dorothy fretted - what would she say to the woman? – and never got around to going. Now Corporal Bailey was missing. She resolved right then to make it up to him. She would do it today.

No one was home when Dorothy arrived at the house she shared with her parents and sister, Frances. This suited her perfectly; there would be no questions. She pulled on her billowing riding pants and cinched the ankles. Then she wheeled her black Schwinn bicycle from the garage and rolled out into the street.

With gas rationing, many people had simply stopped driving, so there was little traffic to slow her down. Dorothy sailed through her neighborhood of neat and tidy bungalows, crossed Superior Avenue and began to pedal south into Cleveland Heights.

The wind was at her back now, which helped, but it was still uphill most of the way. Out of condition from a long winter, Dorothy's legs were aching when she finally found Laurel Crescent, a narrow little street that curved toward an overgrown field.

There were ten houses: four on one side, six on the other. The Baileys lived in the last one on the left, next to the field. White, with dark green shutters, it had a Blue Star – denoting a serviceman in the family – proudly displayed in the window.

The two-story home, with its broad front porch and multiple windows, was twice the size of the Nicholsons' house. Dorothy was thoroughly intimidated, but she hadn't come this far to turn around and run home. She squared her shoulders and knocked – albeit somewhat timidly – on the front door. There was no answer. She knocked again, louder and more firmly.

Then something occurred to her. Why hadn't Warren provided a telephone number? True, many people still couldn't afford one, but someone who lived in a house like this surely could.

Of course, she could have looked it up. Looking things up was what she did. Grumbling to herself, Dorothy walked down the driveway, past the side door, and around to the rear of the house. There she found a small porch and yet another door, but no signs of life. She knocked again, but predictably drew no response.

Curious, Dorothy took a moment to inspect her surroundings. Behind her was a pleasant garden with a path that led to the unpaved alley beyond. Next to the garden was the garage. Dorothy noticed – by standing on tiptoe – that there was an automobile tucked inside. She wondered if it had tires. So many people had donated them to the war effort.

Enough. She was procrastinating again. Dorothy retrieved a pencil and notepad from her bicycle's saddlebag and composed a hasty note.

Dear Mrs. Bailey,

I'm sorry to have missed you. I hope you are well. I'm a librarian at the college and have been writing to your son for several months. In his last letter, Warren asked that I look in on you. I will call again.

Sincerely, Dorothy Nicholson

She tucked it behind the screened door at the side of the house and returned to her bike. Ready to roll away, Dorothy paused for a last glimpse of Warren's house. The curtains moved! She was sure of it. Had someone been watching her the whole time? She was half inclined to go back, but suddenly felt inexplicably uneasy. Dark clouds were gathering overhead and the wind had picked up. A rumble of thunder convinced her. Dorothy pushed off toward home.

Her timing was perfect. Drops of rain began to fall as she walked in the back door. She paused to listen. Coming from somewhere in the house was her sister's rendition of the popular "For Me and My Gal." Dorothy tiptoed to the doorway of the kitchen and peered around the corner. There was Frances – younger by three years – singing and cavorting around the room like a dance hall hostess. Dorothy often thought that Fran could make good money doing just that at a servicemen's club, but Mother simply wouldn't hear of it.

If pressed, Dorothy would admit to being a little envious of her sister. Boys stopped in their tracks to stare at Fran. And why not? She had great legs, a perfect complexion and a talent for arranging her thick auburn hair in the latest styles. Unlike Dorothy's stick straight brown locks, Fran's curls stayed right where she put them.

"What's for dinner?" Dorothy burst into the kitchen, catching the songstress in mid-twirl.

"Spying on me; I might have known!" Fran adjusted her apron with the little red cherries and turned to face her sister. "When did you sneak in?"

"A minute ago. And I didn't sneak, you just didn't hear me."

"Can't hear anything with the wind howling around the house." Fran raised a perfectly plucked eyebrow. "I was surprised you took the bike out. I think it's too cold to ride." She gave a theatrical shiver. "Where'd you go, anyway?" She revolved toward the stove. Fran never walked if she could dance. "I started dinner. Aren't you glad?"

"Maybe." Fran's culinary skills were improving, but slowly. "What are we having?"

"A lovely roast, creamy mashed potatoes, and crisp carrots!"

"Hah! Since when?" Dorothy retorted. "The last meat we had was as tough as shoe leather."

"Why Dofy," said Fran, using the name she created when, as a little girl, she couldn't quite say Dorothy. "Have you been nibbling on your stompers again?"

"Not a chance. Who knows when I'll get another pair?" She tried to match Fran's light tone, but failed entirely.

Fran twisted around and gave Dorothy a critical glance. "What happened? You look awful."

"As I feel." Dorothy ran her fingers through her hair distractedly. "Let me change my clothes and I'll tell you."

"Sure, okay. I'll make you a cup of tea."

"Music to my ears." Dorothy dragged herself upstairs as Fran launched into the next song on her program.

She was still warbling about sitting under an apple tree when Dorothy returned and collapsed into a chair at the table.

"Got to leave at five today," Fran remarked. "I know I should be grateful to you for the job, but it's a bit boring." She waved her arms above her head. "I long for excitement."

Inwardly, Dorothy sighed. She had been afraid this would happen. Not long after being hired at the library, Dorothy managed to work her sister into an opening at the circulation desk. Their mother, Etta, was thrilled that the sisters could be together, but Dorothy knew that Fran would soon grow restless.

"So tell me!" Fran demanded, as she brought over the

tea pot and sat down. She pulled two cups from her apron pocket, which made Dorothy laugh. Fran was ingeniously efficient; you could count on it.

Without comment, Dorothy spread her letters on the table.

"Oh! From those soldiers you write to?"

Dorothy nodded.

"Will you read them to me?"

"After dinner, but I want you to look at this one." She nudged the red-stamped envelope toward Fran. "It was supposed to go to Warren Bailey. You remember, don't you? He's written before."

"Missing." Fran's face fell. "Sure, I remember Warren. I thought he was sweet. He asked you to check on his mother." Her eyes narrowed. "And you didn't, did you?"

"Not then, but after I got this I felt so bad I just went without thinking."

"Why didn't you wait for me?"

"Believe me, I should have."

"Why, what happened?" Fran's blue eyes glowed with excitement. "Tell me everything. Where does she live?"

"Not far. Cleveland Heights. A little street called Laurel Crescent."

"Was she glad to see you?"

"Well, that's just it," Dorothy began. "She wasn't home."

"You rode all that way and she wasn't there?" Fran groaned in sympathy. "Did you leave a note?'

"I did. But here's the strange thing. As I was leaving, I turned around just in time to see the curtains twitch."

"Twitch?" Fran thought for a minute. "You mean like they were doing the shimmy?" Giggling, she jumped out of her chair and shimmied around the table twice before sitting down again.

Dorothy chuckled. "Yes, like that, but not so energetically."

"Maybe it was the dog."

"If they have a dog, he was unnaturally quiet."

"What about a cat?"

"What about she was home the whole time and just didn't answer the door?"

Fran shrugged. "You can't take it personally. She didn't know who you were. Maybe she'd just crawled out of the tub."

"Maybe." Dorothy noticed steam rising from the pot on the stove and pointed. "Speaking of crawling out, whatever it is, please don't burn it; I'm starving."

"Yikes!" Fran was on her feet in an instant. She stirred vigorously while Dorothy set the table and sliced bread.

In a few minutes, Fran approached with the pot in her hands. "Dinner," she announced with a flourish, "is served."

They sat across from each other in the same places they had occupied for years. "I miss Mom," Dorothy said, around a mouthful of stew. "We haven't heard a word from her since she arrived in Philadelphia."

"I know. I miss her, too. But I'm glad she's with Daddy for a while." Two years ago, Walter Nicholson became mysteriously involved in the war effort and was recently transferred to the City of Brotherly Love. What he did there was anyone's guess.

Dorothy took another taste of Fran's creation. "This is surprisingly good."

"Surprisingly? Implying that my food is normally awful?" Fran tried to frown, but ended up laughing instead. "I am trying. Must give me points for that."

After dinner, they gathered in the living room. Before he left, Mr. Nicholson had purchased a new Philco radio for his family. They turned it on now, to listen to news of the war. It was grim and depressing.

"I wish I could help," said Fran, with a wistful look.

"You could write letters," Dorothy pointed out. "The boys yearn for mail."

"I guess, but I would never know what to say. No, I crave adventure. I haven't figured out how to get it, but I will and then look out!"

"No doubt," said Dorothy. She pulled out her envelopes and opened the first of her letters.

Fran gasped. "What happened to it? Looks like Swiss cheese."

"The censors happened, that's what." Dorothy began to read aloud and Fran amused herself by trying to guess what words were missing.

Later, as they got ready for bed, Fran ventured to ask, "Dofy, what are you planning to do about Mrs. Bailey?"

"Nothing, right now," said Dorothy. "Fingers crossed, she'll reach me at the library."

But she didn't. Not that day, nor the next, nor the next.

By the end of the week, Dorothy had become so preoccupied that one of her colleagues was finally forced to comment. John Green, whose desk faced hers, shoved a stack of books out of the way to lean forward and hiss, "What's wrong with you? All week you've looked like someone shot your dog."

John had been both friend and mentor since Dorothy started working at the library. She respected his judgment and valued his friendship, and continually fought the impulse to think of him as something more. But today her defenses were down.

Beckoning him to follow, she led the way to a dim corner at the end of the stacks. It was the only place in the library where you could have a marginally private conversation.

John listened patiently to her story about Warren Bailey and his mother. "Your sister could be right," he said, with an expression Dorothy couldn't quite interpret. "Maybe she just wasn't, well, ready for visitors. But I'm surprised she hasn't contacted you." His brow furrowed as something occurred to him. "I wonder…maybe she got news about Warren and was too upset to talk."

"I hadn't thought of that!" Dorothy lamented, as they walked back to their desks. "I was wondering if she simply didn't get the note."

"Unlikely," said John. "If it was between two doors, it couldn't have blown away. But that brings up another possibility. What if she went away? You know, to visit family. Particularly if she did get bad news."

"Fair point." They had just settled in their chairs when a student approached them. The young woman held an armful of books and wore the tired, frustrated look that students acquired midway through term. Dorothy rose to help her. "But someone was there, John," she whispered. "I didn't imagine it."

"Of course not." John dropped his head back into his work.

But he had not stopped thinking about it. "I've had an idea," he offered, when Dorothy returned. "Let's try Mrs. Bailey again. If you want, you can hide behind a tree and I'll knock on the door. See if I can get a response."

Dorothy couldn't picture herself hiding anywhere and said so, but she was more than happy for John's company. After work, they rode the streetcar east to the closest stop and walked up the hill.

"Is there an alley behind the Baileys' house?" John asked, as they stepped along.

Dorothy closed her eyes, trying to reconstruct the little street. "Yes, as a matter of fact, there is."

"Swell. We can use it as an observation post."

Dorothy smiled to herself. Poor John. His plans to enlist were thwarted last fall when he was struck by an automobile. His broken arm was healing fast, though, and Dorothy knew it wouldn't be much longer before John Green would be in uniform. Don't think about it now, she told herself, and fixed her eyes on John's face.

"Here's what we'll do," he was saying. "You walk along the alley while I walk on the sidewalk. In between the houses, we should be able to see each other. Wait behind the house for me and keep your eyes open. Whadaya say?"

At least someone had a plan. As they approached the Baileys' street, Dorothy stepped into the alley and waited until John made the turn onto Laurel Crescent. To her astonishment, he stopped and began to wave frantically in her direction.

Alarmed, Dorothy raced through someone's garden to reach him. "What's wrong? What's happened?"

John took her by the shoulders and spun her around so she could see for herself. One police squad car was blocking the street. Another was parked by the field. An ambulance stood close by.

Dorothy gasped. "They're in front of the Baileys' house!"

"I had a feeling you were going to say that." John looked grave. "We need to find out what's going on. Maybe she got bad news and collapsed."

"It's possible. I've often said to Fran that if anything happens to Roy, Mother will fall over dead."

John nodded. "But if something else has happened to Mrs. Bailey, you need to tell the police what you know."

Before she could protest, John grabbed her arm and tugged her toward the cluster of people milling about in the street. Obviously, the arrival of the police had caused a great stir. Young boys, who had hopped on their bicycles to follow the squad cars, were now swarming like bees in the Baileys' front yard. A portly policeman was trying to hold them back, but he was clearly being outmaneuvered.

"What's happened?" John asked of the matronly woman standing beside him. Still wearing her apron, she had been torn from her chores by the activity on her otherwise quiet street.

"They won't tell us a thing," she grumbled. "Milkman noticed no one had collected the milk, so he called police."

Dorothy couldn't stand not knowing. Emboldened by

curiosity, she pushed her way toward a policeman who was leaning against his squad car. John was one step behind her.

"Patrolman Connolly, at your service." He tipped his hat.

"Is it Mrs. Bailey?" Dorothy asked. "I write to her son in the service. I stopped by the other day, but she didn't answer the door. I thought it odd because..."

Connolly's eyes narrowed to slits. "Reporter, huh? What paper are you with? The Press? The News? Well, you're not getting a story from me."

"I'm not a reporter. I work at..."

He cut her off again. "Yeah, I heard. You write to their son." The cop looked from Dorothy to John. "Who's this, then?"

"My colleague from work," said Dorothy.

"Right then. Dating a guy in the service and one at work. Fine thing. You dames. All alike,"

Dorothy flushed crimson with embarrassment. "You don't understand..."

"See here," John began. "There's no need to be insulting."

Connolly glared at them, unconvinced.

"I'm worried about her," Dorothy insisted. "My last letter was returned. See? Their son is missing." She rifled through her purse and produced the envelope.

Connolly flicked his eyes over it, but before he could respond he was joined by another officer. The two men held a whispered conference. Connolly turned back to Dorothy and John. His voice was kinder. "Give it to him, Miss." He pointed to a dark-suited man standing in the driveway. "And you need to step away. Right now. Trust me on that."

It was good advice. At that moment, the Baileys' front door flew open and two men carried out a stretcher wrapped in a white sheet. It was clear to everyone that a body – or what was left of a body – lay beneath. The policemen did their best to control the onlookers, but it was futile. Children, small and quick, ducked beneath arms and slipped between legs to catch a glimpse as the stretcher was loaded into the ambulance. "Scram!" yelled Officer Connolly, trying to sound menacing. "Go on now, scram." He knew it was a pointless. In all probability, this was the most exciting moment of their young lives.

Dorothy looked around for the dark-suited man. "He's disappeared." She scowled. "I took my eyes off him for one second."

"Maybe he went around back," John suggested. "Here, give me the envelope and I'll try to catch up with him. In the meantime, try talking to that woman in the apron again. Maybe she'll tell you something she didn't tell me."

John strode off down the driveway, pausing only to open the screened door and peer inside. His eyes met Dorothy's. He shook his head. Then he trotted off toward the rear of the house.

A few minutes later, they met again on the sidewalk. "I have some news!" They both spoke at once.

"You first," said Dorothy, because John looked about to burst.

He didn't argue. "Um, okay. That man was Detective Anderson."

"Did you give him the envelope?"

"I sure did! And he was very interested. Asked for the whole story. And guess what?" John lowered his voice. "He wouldn't give details, but Mrs. Bailey did not die of natural causes. Someone bumped her off!"

Dorothy was taken aback. "Murdered? Are you sure? I mean, is he sure?"

"Yep. And he asked that if we find out anything we should tell him. Look, gave me a card and everything."

"Did he leave?" Dorothy asked, wishing she could have spoken with the detective in person.

"Sorry, yes. He was parked in the alley." John leaned closer. "And there's something else. I overheard one of the cops talking about stab wounds. Blood all around. Sounds like someone really worked her over."

"Oh, poor Warren." Could this day get any worse? "But now you must hear my news. I had a talk with Nora Grainger – that's the apron woman." John nodded. "She lives opposite the Baileys, so she sees who comes and goes. Phyllis – Mrs. Bailey – took in two boarders last fall. She introduced them to Nora as Ginny and Maxine, but – and this is the best bit – Nora overheard them talking one day and those weren't the names they used with each other!"

"Well, blow me down!" John exclaimed. "How did she overhear…?"

"Who knows? She strikes me as something of a busybody."

"I'd say so. Anything else?"

"Yes. One of them disappeared right before Christmas and left owing Phyllis money. No one seems to know where she went."

"That's a killer-diller!" John shook his head. "Gotta be careful letting out rooms."

"You're telling me. Then the other one left a few weeks ago to go back to her family. At least that's what she told everyone."

John rubbed his chin thoughtfully. "When did Nora last see Mrs. Bailey?"

"Well, that's just it! Not for several days, which makes me wonder who was watching me from the window."

"Yes, I wondered about that," John said, as they walked down the hill. "I sure would like to talk to her other neighbors; someone must have seen something."

Fran worked late that evening. It was after nine when she burst through the door, happy and smiling. Her expression changed when she saw Dorothy. With hands on her attractive hips, Fran glared at her sister. "Dof, you've been running your fingers through your hair again and it's standing up all over your head. Really unattractive." Carefully, she removed her hat and jacket. "Something must have happened to get you in such a state, so give!"

"Oh, Fran. It's the worst. Mrs. Bailey is dead! She was murdered in her own house."

Fran's eyes widened. "How do you know?"

"Because John Green and I went to see her. When we got there, they were carrying out her body."

"Her body?" Fran looked ghoulish. "So you got to see her after all?"

Dorothy groaned and threw her hands over her face.

"Sorry, I couldn't resist." Fran tried to appear contrite. "You must be shook up."

"I was, at first. Now I think I'm angry. Who would do such a thing?"

"And why? I mean, people don't just walk down the street, pick a house and decide they're going to clobber the occupant. It was probably robbery, don't you think?" Fran kicked off her shoes and stretched out on the couch. "We should go to the movies." She was the master of the non sequitur. "I want to see the new one with Astaire and Rita Hayworth."

"How can you think about movies at a time like this?" Dorothy griped.

"I can always think about movies, and besides, you need a diversion."

"No argument there. Yes, all right," Dorothy conceded. "We'll go."

"Swell! That's settled." Fran swung her legs off the couch and sat up. "Did you hear the news, by the way? The Brits met up with our boys and captured some important hill. I'm glad Roy isn't there."

"But Warren is. Or was."

"You like him, don't you? Are you hoping he'll come back for you when it's all over?" Fran's eyes twinkled.

Dorothy waved a hand dismissively. "I don't even

know what Warren looks like."

"Funny, I always thought you'd go for John."

"Please stop meddling in my love life."

"That's just it; you don't have a love life."

"No, I don't," Dorothy admitted. "And probably won't until the war is over."

Fran's smile dimmed, knowing it was true for both of them. As usual, her solution was to change the subject again. You had to have your wits about you to enter into a conversation with Fran. "I've been thinking. Do you suppose Daddy would let me stay with him for a while?"

Dorothy's mouth fell open. "Where did that come from?"

"I want a change," Fran replied.

"So you're going to abandon Mother and me? I'm not sure she would approve."

Fran shrugged. "I'd rather try for a job at the Stagedoor Canteen right here in town."

"They'd probably hire you, too," said Dorothy. "But Mother would have a fit."

"I don't really need her permission."

"You do if you want to live in this house."

"Yes, I know," said Fran. "That's the point." And no more was said on the topic.

Friday morning, the sisters searched the newspaper until they found a short piece announcing the death of an unidentified Cleveland Heights woman.

"It says they suspect foul play," Fran noted. "But stop short of calling it murder. I wonder why?" She read the two paragraphs again. "She isn't named, pending identification of the body, I presume." Fran felt authorized to speak since she read more mysteries and spy thrillers than anyone Dorothy knew. "But what if it isn't Mrs. Bailey after all? Did you ever consider that?"

Dorothy slapped a hand to her forehead. "Don't give

me anything else to think about," she said. "The police will do their job and I'm staying right out of it."

That evening, they went to the movies as agreed and came home humming the tunes they could remember. "Don't you feel better?" Fran demanded, pleased with herself.

Dorothy had to admit that she did. But Monday morning her resolve to stay out of the investigation collapsed.

It was around noon, and John was at lunch, when the telephone between their desks rang persistently.

Dorothy spoke crisply into the heavy black receiver. "Reference library."

"Dorothy? Dorothy Nicholson?"

"Why, yes. How may I help you?"

"It's me. Nora Grainger. Do you remember? We met..."

Dorothy almost choked in her excitement. "Of course, I remember you."

"I saw a light!" she said excitedly. "Last night. In the Baileys' house." She paused to allow Dorothy time to digest that bit of news. "I know the police don't believe me. Probably think I'm a crazy old fool, but I know what I saw. I know I didn't imagine it."

Just as I didn't imagine seeing the curtains move, thought Dorothy. "If it's any consolation, I believe you."

"I'm glad of that!" Nora sounded relieved. "You see, Mr. Grainger is in Chicago on business and I was wondering...would you and your handsome young man come over and talk to me?"

The handsome young man took that opportunity to appear and saw Dorothy fairly jumping out of her chair. She quickly scrawled a note for him to read. He nodded vigorously.

"Mrs. Grainger, we'll be there after work."

For the rest of the day, neither John nor Dorothy got much accomplished. They watched the clock. They waited impatiently for the streetcar. And they couldn't walk up the hill fast enough.

Nora Grainger was waiting for them. "I'll make some coffee, shall I?" They nodded and she got to work, chatting all the time. "Frankly, I'm afraid I'll be murdered in my bed. Not every day someone is stabbed to death right across the street."

"So she was stabbed," Dorothy murmured. "I didn't know..."

"Oh, yes, dear. That nice policeman told me. Probably shouldn't have said a word, but I offered him a piece of cake right out of the oven and that got him going." She grinned wickedly. "Used up my ration coupons for sugar and flour, but it was worth it. He said the murder was going to be hushed up, but he didn't know why."

"You don't say." John seemed to turn that over in his mind.

Nora tried to look knowing. "Frankly, I think it has something to do with her husband's job in Washington. Military, you know. And I bet it was one of those women who killed her. Spies they were, I'm thinking."

"They say spies are amongst us," John agreed. "Could be anyone."

"Mrs. Johnson – she lives next door to the Baileys – always thought so. She said that right away. Said both women looked German."

John Green coughed and took a sip of his coffee. He had tucked into a piece of Nora's cake and found it to be stale. He swallowed. "Mrs. Grainger, what time did you see that light?"

"The light?" She looked at him blankly. "Oh, the light! And please, call me Nora." She tried to gather her thoughts. "Let's see, now. Half-past midnight; I checked the clock. You see, I never sleep well when Mr. Grainger's away. Sometimes, in the summer, I'll go sit on the front porch in the middle of the night. Peaceful and quiet it is." Nora rambled on. "Anyway, last night I couldn't settle down. It was too chilly to go outside, so I just leaned on the windowsill and looked up and down the street. And that's when I saw it."

"Where was it," John prompted. "Downstairs?"

"No, dear. It was upstairs. Front bedroom. It bobbed back and forth like a flashlight. Anyway, that's what I thought."

"Did you call the police?"

"I did, but they found no one."

No surprise, thought Dorothy. Nora had probably turned on the lights to make her call and instantly alerted the intruder.

"I wonder what someone was looking for," John mused. "And if they found it." He brightened. "Here's an idea. What about a stakeout? Miss Nicholson and I could stay with you tomorrow night. If they come back, we'll see them."

Nora warmed to the idea right away. "I think that's a fine plan," she enthused.

Dorothy wasn't so sure. "John, what are you expecting to happen?" He wasn't the type to sit passively and watch.

"I was thinking I might break into their garage." John said it so solemnly that Dorothy had to bite her lip to keep from laughing. "I looked at it the other day. I'm not even sure it's locked properly."

Had her mother been home, Dorothy knew it would never be allowed. Spend the night with a man? Only two women in the house? Etta would have put her foot down. But she was in Philadelphia. It took Dorothy only a minute to decide. "Let's do it!" she said.

Fran was predictably peeved. "Another adventure without me?"

"Someone has to be here in case Mother calls. I can't think of any way around it."

"And if she does, and wants to talk to you, what am I to say?"

"You'll think of something."

Fran muttered darkly about being the youngest and always left behind, but Dorothy knew her sister would rise to the occasion.

The following evening, Dorothy dressed carefully for her outing. She borrowed an old brown coat – several sizes too large – from Roy's closet, and stuffed her hair under a knitted cap.

When John arrived, he was similarly attired. Fran snickered when she saw them. "You two belong in a vaudeville routine," she said. "You simply can't take the streetcar looking like that.

"No problem," said John. "I borrowed my old man's Nash."

Fran rolled her eyes. "Well, be careful, then." She hugged Dorothy. "I'll be fine, but you'll pay for not including me."

"Don't I know it," Dorothy said under her breath. And they were off.

Riding along in the Nash, Dorothy stole a look at John. He grinned back in a way that made her heart race. "Our first date and we're dressed like bums," he said.

They burst out laughing at the absurdity of the situation, but Dorothy felt in her heart that something had changed for the better between them. Our first date? She could only hope there would be more.

On Laurel Crescent, John parked the Nash behind the Graingers' house where it wouldn't be seen. Nora ushered them inside. She was clearly in a festive mood. Over lemonade, they discussed how the evening should progress.

"Now don't just walk across the street," Nora warned. "Best go through the back yard and across the field so no one will spot you."

"Good suggestion," said John. "And if I see anything suspicious, I'll flick the flashlight twice as a signal."

At ten o'clock, the time the Graingers normally retired, the conspirators turned off the lights and John eased out the back door. Dorothy and Nora moved silently to the front porch and prepared to wait it out.

It was a perfect night. A heavy cloud cover concealed moon and stars and they sat in total darkness. They watched and waited.

It was well after midnight when Nora Grainger fell asleep and began to snore, to Dorothy's everlasting annoyance. Wretched woman, she thought. All she wanted was our company.

For a while, she glowered at the sleeping Nora, but soon her own eyes grew heavy. She wondered how John was doing. Was he in the garage, or hiding in the shrubs? Maybe he'd fallen asleep like Nora. Dorothy had the notion to wander across the street and check on him, but just then she saw a light flicker twice in the vicinity of the Baileys' garage.

She pounced on Nora Grainger. "Wake up, wake up." She shook the woman more viciously than planned. "Someone's come. John's signaling."

Nora opened her eyes and looked groggily at Dorothy. Then she realized what was happening. "What should we do?" she asked, instantly alert.

"I'm going to move a little closer and risk showing myself. You can stay here where it's safe. If we yell, call the police."

Nora was having none of it. "I'm coming, too," she announced.

The woman was maddening. What if she became excitable and gave them away? But there was no time to argue. "Come on, then," Dorothy relented.

They stumbled through the house to the back door. "Hang on a minute." Nora paused to rummage in a kitchen cupboard and pulled out a cast iron frying pan. "Protection," she explained.

Good idea. Why hadn't she thought of that? Roy's old baseball bat would have been perfect. Instead, she pulled out her flashlight. Thus armed, the two women crept from the house and navigated across the field, making their way from tree to tree. At the end of the Baileys' driveway, they sought cover behind a large maple.

"I can't see a thing," Nora groused. "Can you?"

Dorothy was about to speak when John's light flickered a brief warning. At least they hoped it was John. Seconds later, a dark figure appeared in the Baileys' garden. Nora sucked in her breath and grabbed Dorothy's arm in excitement.

The figure grew closer and then disappeared behind the house. Dorothy and Nora moved forward, trying to blend into the hedge that ran alongside the driveway. They were almost to the garage, when they saw John move stealthily away from it and toward the house. What was he planning?

With her heart pounding wildly, Dorothy broke into a run, with Nora at her heels. They heard a whoop and a shriek. The women rounded the corner in time to see John throw a sack over someone.

Dorothy clicked on her flashlight and saw a glint of metal. "Watch out!" she screamed. "A knife!"

Furious at being ambushed, the figure lashed out, hoping to connect with her captor. To her credit, Nora knew her cue when she saw it. To John's astonishment, she lifted her heavy frying pan in both hands and brought it squarely down on the head of the writhing figure. There was a moan and a last wobble of the knife. John's quarry fell to the ground with a thud.

Over the weekend, Detective Anderson summoned Dorothy and John to the police station. He wasted no time on preliminaries. "You know, I should arrest you for interfering with police business," he pointed out. "But since you bagged the criminal, we can only be grateful."

"You must also thank Nora Grainger," Dorothy reminded him. "Her contribution was vital."

"We acknowledged her last night, but I have doubts about her ability to keep things confidential. What I'm going to say next is for your ears only." Noting their eager faces, Anderson's own relaxed into a smile. "The woman you tackled was a spy. We had been watching her for some time."

"A spy?" Nora had been right all along, Dorothy thought. "Was it one of the women who boarded with Mrs. Bailey?"

Anderson nodded. "Gertrude Klein, alias Virginia – Ginny – Castle. Her friend was Margaret Winkler, who called herself Maxine White. They met in New York at a rally for Nazi sympathizers.

"Sympathizers!" John was staggered.

"As we understand it, the two women were leaked classified documents by a contact they had nurtured in a defense factory here in town. The documents – drawings for a new weapon – were valuable if they could be sold, but it wasn't going to happen in Cleveland. Klein went to Chicago to move things along."

"But Winkler also left, didn't she?" Dorothy asked.

"In a way. You see, our undercover agents let Klein believe that Winkler had double-crossed her and run off with the documents. We had the Bailey place bugged, so we had good reason to believe that was her intent. We pulled Winkler off the street immediately."

"Why didn't Klein take them with her?" John was clearly puzzled.

"She left them behind as security. It was stupid, really. Once Klein heard about Winkler, we were fairly sure she would come back to pick up her partner's trail. Knowing Klein's reputation for violence, we put in a decoy. That's who you saw at the window, by the way." His face clouded over. "We were sorry to lose her."

"Lose her?" Dorothy stared at him. "I don't understand. I thought..."

"It was Mrs. Bailey?"

"Well, of course. Everyone did."

"Mrs. Bailey has been working for us through her husband in Washington. She arranged to casually meet Klein and offered to let rooms to her and Winkler. When we heard

56

that Klein had left Chicago, we put Mrs. Bailey on a late-night train to Washington. I drove her to the station myself."

"Then she's all right? She wasn't murdered after all?" Dorothy was bewildered.

"No," said a voice behind her. "I'm perfectly fine."

Dorothy and John whirled around to see a smartly dressed woman of middle years standing in the doorway. She removed her gloves and held out her hand. "I'm Phyllis Bailey," she said. "Thank you, Dorothy, for writing to my son. And for caring enough to act on his request. I'm only sorry that things got a bit out of hand."

"But Warren...my last letter..."

"Warren was injured and became separated from his outfit. Eventually, he was picked up by another battalion, which is why no one knew where he was. He's going to be fine."

"I'm so relieved," said Dorothy. "And so very pleased to meet you at last." She meant it with all her heart.

A few days later, Dorothy and John conversed across the expanse of their desks. "Mother got home last night," said Dorothy. "Fran came up trumps and never let on what happened. But the real news is that she's decided to enlist as a WAC. Mother is horrified, but Daddy is supportive and I think it will be good for Fran. Of course, I'll have one more person to worry about."

"And another letter to write." John gestured to the pile of recently delivered army mail. "Are those from your admirers?"

"I don't know about that." Dorothy looked sheepish. "I try to think of them as brothers."

"Hmm. Is that how you think of me?" John asked pointedly.

"Yes. No." Dorothy blushed and stammered. "How should I think of you?"

"Oh, I don't know." He avoided her eyes. "Will you

have time to write to me when I'm in the service?"

"John, of course I will."

"And look in on my mother?"

Dorothy laughed. "Happily." Then it hit her. "Oh, no! You're not!"

"I am, but please don't say a word just yet. I got the green light from the doctor yesterday. I plan to leave when finals are over. Don't want to miss the war, now do I?" he added, echoing Fran's sentiment.

"No," said Dorothy. "We wouldn't want that." She wanted to cry.

May was a tumultuous month for Dorothy. First Fran left home, and a strange silence filled the house. Then John Green left the library. With a glowing commendation from Detective Anderson, he was sworn into the United States Army. One year later, as a paratrooper with the 101st Airborne Division, he dropped into Normandy, France in the early morning hours of June 6, 1944. T Sergeant John Green survived the war and returned to marry Miss Dorothy Nicholson, with whom he had shared such a special adventure. They would go on sharing adventures for the rest of their lives.

Christina L. Wilkinson (Chris) has always loved history and mysteries. While researching and writing articles about local history, she frequently thought about writing a novel using stories she had collected along the way. "The Decoy" represents her official transition from non-fiction to mystery. It reflects her interest in the 1940s and WWII, and is loosely based on the escapades of her mother and aunt, both of whom were librarians during that era. Wilkinson enjoys traveling and digging in her garden. She holds a degree in Historic Preservation and Community Revitalization from Skidmore College.

Suffer the Poor

By Harriette Sackler

Horror. That was Anne Heatherton's reaction upon visiting London's East End for the first time. An abundance of descriptors would come to her later. Misery. Poverty. Hunger. Hopelessness. To name a few.

It never occurred to Anne that people could live in such appalling conditions. True, she lived quite a sheltered life on her family's estate near Bath. When she did come to London, she stayed at their town home which was located in the best of neighborhoods, from which she never strayed.

Anne decided to tour the East End with a group of altruistic woman interested in assisting the poor. Her dear friend Mary asked her to accompany the group. While there was a good deal of missionary work being done in 1890, Mary told her that no private efforts existed. Even though Anne was informed about the disgraceful circumstances which the poor were forced to endure, she never could have imagined this kind of squalor.

The ramshackle dwellings and shops that lined the crowded streets of East End appeared to be moments from crumbling to the ground. Garbage and unidentifiable detritus made it practically impossible for the ladies to navigate. Women in filthy clothing sat in front of their lodgings while children dressed in nothing more than rags played or, in most cases, sat near their mothers, too weak from hunger to expend any energy. Men gathered in groups to voice their anger and helplessness at the inability to find work to feed their families. They eyed the group of well-dressed women with contempt.

"So, m'ladies," their guide said to them, "I do believe you have now been introduced to the conditions of life among the poor. But, please, keep in mind, that no matter how great the need, the citizens of the East End are proud people. They would rather be able to provide for themselves, than accept charity. The men want nothing more than to have jobs that pay a respectable wage so they can care for their wives and children. The woman ache seeing their children go hungry and, all too often, perish. Workhouses are detested and considered the last resort. Please consider this as you contemplate what assistance you can provide."

"Well, ladies," Mrs. Pinckney, the group leader, announced, "we have a great deal to think about. But I am truly confident that we can make a difference. I believe it is our moral duty to share the blessings of our fortunate circumstances with others. But certainly not to be patronizing or morally superior. Don't you agree?" The women nodded emphatically and whispered to each other as they moved toward the outskirts of the East End.

During the next several weeks, Anne returned to the slums, ignoring the protests of her parents. While they were supportive of efforts to alleviate the sufferings of others, they were not inclined to allow their daughter to venture into danger. However, they eventually resigned themselves to the fact that Anne had demonstrated, time and time again, that she had a mind of her own and no amount of pleading would keep her from doing as she wished. So they offered their headstrong daughter whatever resources she wished to fulfill her vision.

Every time Anne ventured into this part of town, she came armed with the kinds of supplies that were so sorely needed. She brought food: loaves of fresh bread, jam, milk and cheese. Clothing, bed linens, blankets and pillows. Eating utensils, pots and pans. All manner of items that would make life a bit more tolerable for those who could not afford to purchase them. The carriage that transported her was so filled with items that Anne rode with the driver, a breach of etiquette that would have appalled her parents.

Anne also spent time with the women she met. She sat with them and listened to the stories they had to tell, many more than enough to rip her heart apart. She held their babies. She mourned with them when children died or husbands ran off in desperation. She became their friend.

On one such visit, as she sat on a wooden box, sipping tea in the home of a Mrs. Hale, young Johnny Hale burst into the room in an agitated state.

"Mum," he cried, "another one of the missionaries has been killed. Stabbed in the heart, just like the other two. A member of the Army this time."

Anne had spent enough time in the neighborhood to know that the Salvation Army had a large presence in the area Their recruits went into the very worst of the East End dwellings and drinking establishments in an attempt to enlist followers to the pathway to Heaven. Anne was of the opinion that it was difficult to believe in a benevolent God when your children were starving. But she, nonetheless, admired the Army's efforts to minister to the needy. Who would want to hurt these selfless souls?

"How did you learn about the crime?" Anne asked young Johnny.

"Well, I was playin' dodge with the fellas when the coppers showed up. Ya know we don't see much of them around here unless something bad has happened."

"Are they still downstairs?"

"They are ma'am. Down the street in front of Badger's Tavern."

Anne quickly left the lodging and descended the rotting old stairs with as much speed as she was able without risking life and limb. As she left the house, she saw a large group of people gathered round an establishment a few doors down. In the center of the crowd stood a member of the police force, doing his best to maintain a semblance of order.

"Move along now. There's nothing to be seen here. But if you witnessed anything that can help us locate the bloke who had a mind to murder an innocent young woman, we want to hear from you."

As the onlookers dispersed, Anne moved forward to address the policeman.

"Excuse me, sir. May I ask you exactly what has happened here?"

The officer touched his forefinger to his hat and nodded to Anne.

"Something terrible, miss. A young woman with years ahead of her has had her life snuffed out. She was a member of the Army, preaching the word of the Lord to the sinners who spend their miserable days in the East End. A tragedy, to be sure. When we find the scum, pardon my language, miss, he'll swing in no time."

Anne was saddened to think of the young woman who was victimized in such a heinous manner.

"Sir, I was told that there were others who suffered their demise in similar fashion."

"Yes that's true, I'm afraid. A young man and an older woman, both on church missions down here,"

Anne shook her head. "I'm so very sorry."

"Miss," said the policeman, "may I ask why a person like yourself would be spending time in the East End? This certainly is not a place for a lady as genteel as yourself."

Anne showed no reluctance in responding.

"After touring the area with a group of woman from Kent, I concluded that I wished to dedicate both resources and effort to be of service to those forced to live under such dreadful conditions."

"Far be it for me to tell you what to do, miss," said the policeman, "but the East End is no place for you. Terrible

---

62

things happen every day down here. Bet you heard of the Ripper some years back. Never did catch the fiend. Miss, pardon my saying so, but you need to go home."

"I thank you for your concern," Anne replied. "I certainly will take your advice to heart."

She then turned and walked away.

The next day, Anne traveled to her family's estate near Bath. She hadn't been home for a number of weeks and was anxious to spend time with her parents and older brother. Her work in the East End had taken its toll on her, and the murders of the three missionaries deeply troubled her. Why had their lives been taken when their only purpose had been to be of assistance to the needy? Much like her own intentions.

As the carriage passed through the countryside, Anne saw the familiar surroundings through new eyes. How beautiful and tranquil this part of England was and in such sharp contrast to the filth and despair of London's East End.

Anne was anxious to see her family and talk to them about her experiences. Even though they had been very much against her intentions, they had provided funding for her efforts. They knew, of course, she would have likely gone off without their blessing.

Lord Jeffery and Lady Caroline were thrilled to see their daughter. They both embraced her, then held Anne at arm's length to assure themselves that she had come home to them unharmed.

"Oh my dear, it is so good to have you back." Lady Caroline cried. "We've been so concerned for your welfare."

"Mother I am fine. Truly I am. But I've missed you so. And I do have so much to share with you."

Sir Jeffery smiled at his daughter. "And we are anxious to learn about your experiences, my dear. But now you must be tired from your journey and anxious to rest a bit before we dine. Your brother will be returning from the village shortly, and I am certain he will have a long list of questions for you."

Anne smiled broadly. "It will be so good to see Teddy. And you are right. I would love a bit of a nap before dinner. It has been a long trip in so many ways,"

Conversation over dinner that evening was spirited and focused on Anne. As she observed the quantity of delectable food that had been prepared for the family of four, she felt more than a pang of guilt. Why, this amount could provide a feast for a large number of starving East Enders. Anne's weeks in the slums had dramatically changed her perspective on life.

"Now my dear," her father said, "while we greatly admire your desire to help those less fortunate than yourself, your mother and I must insist that you do so in a manner that is less threatening. I'm sure you can encourage our friends and acquaintances to devote time to set aside worn clothing in good repair or even ask the ladies to join with you to sew or knit blankets and buntings for the babes who have so little. I would be more than amenable to providing a reasonable portion of our crops to your cause. Our first responsibility, you understand, is to our family and all the villagers and tenants who rely on us for their well-being. However, I am confident that we can assist, in some way, the wretched who have become so dear to you."

Anne looked into her father's eyes to judge the sincerity of his words. She wanted to be sure he wasn't mocking her. After all, he had never before expressed any concern whatsoever for those hidden from his view. But it appeared to Anne that he had been troubled by the picture she had painted and was prepared to provide assistance.

It was at this point that her bother Teddy chimed in.

"Sis, I must say I am damn proud of you. You have got backbone and a hell of a heart. And here I am only contemplating my next romantic conquest or upcoming card game. You shame me, little sister. But I will throw in my

---

64

promise to help you out."

Lady Caroline took the opportunity to halfheartedly admonish her son.

"Teddy, I will excuse your coarse language this one time since I know your sentiments are heartfelt. But please remember your manners in the future."

"Now Anne," her father said, "you have your family's blessing to continue your work. Only, however, and I repeat, only, if you will come home and no longer spend your time in danger. We cannot fear for your safety every waking hour."

Anne contemplated her father's words.

"Father, I will agree. But I must return to the East End one more time. There are people I want to see and to tell them they will not be forgotten."

Anne returned to London with a deep feeling of sadness. She would sorely miss the many East Enders she had come to care about over time. However, she understood how selfish it would be to prolong her family's concern for her safety. And, it was with a sense of failure that she acknowledged her own anxiety over the dangers she was exposed to on a daily basis as she traveled about the streets of the slums.

Over the next several days, Anne visited with the East End women and children she had come to know. She assured them that she would continue to work on their behalf and provide as much aid as she was able.

Her last stop was at the lodging of Mrs. Hale and her son, Johnny. The room they occupied on the top floor of the house was not as barren as it once was. It now contained a bed frame and straw-filled mattress, covered with a colorful down quilt. A small table and two chairs, a chest of drawers, and a collection of cooking utensils and dishware had transformed the dismal room into a home. It pleased Anne to no end that she had been able to make a difference in the lives of these two people.

"Oh, dearie, we are going to miss you something awful. Johnny and me have been blessed by your kindness. Your visits have been the bright spots of my days. But your mum and pa are worried sick about you with good reason. These streets are filled with danger. Those that live here have reached the bottom and have nothing to lose. They're angry and have nowhere to turn.

"Oh, I know, I know. But it is beyond me why this can't be changed."

"Maybe someday, dearie, maybe someday."

Mrs. Hale let out a hearty laugh. "Will you listen to the likes of me now? Calling a high born lady like yourself dearie."

Anne reached for Mrs. Hale's hand.

"I would not have it any other way."

After Anne and Mrs. Hale made their teary goodbyes, Anne left the lodging house to make her way to the stable where Hampstead, her carriage driver, awaited her. They would return to her family's London house for the night and leave early next morning for Bath. The help who had accompanied her to London would close the house and follow. They were all going home.

Lost in thought, Anne started down the street. She failed to notice that there were fewer people about at this early hour. East End nights were filled with drinking and debauchery and inhabitants tended to sleep in until much later in the day.

As she passed by one of the many narrow alleys that intersected the main streets, she was jolted out of her reverie by a stifled scream and a scuffling sound. Without thought, Anne ran into the filthy alley to find a man accosting a young woman. His arm around her neck prevented the victim from running away.

"Let go of her! Let go of her, I tell you," Anne ordered him, to no avail.

She then started to scream as loud as she could to summon assistance. But there was no response.

In desperation and with no thought to her own well-being, Anne quickly took in her surroundings and, as luck would have it, found a wooden plank that lay on the ground amidst all manner of garbage. She lifted the piece of wood high above her head and, with all her strength, brought it down on the man's head. With a howl of pain, he loosened his grip on the young woman and then dropped to the ground.

Anne grabbed her hand and ordered her to run. They bolted out of the alley and down the street, screaming for help as they went.

A shopkeeper heard their cries and quickly ordered them to safety inside. Then he went back to the street and proceeded to sound an alarm with a whistle he carried in the pocket of his apron. Within moments, a crowd had gathered outside the shop, followed by a policeman who quickly took charge of the situation.

"Who can tell me what has happened?" he ordered.

Anne, quite shaken and out-of-breath, described what had transpired and several men were quickly dispatched to the alley to apprehend the suspect.

After answering the many questions addressed to her by the policeman and being assured that the young victim was not in a serious way, thanks to Anne's intervention, she hurried to the stable to meet Hampstead, anxious to complete the preparations to return to Bath.

The following morning, Anne insisted on delaying their trip until she paid a visit to the East End police station. She was anxious to learn the details of all that had transpired the day before.

When she introduced herself to the policeman at the front desk and stated the nature of her visit, he quickly rose and addressed her in a deferential manner.

"Lady Heatherton, it is a true pleasure to make your

acquaintance. Your quick action saved a life. You are truly a brave young woman. If you will pardon me, I know Captain Walters will be anxious to speak to you. Please have a seat, and he will be with you momentarily."

Not five minutes had passed before a large, rather rotund gentleman made his way to the bench where Anne was seated. He wore a broad smile on his red-whiskered face and quickly introduced himself.

"Lady Heatherton, I am Captain James Walters, and it is my pleasure to have you visit our station. You have become the talk of the East End as the heroine who saved a young woman's life. Please, if you would, come back to my office, so I can share the details of this case with you."

When Anne was seated in front of Captain Walters' desk, he began to speak.

"The young woman you saved from certain death is Miss Mary Thompson. She is a relatively new member of the Salvation Army, which as you may know, represents quite a large presence in the East End. While many do not agree with their preachings, the Army does attempt to do good work. By the way, Miss Thompson is resting comfortably in the Army's lodgings and is anxious to thank you personally for your bravery.

"The fiend who attempted to murder Miss Thompson, and certainly would have in short order were it not for your intervention, is one Lawrence Foster, the proprietor of the Black Crow Tavern, one of the worst and most dangerous establishments in the East End.

"It seems that Foster had taken offense to the presence of the do-gooders who would invade his tavern, uninvited and unwanted, preaching the dangers of drink and idleness. He vowed to keep them away permanently and had already succeeded in ending the lives of three missionaries. Miss Thompson would have been the fourth. Thanks to you, he has been apprehended and will hang for his actions."

"Captain, I am thoroughly speechless. I acted entirely

on impulse and, had I thought about my actions, I probably would have never interceded for fear of my life."

"Makes no matter, Lady Heatherton, you did what you did."

After warm farewells to Captain Walters and the other policemen who introduced themselves to her, Anne left the station and, with Hampstead's help, settled into the carriage that had waited for her outside.

A very special time in her life was coming to an end. But, she had vowed to continue her work, if from afar. Someday she would be back. That she knew to be true.

Harriette Sackler serves as Grants Chair of the Malice Domestic Board of Directors. She is a past Agatha Award nominee for Best Short Story for "Mother Love," which was published in Chesapeake Crimes II. *In 2013 "Fishing for Justice," appeared in the Sisters in Crime-Guppies anthology,* Fishnets. *"Devil's Night," a tale of life in the ruined city of Pittsburgh, can be found in* All Hallows' Evil, *a Mystery and Horror, LLC anthology.*

Harriette is a member of Mystery Writers of America, Sisters in Crime, Sisters in Crime-Chesapeake Chapter, and the Guppies.

She lives in the D.C. suburbs with her husband and their three pups and spends a great deal of time tending to her duties as Vice President of her labor of love: House with a Heart Senior Pet Sanctuary. She is the very proud mom and grandmother. Visit Harriette at: www.harriettesackler.com

Dead Man Hanging

By Georgia Ruth

Daniel Kanipe stepped out of the mud to duck under the shelter of the porch roof. "Mornin' Charlie. You next?"

"Nah, Mr. Kanipe. I'm just bidin' time." The young farmer moved his chew to the other side of his mouth. "My missus tol' me to come to Marion. I'm drivin' her crazy. Can't get to the fields cause they're all underwater. Nuthin' else to do but set and watch this dadburn rain."

"It's a frog-strangler, that's for sure." Kanipe waved at the barber through the window of the shop next door to the Eagle Hotel.

"Ain't never heard that expression."

"Tennessee boy taught me that when we rode for Custer, rest his soul." Next to Charlie's rocker was an old stool, and Kanipe sat down, his long oilskin drover coat draining on the rough planks. "I was looking for something to occupy my time but Comanche here doesn't appreciate a walk through a hurricane to get my beard trimmed." Kanipe admired the handsome bay whose reins held him trapped in the downpour, his head low.

"He don't know no different." Charlie spat tobacco juice over the sidewalk into Main Street, careful to miss the horse.

Across the street, mighty oak trees drooped and endured. A buggy sloshed past them, its driver sitting under the canopy ramrod straight, mouth grim. Her signature black hat was secure on her head and a high collar showed above her cape. She pulled her horse over in front of the general store, next to the owner's new Ford Model T.

"What's Miz Perry doing out in this weather?" Kanipe wondered aloud.

"I 'spect those young'uns at the orphanage ate all the food, and she needs to restock." Charlie spat further this time.

"One good thing about all this water, it'll go a long way in filling up a new lake."

"First they have to build a dam to hold the Catawba. And right now it's nigh on impossible. I heard tell last night Miz Greenlee saw a house floating down the river."

"The Bridgewater dam is almost finished. I went by there a week ago," said Kanipe. "They'll need another one, too, but there are still a few folks who won't give up their land."

"I'd never sign away my grandpappy's farm." Charlie pulled his old slicker closer to a whitish shirt and stained vest.

"You would if the price was right."

"Everybody wants to poke their nose where it don't belong."

A stranger came out from the barber shop, rubbing his clean shaven face. "Which one of you is Kanipe?"

"That'd be me." His hazel eyes took in the details of this stranger whose hitching gait brought him closer.

"The barber said to tell you to come on in." He adjusted his black hat. "You the Kanipe that was at the Little Big Horn?"

"Could be."

"I'm a journalist from Raleigh. I could do a piece on you."

Kanipe brushed past him, his solid frame filling the doorway.

"Don't want to engage in conversation? Can't say as I blame you. You should be ashamed of yourself for deserting your men."

72

Kanipe shut the door.

The barber continued to sweep the floor around an elevated chair while Kanipe hung his coat on a peg and his hat over it. "Mornin', Pete."

"Mr. Kanipe. Stayin' dry?"

"Not pretending to. A week of rain has me thinking about swim lessons."

"Fifteen inches so far up at Altapass, and I hear the railroad tracks past Old Fort are slidin' off the mountains." The elderly barber shook his head. "Ain't never seen nothin' like this."

"When I passed the depot, a passenger train was unloading. That's the second one stranded in Marion," said Kanipe. "I don't know where these folks are gonna stay."

"Well now, they can't live in a Pullman car without food and facilities."

"We have plenty of room at my place. I could put up somebody for a few days."

Pete motioned to his chair. "Maybe this'll be good for my business."

Kanipe smiled. "You call that capitalism or opportunism?"

"Horse sense." Pete laughed.

The rain continued Saturday into Sunday, and it was a prosperous night for the Eagle Hotel's restaurant and bar. A back room held continual competition in billiards and poker. In the next block the newer Marianna Hotel attracted a higher class visitor with its posh rooms and private baths, and an elevator going up three floors from the lobby's marble entry. On the other end of Main Street was the Fleming Hotel, a two story structure reminiscent of New Orleans with the rooms opening up on to a gallery. At this edge of the Blue Ridge wilderness, the crossroads of the CC&O and the Southern railways, Marion, North Carolina, had no vacancies on July 15, 1916.

The next morning, Daniel Kanipe rode his horse home from services at the First Presbyterian Church. Main Street was as thick as molasses now, too muddy for his wife's carriage, and a deep mire for automobiles. More than one had to be pulled out of town by a team of mules. This day was as gray as every one of the preceding week, but the heavy mist seemed a reprieve. Kanipe didn't even wear a raincoat over his Sunday clothes. He stopped in front of the red brick Eagle Hotel.

"Charlie, you been sitting here all night?"

"Mornin' Mr. Kanipe." Charlie closed the lid of his watch and put it in the pocket of his dirty overalls. "Naw, I got me a room. No need leavin' town when there's nothin' to do at the house."

"Won't your wife be worried about you?" Kanipe crossed his arms over the saddle horn.

"Naw, she likes to be by herself. I'll head out when it dries up a bit."

"That might be next week. I've never seen such a flood."

"In the meantime, I brushed up on my poker playin'." Charlie got out his knife, picked up today's stick, leaned over his knees and commenced to whittling.

"So you won a hand or two last night?"

"Yeah, I did awright. It was a crowd of beginners. Did you take in any stranded visitors?"

"Sure did. A Mr. Duke from the Southern Power Company. This morning I loaned him a horse to check out the river where he wants to put a hydraulic plant."

"I met a Duke last night. He's a terrible poker player. I saw him ride off awhile ago. Tol' me he wanted to check on the pass to Black Mountain. He'll never make it through, and he'll be back. I'll get more of his money tonight."

"Mr. Duke didn't leave my house last night. We talked till late and then turned in."

"Hmmph. Somebody used his name then. A husky

guy, about my age."

"James Duke is almost as old as me." Kanipe dismounted. "Well, now, this has me curious." He secured Comanche to the hitching rail and entered the lobby of the hotel, a handsome establishment with dark mahogany paneling. The twenty-year-old gas lamps on the wall were now in use because the storm interfered with electric service.

At the counter, a large man with full cheeks and tiny eyes chatted with the desk clerk until Kanipe walked up and said, "Good morning, Sheriff."

"Daniel. Appreciate your hospitality to some of these travelers. About forty homes have opened up to them, and it's a good thing. My jail is crowded on account of several disputes last night."

"I'm sure Miz Polly is feeding those rascals real good."

"Ha! My wife feeds the regulars on our good china. I can't convince her otherwise. I just hope she doesn't invite some of them down to our first floor rooms."

Kanipe laughed. He knew it was a possibility for that good-hearted woman. "Sheriff, I'm glad to run into you. Seems we have a bit of a mystery here. The Case of the Stolen Name."

"Tell me 'bout it."

"I have a guest at my home named James Duke. And my buddy Charlie said he played poker last night with a gentleman of that same name."

Kanipe was interrupted by a scream. He and Sheriff Laughridge glanced upward, and at the same time headed for the stairs. On the second floor a black maid ran toward them, eyes wide, mouth twisted. "Sheriff, come quick. Mistah done hanged hisself." And she continued to wail while she escaped to share the news.

The two men entered a room's open door, stepping over scattered linen. A lean man with a mustache was suspended from the chandelier in the center of the comfortably appointed room. Underneath his dangling legs, a chair was turned over.

Kanipe felt the man's pulse and shook his head.

Sheriff Laughridge walked over to a desk where a note lay. "This here says he was sorry he lost all the company money in a poker game, and he's too ashamed to face his family." The sheriff glanced around the room. "Don't see a wallet. Or a room key."

The two men got the body down and on the bed. The sheriff examined its hands and face and then went through the clothes neatly laid in the drawers. He put the note in his pocket.

"What are you doing?" asked Kanipe.

"Detective work."

"What's to detect? There's a near empty bottle of whiskey right here. A local distillery brand."

"That's the problem. He might have passed out before he was hanged." The sheriff carefully checked an empty suitcase left in the closet and searched the pockets of a suit coat. "Wonder how much money bought a ticket to hell."

Kanipe walked to the window and pulled aside the curtain. Rain slashed against the glass.

Sheriff Laughridge said, "C'mon. I'll call Cliff to come get him, and then I'm gonna ask around."

In the lobby, the sheriff tried to ring the operator, but the phone lines were down. He wrote a message on paper and handed it to Kanipe.

"Find Cliff McCall and tell him I need him up here. He might be at the Methodist church or he might be down to his store. I suspect his undertakin' skills are taxed right now, but the hotel would be pleased to have this room vacated."

When Kanipe came out of the hotel, Charlie sat in the same spot. "Did you solve the mystery?"

"No, it got bigger. Now it's the Case of the Dead Man Hanging." Kanipe hovered over the farmer.

"You don't say." Charlie kept chewin' and spittin' and whittlin'.

"Charlie, when you were playing poker did you notice anyone suspicious? Like strangers hanging back on the edge of the crowd watching everybody, unfriendly like?"

"Besides some Cross Mill workers with new payroll to burn, most everybody was a stranger, passing through and stalled by the flood. The real money was probably in the gentleman's game at the Marianna. I can't afford to walk into that place." He snorted. "Naw, at the Eagle, it was just the regular guys aimin' to grow their holdings." He paused. "Except for the man who walked with a limp. You met him at the barber shop. Could be he deserves a second look." He kept his eyes on his whittling.

"How's that?"

"He sat in a corner with his black hat tipped down over his eyes and held his drink close. Didn't speak to nobody. Come to think of it, when that land agent lost big time and called it quits, the man in the black hat left shortly after that."

"You said he lost big time. Where did he keep his money?"

Charlie looked up into Kanipe's scowl. "In a wallet, inside his jacket pocket. He wore a suit, and I thought he was a high roller, but he was only a front man owned by the power company."

Kanipe went back inside to report to the sheriff, who had already gone out through the kitchen. He stopped at the counter. "Were you on duty when a thin man with a moustache checked in? Maybe yesterday, maybe the day before."

"Sure was. He wanted to put his satchel in the house safe on Friday, but I recommended the bank next door when he told me its value."

"So did he leave it at the bank?"

"I don't know. When I saw him again, he wasn't carrying it."

"When was that?"

"Last night, he was coming down about five and went

into the restaurant."

"Which room was he in?"

"204, Mr. Kanipe. He was the guy who hanged hisself."

"Were you here when he went up to his room?"

"No, we'd closed the lobby by then. Sir, I already told the sheriff all this."

"All right then, thanks." He pushed away from the counter.

"No problem, sir."

"One more question. How much money was in that satchel?"

"He told me five thousand dollars."

Kanipe whistled.

On Monday the rain was letting up, but the rivers plunging down the mountains were higher. Kanipe saw more townspeople out and about. He made a point to go into the Red Iron Racket dry goods store to get a few sundries. He always enjoyed chatting with Mrs. Geer, and he knew he could get an update of local news from her. She also owned the Marion Café where he and his family of twelve frequently dined.

"Daniel, so glad to see you survived this beastly weather. Such tragic news coming in from Asheville and Black Mountain. I've talked to some of the railroad men." Mrs. D.R. Geer straightened a pile of men's shirts as she talked.

"What have you heard?"

"Stories about children lashed to trees having to watch their parents swept away. Rescuers losing their lives. Farmland along the river is scrubbed clean down to the bedrock and littered with livestock, household furnishings, automobiles and what-all. The Greenlees lost their wheat crop, but they're not the only ones." She paused to take a breath. "We had to prize our mule out of quicksand with a fence rail. Silly thing was up to his belly."

"Folks will tell tales about the flood of 1916 for years to

come."

"I hear that young Mrs. Vanderbilt in Asheville stayed at the river offering coffee and sandwiches to the rescuers. And loaned her car to take folks to the hospital. She's a pip, that one."

"So have you heard anything about the mystery right across the street?"

"That sad young man hanging himself? Of course. I could write the headlines and front page for the Progress today if I had the time."

"Did you see him at all on Friday or Saturday? He was a lanky guy with a mustache."

"Not sure if I did. The downpour made it difficult to see the street, much less across it. But I did notice Charlie seemed to be in dispute with somebody late Friday afternoon. And I can't say for sure, but it seems that the hanged man fits the bill."

Kanipe thought for a minute. "Where was that?"

"Outside the Eagle."

"Did you see a stranger with a black hat this weekend?"

"Lots of them. Before you went into the barber shop, you about knocked down somebody wearing a black hat." She raised an eyebrow at him.

"He felt obliged to comment on my military record. I won't argue with ignorance."

She looked out the window at the increased activity on the plank sidewalk. "When did Charlie get a pocket watch?"

"Probably won it last night at the Eagle."

"Maybe he'll clear up his account with me. I better mention it today before he gets into another game."

Daniel Kanipe glanced her way. "Does he owe a lot?"

"Not a large amount, but he's not the farmer his grandpappy was."

"Do you think he'll sell out to the power company?"

"He oughta, but I don't know. Pride goeth before a fall,

the Good Book says."

Kanipe put his hat back on. "I better be movin' on, Miz Geer. When this rain stops, me and Annie will be around to celebrate with your world famous pot roast."

"I might not have any left. No tellin' how long our tourists are going to be stuck here. Mind ya, I'm not complainin', but with no electricity, I have to go back to refrigerating with ice. And that's a mean trick, that is."

"The flood's been a boon to some." He saw McDowell County's top lawman slowly making his way toward the courthouse. Kanipe saluted Mrs. Geer and headed out into the drizzle to mount his horse. Comanche seemed glad to be on the move but the mud sucking at his hooves slowed his pace toward the sheriff's office. Kanipe tied him off next to a roan and went inside, stepping right into a domestic dispute.

"Now, Jay, it don't make no sense you sittin' around in them wet clothes. You just come on back and get dried off. You won't be no good to nobody if you get sick." The pudgy woman had her fists on her hips.

"Polly, it's July. I'm not going to get sick." The sheriff looked up as Kanipe walked into the office. "Daniel, help me out here."

"I know better than to argue with a pretty lady," said Kanipe. "Where have you been, anyway?"

"I was talking with the folks targeted by the power company. The holdouts. Didn't learn anything I didn't know already. Southern Power wants to buy land to put under water, and the farmers don't want to sell." He removed a boot and dribbled out a muddy stream into the metal waste can. "Polly, I believe I might like some coffee. Daniel?"

"Sounds good."

Polly fussed and muttered out the door and down the hallway.

"Did you get a name on the deceased?" Kanipe sat in one of the oak chairs by the window looking out on Court Street that oozed downhill like a river of mud. The horses huddled, heads together.

"Yeah, the phones might be down, but the telegraph works. His name is John Vickers, with relatives in this county."

"One of our own then, raised in this area. Southern Power isn't run by ignorant men. They chose a representative who knows how to talk to country people who don't trust outsiders."

"Daniel, you're talking like a detective. I might have to deputize you since Miz Polly doesn't want me to go out in the rain." The men shared a laugh.

"Jay, I heard that," said Polly as she backed into the door she had left ajar. She held a tray with a sterling silver carafe and two cups and saucers. And a plate of molasses cookies.

"This isn't a social occasion," grumbled her husband.

Kanipe hastened to take the tray and place it on the corner of a sideboard piled with papers.

"It isn't every day that we have the honor of seeing Mr. Kanipe. A little rain shouldn't keep us from remembering our manners, dear." With pinky held high, Polly poured coffee and offered cream and sugar to Kanipe, which he declined.

"Lord help us," said the sheriff, but he smiled at his wife and winked at Daniel when her back was turned.

"Up until now I thought the deceased was a stranger. Do we know any of his kin?"

"Better than that. We know Miz Perry. John was raised at Elhanan Orphanage."

The two men agreed on a plan of action. When they met later that afternoon in dry clothing and on fresh horses, they headed south from the sheriff's office in the courthouse and then cut over on Morehead Street. Swirling dark clouds above Mt. Ida continued to drench the area.

"Mattie Perry is a woman of prayer. We might ask that she pray for the rain to stop," suggested Kanipe.

"One thing at a time. I want to solve this murder."

"She's a remarkable woman, Miz Perry is. Claims God healed her of all infirmities. Her folks were missionaries, and she dearly wanted to go to China. Said it wasn't to be."

"What kind of infirmities did she have?" Sheriff Laughridge asked.

"She was blind." Daniel looked over at his companion to make sure he had heard him.

"Hmmm."

Sheriff Laughridge and Daniel Kanipe hitched their horses and walked up the steps to the front entry of the unusual three story orphanage.

"Looks like a Victorian mated with an Arab. The baby turrets are of different architecture," muttered the sheriff. He pointed to the edge of the clearing. "Don't know why they haven't cleaned up that mess from the dormitory fire two years ago."

"Maybe they use the lumber for heating this old place."

"Seems I remember this was planned as a 125-room hotel with lots of extras suggested by a passel of folks, but nobody was happy and construction was abandoned."

"No matter what it looks like, it was an ideal place for Miz Perry. She's done a good work here for more than ten years, giving these kids a home and education they wouldn't otherwise have," said Kanipe.

"I know. She preaches tolerance and forgiveness," said the sheriff.

"Not always practical, is it?"

A neatly dressed young woman greeted them at the door and escorted them to a parlor where they awaited the arrival of the dynamic Mattie Perry. She swept into the room with efficient stride swirling her skirt.

Miss Perry came right to the point. "Gentlemen. I am honored to have you call upon me. I trust you are not here to discuss a problem about my children."

"I'll hasten to explain this does not involve Elhanan. We're looking for information that will close the file on a grievous situation."

"Please don't beat around the bush, Sheriff. Why are you here?" Miss Perry stood as tall as five feet allowed.

"Sunday afternoon, the body of a young man was found swinging from a chandelier in one of the rooms at the Eagle Hotel."

"Oh Lord." Miss Perry put steepled forefingers to her lips. "This is extremely serious. Gentlemen, please have a seat." Suddenly she looked her fifty years.

Daniel Kanipe stepped in. "Excuse the Sheriff for being so abrupt, madam. We didn't come to shock you."

"I heard gossip."

"We want to ask if you know anything about the victim, John Vickers."

Mattie Perry's eyes widened. "I was hoping I didn't, the poor soul." She looked across the formal room with its heavily carved English manor furniture. The windows were draped with dark velvet, drawn against the storm. The dampness of two weeks of rain in July elevated the humidity. A fire in the hearth would have seemed appropriate.

The sheriff gave her a few moments to collect her thoughts before he asked. "What can you tell us, Miz Perry?"

"John was a resident here for several years. He was a very bright boy whose parents were deceased. No close relatives were willing or able to care for a ten-year-old, although he had a brother taken in by an uncle in the nearby Dysartsville community. A few times they came to visit or take John to their home for a weekend. I fear that only increased his feeling of abandonment. He was a sensitive child, prone to periods of silence. One day he just left. He was sixteen. There was little we could do." She looked at Kanipe, her expression showing great distress.

"You did your best, Miz Mattie," soothed Kanipe. "You don't need our forgiveness."

"I ask that you understand John, not myself." Mattie Perry glanced at her folded hands. "I concluded that this young boy was not naturally attracted to our young ladies. At the time, that seemed a blessing because we endured continual intrigue among our teenage residents. John became very good friends with a young man we had hired as a dormitory assistant."

"So you witnessed a compromising situation between them?"

"No, I did not. They developed a close friendship that brought joy to their faces when they were together. That is all that I witnessed. Soon after that, the young assistant went to Raleigh to attend classes in theater arts, and John disappeared without a word. I was left to apologize to his family for his abrupt departure. But he was of an age to accept an adult role."

"How long ago was that?"

"Seven years ago, I believe."

"That seems to be the right age of our victim," said Kanipe.

"And how does that help your investigation?"

Sheriff Laughridge stood. He gazed around the formal room. A desk in the corner held a ledger placed squarely in the center. A side table to a wingback chair held a large Bible. "Miz Perry, I know you did your best by this young man. His choices do not reflect on this institution. Although there is a chance they may have caused his death."

"You're not passing judgment on him, are you Sheriff? I think that is out of your jurisdiction." Mattie Perry drew herself up to an indignant posture before turning, tight lipped, to escort them to the door. The two men followed without comment.

As he mounted his horse, Sheriff Laughridge remarked, "Most early deaths are caused by bad choices, ma'am."

"Sheriff, if John's body is not claimed by next of kin, I would be proud to provide a final resting place here at Elhanan." She stood stiffly.

The sheriff touched the brim of his hat, and the two

men rode off.

Back at the Eagle Hotel's restaurant, they attempted to discuss their next move over cups of soup and homemade bread. Kanipe found it hard to put the hotel death of a stranger in context with the destruction experienced by neighbors. He and Sheriff Laughridge sat in silence listening to the stories swirling from table to table shared among friends and stranded rail travelers.

Eighteen workers were lost when the Mt Holly bridge had been swept away by a monstrous river. East of Marion, the cotton mills on the Catawba were destroyed. West of town the passenger depot in Asheville was underwater. Two men drowned trying to get food to the marooned guests in the Glen Rock Hotel. Newspaper reporters thickly populated the restaurant, interviewing survivors and writing articles about tragedy. The rain may have stopped but major damage was being revealed. And the rivers were cresting.

"Sheriff Laughridge, perhaps we need to identify the man that Charlie saw follow Vickers."

"I understood the man left the room, no proof that he was following anybody."

"Maybe so, but I think it needs to be checked out. There's also the matter of the five thousand dollars."

"The bank confirmed that they have the satchel in their vault. That is no longer an issue."

"Then why did the note suggest a mismanagement of company funds?"

"Perhaps Mr. Vickers was entrusted with more than five thousand dollars and some of it was lost at the gaming tables. He may have had more than one weakness. When Mr. Duke arrives back at your home, request that he determine exactly how much company money Mr. Vickers was carrying."

"I expect him tonight."

"Good. I have to confess it's difficult to concentrate on this hanging with tragedy all around us, and more on the way. I put Anderson in charge of a rescue operation up near Altapass. They had twenty-two inches of rain in twenty four hours. Little Switzerland is cut off by surrounding high creeks. The locals know what to do, but this is the height of tourist season." Frown lines in the sheriff's face were deeper. His eyes topped dark shadows. "I apologize for leaning so heavily on you, Daniel."

"I understand. I'm happy to be of service. At my age, there is not much I can do but ask questions and carry water to the troops."

"Don't need no water, Daniel." The sheriff managed a slight smile. "I'd better go check on my jail. Miz Polly might decide to pardon all prisoners if they promise to help."

"Not a bad idea, actually." Kanipe paid the waiter who stood nearby, no doubt hoping to get new customers at this table.

The sheriff pushed his chair back and was immediately approached by a passing constituent bent on conversation.

Kanipe took the moment to make his way through the crowd that had gathered. He waved at the Eagle's owner on his way out. Another happy businessman.

The chairs outside the hotel were occupied by strangers. The warmth of the sun generated steam rising off the thick puddles. Kanipe removed his coat and tied it behind his saddle. "Okay, boy, we're going to the barn." He patted his horse and gathered the reins. When he swung into the saddle and turned Comanche's head toward home, he noticed Charlie in front of the bank within the shade of a chestnut tree.

"Your woman is going to run off if you don't get yourself to home, Charlie."

"Truth is, she already has." The scruffy farmer kept on whittling then spit into a red clay puddle.

Kanipe dismounted, tied his horse to a hitching post, and squatted next to a man who, by country vernacular, was his neighbor.

"What happened?"

"Not much to tell. I done run outta luck. While I's up here making a few dollars, that agent man was at my farm talking my wife into selling our land."

"I thought it belonged to you and your family."

"It did, but the missus always thought I'd gamble it away. A few months ago she started in on me 'cause I'd been drinking a bit. So to prove I wouldn't lose the farm at poker, I sold it to her legal like for one dollar. Thought I was doing right by her."

Kanipe didn't know what to say. So he was silent. Comanche stomped the red clay spattering mud up on the walk in front of them.

"Saturday night I went home, proud of my pocket full of money, and found an empty house and a note tellin' the tale. That power company agent paid her a thousand cash for land worth ten times that. So I come back to town and go straight to his room, and we have words. I already told him the day before I wasn't selling, so I was madder 'n hell." Charlie coughed a bit, and slid his chew to another corner in his cheek. "But he was alive when I left his room. He had a full bottle of whiskey there and offered me a drink, sorry-like. I declined. He said he had to please others if he hoped to survive. He said it was nothing personal." Charlie snorted. "Maybe not to him. But it was to me."

"Did you see a wallet or a room key?"

Charlie paused, looked out across Main Street and spat. "Yeah, yeah, they was on the bureau."

"Then what did you do?"

"Only thing I could. I got me a drink and sat in on a poker game. I might have had a few more drinks till I got to winnin'. I stayed late."

"And you had a room?"

"Naw, I slept in the livery stable. I expect the sheriff to get around to askin' me questions. He probably thinks I killed him, but I didn't. I'll swear it on the Good Book. Maybe you could kinda tell him my side."

"So why did you stay around last night?"

"I was tryin' to make a little money, now that I don't have no house. And besides, it was still rainin' hard."

"Don't you have stock at home? You might could sell some of it."

"Sold my cows to get through the winter."

"Don't know what to tell you, Charlie." Kanipe stood and stretched his long legs.

"It's a mess, shor nuff."

"Tell you what. You take ole Comanche back to the barn for me and get him comfortable. Then come pick me up at the sheriff's office with my black mare and buggy. My sons are grown, and I could use some extry help around the place."

Charlie looked up in surprise. "Thank you, Mr. Kanipe. Thank you kindly. I won't let you down." He jumped up, startling the horse who jerked his head away.

"Ahh, Charlie. Comanche doesn't take to strangers. You'll have to walk him home." Kanipe grinned.

"Yessir. That's okay. We'll get to be friends." He patted the horse's shoulder and crooned to him. When Charlie tugged on the bridle, Comanche followed him through the puddles.

Kanipe called out, "Charlie, what about that pocket watch you won?"

Charlie turned around. "I still have it, right here. You want to take it?" Charlie removed the timepiece from his overalls bib pocket.

Kanipe saw that the watch was not as valuable as he thought, but it did have an inscription. "You mind if I show this to the sheriff?"

Charlie hesitated. "If you think that's best, okay then."

Sludging across Main Street towards the courthouse and then down to the back where the sheriff's office was located, Kanipe contemplated the case of the dead man hanging. He scraped his boots as best he could in respect to

Miz Polly and then opened the scarred door, jangling a bell when he entered. The sheriff was not at his desk, but his wife soon appeared.

"Mr. Kanipe, I'm glad you're helping Jay. This has been a busy weekend for sure. So many people with problems, I don't hardly know where to carry extry meals. And now we don't have city water. Don't know what we'll do."

"The folks of Marion are accustomed to handling crises. We'll manage. I'll share some good news. At the Eagle, there was talk of the McGhee infant riding down the river on his mattress which eventually lodged in tree branches. When the floodwaters went down, his parents found him alive."

"What a blessing!" Her eyes filled with tears. "I shouldn't carry on so. I've heard tell of so many mountain folks losing their people." Polly motioned toward a ladder backed chair. "You rest yourself now, and I'll get you some coffee."

"I can wait outside if you don't think he'll be long. That way I can soak up a little sun. I forgot how good that feels."

A half hour later, the sheriff ambled down the sidewalk lined with large maple trees. "Been waitin' long? Come on in." Announced by the door bell, they trudged into the office. The sheriff called out to Polly that he was back and then plopped down in his big rolling chair behind the desk. He tossed his hat on his paperwork and put his head back. "Whew. I'm done in."

Daniel let him have a moment of silence, knowing that his cup of coffee would soon be there. Soon it was, along with Polly's cheerful banter and a pat on the shoulder. "Mr. Kanipe, I brought a cup for you, too. Black. We're running low on supplies."

"Thank you, ma'am. Much obliged."

The sheriff held his silence until she left the room. "Well, I solved one mystery today. The heavy man Charlie said called hisself Duke was found this morning drowned in a collapsed railroad tunnel. He was probably seeking shelter.

He had a hefty wallet with him belonging to John Vickers. I'd say we have our killer."

"Maybe. Maybe not," said Kanipe. "That just proves he stole a wallet."

"So, what's your story, Daniel?" The sheriff slowly raised his head to look at his guest detective. And he heard about Charlie's sad tale of betrayal and confrontation. "What's that in your hand?"

Kanipe held up the chain dangling the pocket watch taken from the poker game. "Charlie told me he won this from a man in a black hat, the same fellow he saw earlier in the day who left the game room after Vickers. Charlie noticed him limping upstairs at the Eagle when he hustled out the door to go home. Charlie was in a hurry to tell his wife about the money he won. But she had gone. So Charlie rode back to the hotel and had words with Vickers over his grandpappy's farm, in his mind, stolen by the power company. Then Charlie jumped into another game to assuage his bruised ego."

"But Vickers wasn't killed until later because he opened the door for a man who called himself Duke. He stole the wallet. I think he killed the agent," pronounced the sheriff.

"My theory is that Mr. Black Hat built up his courage or rage, and it was later that night, that he went back to Vickers' room to kill him. He stole the key on his first visit. By then Vickers had consumed most of the whiskey because he was in big trouble with his company. He had to replace the money that he lost in the poker game. The money he had left was in his wallet. And it was stolen by Duke, not his boss James Duke, just a guy who might have used the name to get in the door. He spent the night at the Fleming."

"Why didn't Vickers report the theft to the hotel staff?"

"He wasn't supposed to have that money in the room. He was using it to gamble, so he had a lot of explaining to do to the company. It was easier to drink and complain to an old friend."

"You think this phantom in a black hat was an old

90

friend?"

"I think a few questions might be in order."

"We already asked the people staying on second floor if they'd seen anything. And they hadn't."

"We asked about seeing something unusual in the afternoon and early evening. If Black Hat made a second visit, after the wallet was stolen, it could have been later that night. I think he had a key to the room. Somebody might have heard arguing or scraping noises."

Sheriff Laughridge laid his head back again. "Well, I don't have time right now. First I have to look into a shooting at the Marianna that involves a county commissioner."

"Did you see the initials engraved on this watch: 'JV to AB'? I don't know what this could tell us, but the desk clerk at the Eagle said they didn't have anyone registered by a name with AB."

"You don't think Charlie did it, do you?" Sheriff Laughridge smiled, his eyes shut. "Well now. We got the money back for the power company. The thief was caught, drowned in his sins. And the rest was lost to a poker game." The sheriff raised his head. "Some people just live their lives askin' for trouble. Why don't we just let it be?"

"I might be new at this, but I think we owe it to Vickers to investigate as best we can. If you don't mind Sheriff, I'm gonna talk to Miz Mattie again. To get the name of that theater fellow who was Vickers' friend."

"I don't want to sound un-Christian, Daniel, but if Vickers was involved in some kind of perverted relationship, I don't have time for him. I have too many innocent God-fearing folks around here who are in trouble, and I need to watch out after them first."

There was an uncomfortable silence.

"You're not making a judgment on another are you, Sheriff? We all wrestle our demons of greed, lust and excess, but every man has worth."

"I'm not going to look into it further. I could arrest

Charlie, but I don't know where to put him."

Daniel Kanipe considered his friend's position. "The way I see it, we all have a small role in a big picture. At Little Big Horn, my assignment was to ride back to deliver a message to the supply train. I did that. Don't deserve a medal, don't deserve condemnation. I did my job."

Through the window, Kanipe saw Charlie arrive in his buggy. "I talked to James Duke. He said Vickers had eight thousand in company money."

The sheriff said, "Sounds right. There was five thousand still in the bank vault, one thousand to Charlie's wife…"

"Ex-wife soon. And the rest he gambled away or had in his wallet that was stolen and recovered."

"I'd say you did a fair amount of detective work, Daniel. I'm gonna double your wages."

"No thank you, Sheriff. I'm gonna go back to farming." Kanipe opened the door and motioned to Charlie.

Charlie came in with hat in hand, wide eyed. "Got ole Comanche taken care of, curried and fed."

"Thanks, Charlie," said Kanipe. "I want you to tell the sheriff about winning this pocket watch."

Charlie gripped the brim of his hat and turned it round and round. "Well sir, I was recovering some of my good spirits when a man wearing a black hat joined my table. He had a whiskey in his hand and a frown on his face."

"When was this, Charlie?" asked the Sheriff.

"Sadiddy evenin' after dinner time. Don't know exactly."

The sheriff nodded for him to continue.

"This fella sat there quiet for a couple rounds and a couple more whiskeys. Then he started muttering to hisself and pitching his bets hard. Another player said 'You might consider a more relaxing pursuit, friend.' And ole black hat snapped, 'Not looking for friendship from a man who would sell his soul for a dollar'."

"What do you think he was talking about?"

"Nothing to do with poker, so I didn't worry it." Charlie appeared to study the framed credentials on the wall. "Nobody spoke for awhile 'cept about the game. A couple players folded. Black hat was losing but he stayed in, and the more he drank the bigger his words got. Like he said something about he was owed because he didn't rat out a confidant." Charlie shrugged. "And the more he lost, the madder he got. In that last hand, where he threw his watch into the pot 'cause he'd run out of money, he ranted about worthless gifts. And the "perfidy of the capitalist." I kinda liked that. It reminded me of that agent man who stole my land." Charlie nodded, seeming to remember the scene. "His mind weren't in the game. And after he lost, he slammed his chair backwards and limped out of the room."

The sheriff eyed him hard. "What did you do then, Charlie?"

"I took my winnings and went to the livery to get my horse." Charlie grinned sheepishly. "To tell the truth, I must have passed out in the stall with him cause that's whur I woke up on Sunday. With this here watch. I didn't kill nobody, Sheriff. And that's the Good Book truth."

"Didn't say you did, Charlie." The Sheriff stood and stretched his neck and back. You better get Mr. Kanipe home now. I think he's tired of detective work. And I can't say as I blame him."

Two days later, Mr. Kanipe and his house guest Mr. Duke followed the undertaker to Elhanan, alongside the remains of John Vickers, being transported in the county's first hearse. It had been overly used in the past week. They took the lane that passed the orphanage and ended in the grove of sourwoods and cedar trees surrounding a private cemetery. After the burial, Duke rode off and Kanipe approached Miz Perry.

"If I may, madam, I'd like a word with you."

"This is as good a time as any, Mr. Kanipe. What can I help you with now?" Mattie Perry's mouth was a straight line, her gaze direct.

"My friend showed me this watch that has initials engraved in the lid. I thought I would ask you if you know of a gentleman with initials of AB?"

Miz Perry sighed. "Yes, Mr. Kanipe, I do." She looked over his shoulder at Mt. Ida, lush and green in the sunshine. "Alfred Baldwin was the dormitory assistant who took up with John Vickers and later went east to be involved with a theater group. It's not a coincidence that his watch is here in town, is it? At the same time that his friend was killed."

"I think not. But I wonder about that friendship. I had assumed the older boy compromised the younger. I now consider it may have been the reverse."

"I think you may be correct." As Kanipe walked Miz Perry to her buggy where a young student held the reins of her horse, she said "Sir, I have a confession to make. A sin of omission, because I didn't tell you everything I knew at your last visit. Alfred came to see me Saturday afternoon. As a journalist. He wanted to write an article about Elhanan surviving the flood. He thought since he once lived here, he had an edge over the competition. I told him the story was up in the mountains, among the witnesses. Not around here. He became quite belligerent. He claimed his position was in jeopardy, and if he didn't write an article, he would be fired. Mr. Kanipe, I couldn't relate second-hand stories to help him save his job. He needed to do his own work. He said he had protected a student's secret for years, and it was time for retribution. I told him I didn't owe him anything. He left angry."

"So it sounds like his next attempt for an article was from his old buddy Vickers who didn't want to be quoted for fear of losing his job. Alfred was trying to get a story angle about the Southern Power Company taking over farm land to build a dam. Alfred felt he was owed because he kept quiet about their former relationship. This may have been about revenge."

"Alfred Baldwin had a weak character, and no self-motivation. He wanted to find an easy road and blame others for his failures. John was consumed by guilt and drank to forgive himself. Those two certainly brought out the worst in each other. Alcohol brought them together and destroyed them both."

Daniel looked back at the fresh grave. "In the wake of the storm with resources stretched thin, John's killer may go unpunished."

"Only by man, Mr. Kanipe. I doubt we will ever know the whole truth, but Mr. Baldwin's family was stockholders in Marion's textile industry. They will meet his earthly needs. I will pray for his soul."

Kanipe said, "In my lifetime, I've observed that everybody has a part to play. Even though we might not be able to see the whole story, there is an end. And when I face mine, I aim to know I did my part the best I could." He helped her into her buggy, next to the young driver ready to take her home. "For now, I'm headed back to my farm."

Miz Perry's smile followed him.

Georgia Ruth lives in the historic gold mining foothills of North Carolina where she records and shares the real stories of neighbors who can trace their roots back to Wales, Ireland, and Scotland. Her website is http://georgiaruthwrites.us. Georgia is a member of Sisters in Crime and the Short Mystery Fiction Society. She has fiction published online and in print. All of the dialogue and situations portrayed in fiction are either products of her imagination or are events used fictitiously. "The Blue Ridge Wreath" was published by Stupefying Stories *online last year. It will soon be available in print. "Dear Courtney" was published by Buddhapuss Ink in* Mystery Times Ten 2013. *A new anthology will be released soon by Wildside Press, and Georgia's story "The Mountain Top" will be included. Her former careers in family restaurant management and retail sales provide an endless resource for fictional characters and conflicts.*

Sputter from the Flames

By Kristin Roahrig

Caterina had lived in Rome all her life and had never yet grown used to the summer's heat. Ever since the Pope had left the city in 1305, Rome had been slowly decaying. She stood in the shade of a tree in her courtyard, brushing the sweat off her face with an old cloth. Her daughter Beatrice stood near her by the gate, oblivious to the heat. She was supposed to be mending old fabrics, but Caterina knew she was watching the people passing. Without having to see the unfinished fabric that should have long been completed, Caterina knew what her daughter was doing, especially when one of the passing people was a handsome boy. Her daughter would lean forward by the gate, moving her hips in a way that showed her figure to its best advantage. Beatrice resembled Caterina much at the same age. Her hair was the shiny darkness that was highlighted with red and an olive complexion. But surely, Caterina thought, she hadn't as a young girl stalked every man that passed and posed her body in such a way. She would have to keep a careful eye on Beatrice.

To do this, she set down her bowl and joined her daughter at the gate. The view of the street wasn't ugly, for all its flushed out appearance. Their city may have been the center of an empire once, and the apostolic seat, but the Pope had fled to France years before. And Rome could hardly now be considered one of the great cities. Buildings crumbled and were never restored. The pavement on streets cracked, grass growing through the gaps.

There was little semblance of law in the city. Bands of marauders were easily found. They often hid near the cities gates to steal from pilgrims who traveled to the holy place. It wasn't unusual to find a body in an alley or the river. Protection fell to each neighborhood.

In one of the old homes, Caterina had seen a mural on the wall as was popular before Christian times. The piece was faded and chipped in many places and thin dirt covered it. Still, one could see the lounges and a table with fruit piled on plates. A woman's figure on a lounge showed though her hands were gone, leaving two holes in its place. Rome now resembled the mural. Chipped in many places and faded from what it was yet through the dirt and broken pieces there was some semblance of what they once were.

The pilgrims currently were their only source of trade. There was no reason to come to Rome except for religious purposes. That was how her husband Gustavo made his money. He sold fake holy relics to the passing pilgrims. A bit of the cross Our Savior died on, which was actually the cross that came from scraps of wood she bought. Or a piece of the cloth of one's saint of choice. Little pieces that he sold for exorbitant prices. He had a gift for presentation, so he was able to draw pilgrims from other so named relic traders. With the good trade, they had one of the best houses in the neighborhood. Granted, a back room was closed off due to the roof falling in a month before. But despite the roof, their home was better than most of the other buildings on the street.

Once she asked, when they were younger, if there wouldn't be a retribution for the false sale of relics.

"There are plenty of bandits waiting outside the city gates to take their money. We're just giving them a better chance of survival by taking their money ourselves," he had said. "Besides, how else will we eat?"

Caterina remembered how his sister Julianna laughed

when he said those words. She was younger than him by many years, only a little older than their daughter Beatrice. Three years after their marriage, his parents died and they took Julianna in. The girl became a second daughter to Caterina; a daughter she missed now that Julianna was dead.

At the thought of Julianna, Caterina said, "We should go light a candle for Julianna."

Beatrice jerked her head around, simultaneously trying to watch the street and listen to her mother.

"We can't light a candle for her," Beatrice said. "Not for a suicide."

Caterina wished her daughter hadn't used that word. It might be true but she found herself unable to believe it. Julianna was one who appeared to always carry a radiance within herself and never showed morose tendencies.

"That doesn't matter," Caterina said.

"She's damned, Mother. No amount of candles will help her."

"Beatrice, lighting a candle won't hurt you."

The family had each reacted in different ways to Julianna's death. While her husband accepted her death as he accepted all else in this city, Beatrice had quieted, never saying a word. It was only recently she had become more the way she was before the death.

"I don't understand any of this," Beatrice said.

"She had no troubles," Caterina agreed.

"They could have easily been fixed..." Beatrice cut herself off, her face reddening.

"She had troubles I wasn't aware of?"

Beatrice kept her mouth shut in a thin line. She tried returning to her work that she given scant attention to only moments earlier. Caterina took the fabrics away from her.

"What troubles?" she asked.

"None that the rest of us here don't have," Beatrice said.

She was lying. Caterina couldn't always tell a liar, but

she recognized when Beatrice lied. Caterina had already seen every useless trick her daughter provided to keep her mother from guessing the truth.

"Would you rather speak to your father about this?" Caterina asked.

"No, no," Beatrice said hurriedly. "I suppose it's no longer a secret anyway if one is dead."

"What secret?" Caterina asked.

She tried keeping the impatience from her voice. Sometimes her daughter could take a mountain's age to tell a story.

"Julianna was with child," Beatrice said.

"She-what?"

It was a good thing Caterina had already set her bowl down earlier. Otherwise she would have dropped it, scattering it in pieces.

"She was going to have a baby," Beatrice explained.

"I know what with child means," Caterina snapped. "Are you sure?"

"She told me."

"Who's the father?" Caterina asked.

"I don't know," Beatrice said.

"What do you mean you don't know? Didn't she ever tell you? Or did you see her with anyone at least?"

"No. Well, there was a man she was with once, a cousin to the family" Beatrice said.

"What were they doing? How were they behaving towards each other? Is there anything in particular you noticed about him? And what's his name?"

The questions were tumbling from Caterina in her haste to understand what her daughter had just told her about Julianna. If Beatrice announced she found a donkey with three horns, she wouldn't have been more surprised than by the news of Julianna's pregnancy. Caterina didn't know why she should be surprised; a pregnancy was not an unusual occurrence whether the girl was married or not, but surprised she was.

"I don't quite remember his name. Ludovico, Luciano, or something of that sort. He was very handsome," Beatrice said.

Caterina sighed impatiently. There could be a reason found to Julianna's death with this man, however remote that might seem at present. And the only thing her daughter remembered was that the man was handsome. Surely Caterina wasn't so silly at her age. Was she?

"Have you ever seen this man before?" Caterina asked.

"Only the one time," Beatrice said.

"And?"

"And what?" Beatrice asked.

"And what else was there about him that you remember so well? What were they doing?"

"Talking," Beatrice said.

"About what?" Caterina asked.

"I don't know, I was too far away. They spoke for a good while. Then Julianna saw me watching her and walked away," Beatrice said.

Beatrice pointed to a home that was a few yards from them. The dwelling was where Bachio lived with his wife and children; two daughters and one son. Caterina didn't know them well and preferred to keep it that way. Bachio was in a constant argument with anyone he came across.

As if hearing Beatrice speaking of them, a shout was heard from his home: Bachio yelling at his son. Looking over to his place, she saw him taking a hold of his son by the scruff of his neck and telling him that the room wasn't to be used as a pissing chamber and to do his business out of it. Caterina sighed, wishing circumstances would take the whole family to a different city. Preferably one that was in another country.

"Does the man live there?" Caterina asked.

"I don't know. I've seen him in the courtyard behind their house. I was able to peek through the wall when no one was watching," Beatrice said.

Caterina should have reprimanded her for spying, but was too curious to find out more information. Instead she pressed more questions to her daughter. Beatrice didn't have anything to tell. Caterina could hardly believe Julianna would have something to do with that family. Beatrice was answering truthfully, but her eyes kept shifting to the ground. Her daughter balanced on the balls of her feet in the manner she did whenever she wanted to leave. There was no reason for her daughter wanting to leave her place by the gate. How else could she watch the street then? She had told the truth but kept a piece to herself, a part Caterina hadn't asked.

"In your opinion, what do you think he was to Julianna?" Caterina asked.

"A good friend?" Beatrice suggested.

"The truth, Beatrice."

"She was carrying his child? Why are you so interested in him?" Beatrice asked.

There were many reasons Caterina was interested in this man. Thoughts raced through her mind. Each piece scrambled without making sense. How did such a thing escape her notice? Did Julianna commit suicide because of the child? Or what if the father of the child killed her? Caterina latched onto this possibility, no matter how slight. When she spoke this out loud, Beatrice only shook her head.

The next day Caterina continued thinking about the possibility that Julianna might not have killed herself. Since Julianna's death, she had been haunted by the knowledge Julianna's soul was cat out beyond God's grace and shoved into eternal hell and damnation. Whenever this fear crept into her mind, she would recall holding the little girl that Julianna once had been in her arms, never imagining such an ends for the girl. She was murdered by the hands of the baby's father or someone who didn't want the child. It was a small chance but one Caterina couldn't shake away. Julianna might have been murdered instead, and not damned. If murdered, Caterina intended to find out. Julianna's suicide was never far from Caterina's mind. She felt that however slim the possibility was, she had to set out to prove it was a murder rather than suicide. Her mind wouldn't accept the thought that Julianna's soul was damned. But what she wanted most of all was the truth. What was the truth behind Julianna's death?

Caterina didn't consult her husband on this. There was no need for Gustavo to know of the baby at this time. She decided to see Giovanni. Each neighborhood had an organization of sorts set up to try keeping the violence somewhat under control. Giovanni was the one in her neighborhood whom people went to have disputes settled or called for when they were robbed. As anyone else in the district would do, she went to him.

At the door to Giovanni's home, she saw a hand that belonged to a thief, along with a tongue that was from a slanderer and murderer nailed to his door. Giovanni nailed such relics from those he had to deal with as caution for any stranger who considered doing harm to his neighborhood. She didn't find him at his home, and was told by a servant he had gone to one of the buildings by the convent of San Lorenzo only a half hour before. She hurried straight to there, taking care there were no factions marauding through the streets looking for trouble.

She dodged the people and animals. Soon she reached the convent. Birgitta, a woman from Sweden whom some claimed to be holy, was standing outside her usual place beside the convent. She was making her predictions to anyone who'd listen. She stepped into Caterina's path, taking her arm.

"You appear in great distress my friend," Birgitta said. "But do not worry, for the time will come soon when Rome will no longer be a wasteland. The Pope will return, and Rome will once again be a city to be proud to call one's own. I know, for Mary came to me and said-"

Caterina pulled her arm from Birgitta's grasp. She heard these predictions so much, she wished one of the Popes would return from France simply so the woman would quit following her down the street every time Caterina stepped in it.

She searched through the faces in the crowd until she spotted Giovanni in front of a house a few feet away from where she stood. He wasn't a large man, but had a solid built that gave the appearance of strength. His face looked perpetually tanned, as if he been in the sun too long at one point. It was impossible to tell his age; his face looked neither young nor old. More timeless, weathered, similar to the stones of the broken statues of the gods and goddesses people no longer believed in.

Bachio was already standing by him. His hands were gesturing widely and his mouth moving even faster. Giovanni only nodded occasionally, watching the crowds. He looked to be paying the man's words as much mind as anyone in the neighborhood did, which was very little.

When Caterina moved closer, she heard the conversation.

"You need to do something; I have witnesses," Bachio was saying. "I knew the man was coming to beat me, so I stationed a witness to see it."

"So you let this person beat you, then?" Giovanni asked.

"Yes."

Caterina thought that was one of the more idiotic things she'd heard Bachio say. Evidently Giovanni believed the same, for he only told Bachio he would look into it later. Bachio began trying to argue, but Caterina interrupted. She didn't intend to wait all day while Bachio complained of injuries he probably deserved.

"I need to speak with you," Caterina told Giovanni.

"Wait until I'm done, woman," Bachio said.

"No, you've been standing here long enough," Caterina said.

Caterina could bully just as well as Bachio when she

needed. Her straightforwardness helped get better deals on the purchase of supplies her husband needed to create his "relics". Better deals than even he was able to do, despite the silver-tongued ways that sold his items so well.

"No, you wait--" Bachio began to say.

Giovanni interrupted, stepping between Caterina and Bachio.

"As I said, I'll consider what you've said. There is nothing more I can do at this moment. I'll let you know if I need anything else from you," Giovanni said.

Bachio stared at him a long moment before stepping back and leaving.

"What can I do for you?" he asked Caterina.

"I need you to look into a death," Caterina said.

"A death in the city? Which one?"

The ironic humor was not lost on Caterina. Normally she wouldn't have minded the humor, but today she was in no mood for anything, humor, idiots, or otherwise.

"My husband's sister, Julianna," Caterina said.

"The suicide?"

"I want you to look into her death. I'm willing to pay, of course."

"It was a suicide; there is nothing further I can find about it. She died by her own hand," Giovanni said.

"I'll pay you well," Caterina continued.

"There is nothing for you to find about her," he said.

"I don't care. Losing her was like losing my child. And I learned something that may prove otherwise. I will pay good money. And more, if my husband doesn't learn of this."

"Very well," Giovanni sighed. "How was she found again when she died?"

"On her bed, with an empty cup. There were pieces of wolfsbane mixed in it, making the drink poisonous."

"I'll see what I can do. I warn you, I'll find nothing."

Caterina nodded and left him, certain she made the right decision. She would learn who killed Julianna. When she discovered who, she wasn't certain what she would do with the information.

Leaving the square she heard the familiar words of Birgitta saying, "The virgin has spoken to me. The Pope will return to Rome, and when he does there will be salvation for the city."

A few days passed, and there was no word from Giovanni. She spent more time than usual out in the yard, always watching Bachio's family. Julianna was once seen with a stranger there. Caterina couldn't help but wonder. She never saw his two daughters, instead watching Bachio's son more than anyone else. The young man who had barely left boyhood behind slinked around his own home as if he were a burglar instead of a member of the family.

She was becoming anxious and impatient. Even her husband, who never noticed anything that didn't have to do with his relics or food, noticed her new-founded interest in the family.

"Why do you keep spying on our neighbors?" he asked one day. "Quit doing that, or we'll have that Bachio on our doorstep."

Caterina considered telling him what she had learned, but decided against it. He would only believe she was keeping other things from him. She would be causing more trouble than necessary. Instead, she merely shrugged her shoulders, asking him what else was there to do, besides watching goats eat grass between the cracks of the pavement in the city?

While she watched Bachio's son, she realized she'd never learned his name. She had spent so much time trying to ignore the family, she didn't know the names of Bachio's children.

"You boy, come here," Caterina called him when her husband had left her alone one day.

Bachio's son was walking past her house. He looked around, uncertain where the call came from.

"Yes, you, Bachio's son. Come here," Caterina said.

The boy's eyes widened when he saw it was Caterina who called for him. He began to back away in a guilty manner, which made Caterina sigh impatiently. She'd never even spoken to the boy before; why should he be afraid of her?

"I'm sorry, I, uh can't. I have things to be done," he stumbled over his words.

"They can wait, I only have a question," Caterina said.

The boy came to her. This was the first time Caterina had seen him close. There was nothing about the boy to make him stand out from any of the others. He was slightly built, but had some pleasing features. His mouth turned up in the corners, forcing a natural smile on his face. His dark eyes were large and his nose a perfect aquiline. If she had liked the family better, Caterina might have said he had potential.

"What is your name?" Caterina asked.

"Um, Marcus."

Caterina decided to get to the point and ask Marcus what she wanted to learn.

"How often does the man come to your house?" she asked.

"What man?"

"The handsome one. He sometimes comes to your home, and you know very well who I mean," Caterina said.

"My cousin Lucian? I...I can't really talk about him," Marcus said.

"Of course you can. When will he next come to your house? I have business with him."

"He comes tomorrow, but you didn't hear it from me," Marcus said.

"What business does he have with your family?" Caterina asked.

"Don't you know?"

His tone began to show signs of worry.

"I know my own business with him. What does he

have with your family?"

Marcus glanced to either side of him. Leaning forward, he said solemnly, "The church's business and that is all I can say."

"Church business?" Caterina couldn't help asking incredulously. "And what sort to be so secretive about?"

"It is secretive," Marcus insisted.

"And what is it, then? Your father hiding the Pope under his bed?"

Marcus didn't answer Caterina's question. He only looked momentarily confused. Caterina was beginning to believe he wasn't too bright. Instead of answering, he turned stiffly from her and continued on. She let him go, having no more use for him. The stranger would be at Bachio's home tomorrow. She needed to tell Giovanni of this. Caterina wanted him with her when she went to Bachio's home tomorrow to confront the man.

She found Giovanni at his home. The hand and tongue were still nailed to the door. Caterina was used to seeing limbs nailed to doors and bodies in streets and rivers, but she crinkled her nose at this sight in distaste. When the servant answered the door, he tried keeping Caterina from entering.

"He's very busy," the servant said.

"Busy doing what? I have information for him on a matter I hired him on," Caterina said.

The servant only backed away when Giovanni's voice called out to let her in. Caterina pushed forward into the building. She stopped for a moment, standing in the near darkness of the room. She had never been in here before, and it was difficult to see clearly. Giovanni stepped up to her.

"You have some information for me?" he asked.

"There is a man I suspect to be involved with Julianna's death. He'll be at Bachio's home tomorrow."

"I know," Giovanni said.

"How come you haven't told me of this?" Caterina

asked.

"Because I don't know if there is anything to report yet; I haven't met the man. I planned to go there tomorrow", Giovanni said.

"I plan to go there as well."

"No, I will go on my own."

"I'll go, and there is no way to dissuade me," Caterina said.

Giovanni's eyes narrowed. He walked around her to the entry. Dismissing the servant, he stood in the opened doorway, facing the street.

"Why are you paying me, and yet insisting on doing the work yourself? Let me do my job and I'll report anything important to you," Giovanni said.

"I'm going with you," Caterina said, not bothering to hide the stubbornness in her tone.

"I can't promise to be able to keep you safe if you're with me," Giovanni said.

"I hired you, so you can't tell me what I should do, I'm going with you."

"Very well, but remember what I told you. I can't promise to keep you safe."

"I understand, now, is there anything else you learned about the matter I hired you for?" Caterina asked.

"Julianna had been found on her bed with a cup, drained near completely of drink. So I went to different sellers of herbs and medicines, giving a description of each member of Bachio's household."

"And?"

"I finally found one woman who recognized the description of Bachio's son."

"Was Lucian with him?" Caterina asked.

"No, but after I gave her a few coins she was able to recall Marcus had bought the ingredients of wolfsbane from her only a few days before Julianna's death. He also bought a tiny amount of tansy."

"Tansy? Whatever for?"

Giovanni shrugged. "I'm only telling you what I've learned so far. I confronted Marcus about it, who admitted to this, saying he bought them for a cousin who would sometimes stay at their home."

It was exactly as Caterina thought. She nodded, more certain than ever that this man who her daughter saw was the one responsible for Julianna's death. Caterina and Giovanni agreed on a time to meet the next day before going to see this stranger. Caterina looked forward to it, hoping that by this time tomorrow she would find the true cause of Julianna's death and clear her from the charge of suicide.

The heat of the following morning was worse than Caterina had experienced so far this summer. Dipping her hands in a basin of water, she splashed the liquid on her face, trying to get comfort of any sort from the oppressive warmth. Straightening her sleeves, she stepped outside, nearly tripping over a rat that was hiding near their doorway. With an oath she kicked at the rodent, watching it scurry away. She would have to tell her husband to start watching for rats. She didn't want their home to become like some of the abandoned churches that became so infested with rats one was sure to trip on one with every other step they took.

She met Giovanni by the back entrance to Bachio's home at their agreed upon time. He only simply nodded to her before Marcus met them at the door. He backed away, letting them enter. Caterina looked around, seeing they were only in the kitchen. Two girls Caterina guessed to be Marcus' sisters were working. Across the room was a fireplace that was lit to a blazing warmth. What looked to be a duck was on a spit turning slowly. Flies buzzed around the table where a partially eaten loaf of bread was showing signs of mold. Marcus disappeared to their left. She followed and found herself in a small room with no window. Large candles were lit on a roughly made table that stood in the center of the room. The flames lit up the area well so it was easy to see in the enclosed space.

A tall man whom Caterina instantly realized must be the one her daughter saw stood across the room. His back was turned to them while he was packing a few items in a sack. Turning, he swore and demanded Marcus tell him what these two people were doing in this room.

"They claimed to have business with you," Marcus said. He stood near the door of the room, looking to bolt at the first sign of trouble.

"You were told to keep out of here, not only by me, but your father if I recall rightly. I have no business with them," the man said.

Giovanni stepped forward. "We only have a few questions, Lucian, and then we'll be on our way," he said.

Giovanni walked around the table towards the man.

"Do you remember a girl called Julianna?" Giovanni asked.

"Who?"

"Julianna, she lived on this street," Giovanni said.

"Never met her," Lucian said.

"According to witnesses, you spoke with her for a good while at least once. She was a young girl, around Marcus' age."

"I suppose I may have, it's not impossible. Why do you ask?"

"Did you have a relationship with her?" Giovanni asked.

"No."

"Are you sure?"

Lucian smiled sardonically. "I think I would remember any liaisons I had here. But I'm sorry to disappoint you, there were none."

"Then why did you send for wolfsbane to be purchased?"

"Wolfsbane? Yes, it was only a little. I bought it for some pain I've been having in my hands. Is that what you're thinking? That I harmed this girl? This Julie, Julia-"

"Julianna, yes," Giovanni said.

"Why?" Lucian said, appearing confused. "I hardly knew the girl."

"So you're not the father of Julianna's child?" Giovanni asked.

"Child? No, I have no child. Of course there could be plenty of them as well that I don't know of." He laughed at this. Caterina didn't find it amusing. She couldn't decide whether to believe him or not when he claimed he hadn't been in any sort of intimate relationship with Julianna. Giovanni studied him, scrutinizing him for a long while.

"Is wolfsbane the only herb you had Marcus buy? Any other herbs?"

"No. Is there anything else I may help you with? I do have business to be taken cared of here," Lucian said.

"Yes, what are you doing here?"

"How is that your concern?"

"It's my street; I want to know who comes and goes and why. What are you delivering?"

"I deliver nothing."

"Not to here, but you carry messages. I've watched you. What are they?"

Lucian appeared ready to argue. Giovanni started to draw out his sword. It was a falchion sword; its blade could easily slice off an arm. Lucian scowled, saying it was no information to be killed over; it would soon be common enough news if it wasn't already. He took a small folded paper and handed it to Giovanni.

"When you are done reading it, I would appreciate to have it back," he said.

Giovanni read the words. Caterina was surprised he was literate.

"The Pope is to return to Rome? I heard that he was,

but thought they were only rumors."

"He is traveling here now. If each Pope keeps staying in Avignon over in France, they could lose what is theirs here in Rome. May I have the letter?"

Giovanni tossed the letter back to the man.

"You can leave," Giovanni said.

After Lucian left, Giovanni turned towards Caterina.

"That man wasn't lying and I know when a man is lying. I'm sorry, but it appears Julianna took her own life," Giovanni said.

Caterina shook her head, despite the lack of evidence pointing to her belief. She followed him out of the room. By this time, Marcus was in the kitchen with his two sisters. She watched Giovanni. By the posture of his back, he appeared to be concentrating on a thought. He stopped by the door and Caterina followed, standing beside him.

"Why did you buy the tansy?" Giovanni asked Marcus.

"Lucian asked me to," Marcus said.

"That man only wanted wolfsbane. The herb lady said you also bought tansy."

"Why would she?" he asked.

"Because it's the truth?" Giovanni suggested. "Tell me what happened."

"I told you all I know," he said evasively.

Giovanni grabbed Marcus by the throat.

"Tell me what happened to Julianna," Giovanni said.

"I don't know," Marcus said, his voice tightening. "How would I?"

"You tell me. Why did you buy the tansy? You bought it for Julianna, didn't you?"

He pressed his hand harder. Marcus' face slowly changed colors, growing pale.

"She was pregnant with my child and wanted to get rid of it. I've heard it would help but it didn't so I gave her some of the wolfsbane. Thought it would help her get rid of the child."

"Stupid children. You two should have gone to someone who knows the business," Giovanni muttered, releasing Marcus.

Staring at the boy, Caterina wondered what on earth would have attracted Julianna to him. As Caterina gazed at him, a fierce rage rose up within her. With no further thought she went to Marcus and began slapping him across his face.

"Idiot boy, what were you thinking? Wolfsbane? That's a poison that's known to kill if not taken properly. Stupid boy, you killed my girl, leaving her for a suicide and made the church damn her from God!"

Marcus only held up his hands, trying to ward her blows away. It was Giovanni who finally separated Caterina from Marcus.

"It was a mistake, her death was a mistake, an accident," Giovanni said.

Unable to force any more words out of her mouth, Caterina began shivering and hurried out of the kitchen, holding her hand to her mouth. It was not the first time she had heard of such a situation, but the abruptness of hearing the truth with her pain over Julianna's death made her stomach heave. She kept walking until she reached her own home. Once in the familiar courtyard, she threw up. Continuing to shake, she then slumped against the wall of her home, enjoying the warmth of the stones and glad for once of the summer's heat.

"Did you hear the news?" Gustavo asked.

"What news?" Caterina asked. She said the words more for an expected response than actual interest. They were eating dinner. Caterina ate little, mostly watching her husband and daughter eat the meal.

"Giovanni believes my sister didn't kill herself; that she tried ridding herself of Marcus' child. What was the matter with her?" he said.

"It was Marcus' child?" Beatrice asked. "Him? When

there are so many others of better worth and looks?"

Caterina's husband gazed sternly towards Beatrice at her words. "Take care and don't get any ideas from your aunt," he said.

"I want to go to market tomorrow," Beatrice said.

"Whatever for?" Caterina asked.

"A few errands," Beatrice said evasively.

Caterina suspected the few errands to be trying to get a new boy's attentions. Well, let her. Caterina would be right there watching.

"Julianna was a foolish girl, like any woman is," he said. "I do have other news to share, better news. The Pope will be returning."

Beatrice only stared at him before she burst out laughing. She asked if he had been listening to that Birgitta so much he actually believed the woman's words. Caterina pushed her plate of untasted food away, marveling at Gustavo's ability to so easily change the subject of his sister's death to other news.

"No, it's true, not just rumors," he insisted.

"It is true. Maybe it'll be as Birgitta says: when the Pope returns to Rome, there will be redemption for the city," Caterina said.

Gustavo stopped laughing, considering her words. "Do you really believe that? You believe it's possible? Redemption you say?"

Caterina pulled out a pouch she always carried, counting the number of coins in it.

"What are you doing?" Gustavo asked.

"I'm making sure I have enough coins to give the church so I can light two candles at church tomorrow," Caterina said.

"Why two?" Beatrice asked.

"For Julianna and her child."

By the small weight of the bag, she knew there would be enough.

"What you said earlier about redemption for the city... I was thinking when the Pope returns, there will be even more pilgrims. How about something new to sell: a healing cloth from Lazarus' shroud? People would buy that I'm sure when the crowds start coming," Gustavo said.

Caterina only shook her head. Redemption or not, some things would never change.

Kristin Roahrig's poetry and short stories have appeared in various publications. She is also the author of several plays and lives in Indiana.

Tell Me Where He Lies

By Greg McWhorter

New Orleans that summer was a sweltering armpit that festered with vice and corruption. The denizens of the swamp mixed with the urbanites on the streets of the Big Easy. Bourbon Street, in the French Quarter, was the official, unofficial, heart of the city. New Orleans was a living, thriving place. It breathed the invigorating and fresh sounds of jazz, but every so often it started to wheeze and cough pestilence like a long-time smoker. This pestilence stemmed from years of pagan rites in the name of voodoo, a religion with roots in slavery and bred on soil soaked in blood.

Max Wheland had seen voodoo and blood many times over the last twenty-five years as a petty thug and grifter. The 1950s had been a great decade for his dirty work, but now that a new decade had begun, things were not quite the same. It was now harder to get things over on the cops. The grifters and the cops had each learned each other's tricks of the trade and it was now more expensive to operate. Bribes were higher and you had to have greater investment in lucrative schemes and so on. Max was a survivor, though, and he continued on with the old ways, which were all he knew and the changing times meant little to him.

Max sat in an old bar on Bourbon Street, sucking back a few two-bit beers as some lazy flies tried to give him a hard time. His hat and his shirt were both sweat-stained and his skin was sun-tanned. The once handsome face was now cracked with wrinkles, but his eyes still had that spark that showed he was ready for some easy action whenever it presented itself. He was a good man to know when you were in a spot. He was not afraid to cheat, steal, or kill, if the money was right. He knew the habits of every local cop and he also knew which ones could be tapped for a few bucks. He also had intimate knowledge on where many bodies were buried. He had helped some of them into their graves.

One particular day, Max had been contemplating life. He knew he was getting older and needed to figure out a big hit, but for now he was still content to take whatever might come his way. His mortality kept nagging at him, though. His survival instinct was stronger than his conscience. He ordered another beer and continued to sit and dream of the big score. He didn't notice the big black man that walked in quietly and sat down next to him. The man was clean cut and wore a black suit with a white shirt and tie. He was also wearing patent leather shoes and looked a little better off than most of his brethren.

"M-m-m-mister barman! B-b-b-bring me a beer. T-t-tap," was what the dark black man stammered out. Max took a quick look at him and realized that he was not a local boy. Max figured that the old ways of Jim Crow were falling away to the new Civil Rights movement and he better damn well get used to it. The barman brought the beer and the black man guzzled it down quickly and asked for another. The black man had such a terrible stuttering problem that Max had to listen and translate in his mind what the man was saying, which turned out to be:

"Yes sir. Sure is hot. That beer is mighty good. Really uplifts the spirit."

Max decided to talk for the sake of diversion from his

thoughts. "The beer's okay, buddy, but I don't know about the uplifting of spirits part. Usually beer seems to get most people laid out on the floor around here."

The two men exchanged a quick chuckle.

The black man smiled and stuttered out, "M-m-m-my name is-s Obediah." Max had to continue translating the stuttering in his head.

"My name is Max, partner. Are you new in town?"

"Oh y-y-yes. I's h-h-here on b-b-business."

"Yeah? What kind of work do you do?"

"Ha ha ha...I don't m-m-mean w-work. I-I-I'm h-here to find m-m-my b-b-brother's grave."

"Find your brother's grave? That sounds unusual. Can't you just go to the cemetery and ask an attendant where he's buried?"

"N-n-no. I know h-h-he m-m-must have b-b-been b-b-buried where he was k-k-killed. H-h-he w-was l-l-laid to r-r-rest in u-u-unconsecrated grounds. H-h-he comes to m-m-me in m-m-my d-d-dreams. H-h-he d-d-does not r-r-rest. I n-n-need to f-f-find h-h-him and end h-h-his unrest."

Max had now turned to face the black man, deciding that he was an interesting diversion after all.

"Okay Mac. I get that your brother was iced and planted somewhere, but what do you mean by his 'unrest'?" Max realized as soon as he asked, that this man must believe in voodoo. It was practiced by many blacks around town and even out into the swamps. He knew they usually kept it to themselves and didn't interfere upon white people with their silly superstitions. Max found himself intrigued that this man was so open about his beliefs. It was probably the newly animated countenance of Max's that made the black man bow his head down and look away from Max in apparent shame.

"W-w-well S-s-sir...I's s-s-sorry...F-f-forgot m-m-myself."

"Naw. It's all right with me, bud. Every man has the right to his own religious beliefs. That's what makes America unique, right? We got freedom of religion. Hell, I was raised Methodist myself. Haven't been in a church since I was a kid, but I believe you got a right to believe what you want."

"T-t-thank y-you sir," stammered the man before drinking more beer and sitting in silence.

"So what was your brother's name? Maybe I knew him."

The black man lowered his head and almost whispered, "M-m-manny Gumms. M-m-manuel Jacque Gumms."

Max knew the name all right, but not a flicker of recognition crossed his face. He was a good poker player and never gave away a hand. He knew that one never knew where or when an opportunity might present itself.

"Name sounds familiar. Was there something in the paper about him?"

The black man started stammering out a story of his brother's corruption. Max didn't listen. His mind was going over what he already knew. Manny Gumms was a petty bootlegger. He came from the swamps and set up a still in town. He tried to compete with the bigger gangs. He tried to expand into prostitution and drugs and had been pretty successful servicing the black population. His mistake had been in realizing that the big money lay with the white population. He started squeezing in on the big boys and got chopped down one night. Max knew all this. Max was with the gunman that night. He had been paid to hide the body quickly. Max knew where Manny's body was. He planted Manny.

The black man ended his story by saying that since Manny's body had not been found and buried properly, his soul would not lie at rest until a special token was placed in the grave with him. Max's attention came back to the man.

"And what is this token that you need to put in his grave?"

"T-t-this," said the black man as he took a small wood box from out of his suit coat pocket and opened it toward Max. The glow almost stunned Max at first. He couldn't believe what he was seeing. It was a huge gold nugget. It must be worth an easy thousand or more, he thought. It was almost the size of a human heart. Then he realized that it wasn't a gold nugget. It was gold molded into a replica human heart. Max realized that this must be some sort of pagan icon and didn't want to press for details. After all, he had just told this man that everyone had the right to their own beliefs.

"Is that for real?"

"Yes, sir! Cost my family everything. Manny will not be at peace until he has this token to ease the obsession that he faced in life."

At least this was a close approximation of what Max had been able to translate through the stammering and spitting.

Max realized his luck. This wouldn't be the big score that he dreamed of, but it would put him on easy street for a while. The whole plan only took seconds to sink in. Max would take Obediah to his brother's grave and help him slip the gold in. Max would then come back later and dig it up. Max figured that he would get a cool thousand for just a little digging. It was too good for him to pass up. Max also realized that the best part was that he wouldn't have to kill Obediah.

"Tell you what, Obediah...I'm gonna help you. Families and their religious beliefs are important. I get that you want to ease your brother's suffering in the afterlife. That's what I call noble. Yes sir. A gentle act of kindness for a departed loved one. I'll help you find your brother. We'll find his grave."

Obediah had a naïve and somewhat shocked look on his face as he stammered out, "H-h-h-how? I-i-i-is it possible? C-c-can you r-r-really tell me where h-h-he lies?"

"Sure."

Max told him that he was a freelance reporter and that he had access to the paper archives and could tap the police files, too. He told Obediah that he might not be able to find the exact burial spot, but with some luck, they might get close enough to find some clues. He quickly added that in his investigations of news stories, he sometimes made contact with gangsters and that maybe they might tell him something. Obediah listened intently and appeared thankful and stunned. Max realized that a white man helping a black man for nothing might seem odd to Obediah, so he asked if he could do a full report on his brother's death and use any information he got. Max let him know that he didn't want any compensation other than the story. Max told Obediah that he would, of course, leave out the part about the gold heart so that no one would disturb his brother's rest. The day wore on and Obediah and Max made their arrangements to meet around eleven o'clock that same night.

Max rested up for most of the day. He later put a couple of shovels and some flashlights in the trunk of his car and found some old clothes that he could wear and not worry about getting dirty while digging. Max thought to himself that when he met up with Obediah later, he would tell him that he had spent all day searching the archives and talking to various street toughs. Max couldn't help thinking how easy this job would be and even made a mental joke about how appropriate the nickname was for the city: The Big Easy.

Max was a little taken aback that Obediah wanted to meet at a cemetery at night, but he understood that the black man had his religion and therefore he must have other dead relations to visit. Besides, at night it was cool enough to walk around the city in comfort and Max readily knew the cemetery which Obediah had picked. It was typical of the kind built around New Orleans with crumbling above-ground tombs, which were built that way due to the high water table in the region. It contained many high-rising sealed tombs and bricked-in vaults that protected the remains of the city's earliest citizens, both good and bad. Max was glad they were to meet outside of the cemetery, as he knew of all the late-night muggings and deaths that still happened within its brick white-washed walls adorned with wrought iron crosses and fleurs-de-lis.

At eleven o'clock, Max had parked his car and was already waiting at the rendezvous spot. The sweltering heat of the day had vanished and been replaced by a damp coolness supplied from the gentle off-shore breezes from the Gulf of Mexico. Obediah picked the front gate of the Saint Louis Cemetery on the outer edge of the French Quarter in what used to be Storyville a few generations back. He told Max that he wanted to pay his respects at the tomb of Marie Laveau, the first high priestess of voodoo. Max waited at the gate. He enjoyed the damp breeze that vaguely smelt of fresh earth. He heard the eerie sound that the breeze made as it wound through the cemetery, like a low unending moan of anguish. He waited only a few minutes at the gate before Obediah appeared. He told Max that he had marked three X's on Laveau's tomb so that she would grant his wish of finding his dead brother and placing the token in his grave. Max pretended to be interested, but he was just acting. Max thought to himself that this whole night would take a bit of acting, but it should be a snap.

Max told Obediah that it took a lot of digging around and asking the right people, but he thought he knew the location of his brother. They would have to take his car a few blocks south to Decatur Street. On Decatur there was an abandoned warehouse with the name "Spivey's" at a certain address. Inside, they would find that the basement had only a dirt floor littered with old junk. In the basement is where they would find the resting place of Manny Gumms...If the information Max got was correct, that is.

They got in Max's car and Obediah produced a brown grocery sack. He told Max that this would have to be done right. Candles would have to be placed and some chants would have to be said before they could place the gold heart and leave. This irritated Max, who wanted to just get this over with as quick as possible, but he knew that he would have to play it Obediah's way in order to get his plan to work and thus resigned himself to it.

They arrived quickly at the warehouse, but Max drove past it once on purpose to make it seem that he didn't know the area too well. He let Obediah point out the faded sign that bore the name "Spivey's". The warehouse was a two-story brick affair that had been built in the late 1880's. The arched brick windows were all boarded up and the once whitewashed red brick was flaking away, leaving the building in patches of red and white.

"You've got good eyes, Obediah. No one seems to be around, but let's park in the alley, just to make sure that we are not followed inside. You never know what kind of thugs might be around. Winos are one thing, but petty crooks might try to mug us." Max switched off his headlights and glided the car into the side alley.

Max was happy. All was going well. Just another hour or so of work, and then the gold would be his. They parked between some dumpsters and got out. Getting in was easy, as the old building was almost all skeleton now. Years of neglect had left it stripped of anything of use and now all that remained was for the wrecking ball to come and do its job.

Max knew where some loose boards were that had once allowed him access to the building. He hoped they were still loose and that no homeless men had snuck in, as they would complicate things. His luck held as he found the loose boards and bade Obediah to follow him inside. Just inside, the two men turned on their flashlights and began walking around the cavernous first floor of the ancient warehouse. Although the walls were brick, it had a wood floor and there were massive wood beams that supported the upper floor, which was also made of wood. They saw no signs of anyone having been there recently, as the dust on the floor was undisturbed. Their footprints were the only ones.

They located a staircase and descended with their flashlights still on. This just happened to be one of the few buildings in town that had a cellar built in it, as most of New Orleans was below sea level. Max had picked this building for that very reason when he brought Manny here a few years back.

They landed on the basement floor and saw that it was an all-dirt floor. There might have been some tiles, or floorboards, at one time, but not now.

"Okay, Obediah. Take your flashlight along the right wall and I will go along the left. We'll meet at the other end and decide how else to search from there."

Max was no fool. He knew that Obediah would find the grave along the right wall. He knew he would find it because he had marked the spot with an empty whisky bottle, shoved upside down in the ground, marked with a black "X" which was a little joke of Max's. He always left his burials with a marker of some kind.

"M-m-m-Max, sir! I-I think I found something!"

Max suppressed a chuckle as he ran over to see what Obediah found. And as Max had suspected, Obediah had found the bottle marker with the "X."

"Obediah! This must be it. That has a gangland look to it, all right. Some bastard's joke I guess. Let's try here."

They each took a shovel and started digging. It wasn't long before they found the decomposing remains of Manny

Gumms in his shallow grave. They had only dug down about two feet before they found a large piece of canvas, and underneath was the rotting body. The eyes no longer remained and only empty sockets remained in which earthworms greedily ate. The body was showing lots of bone as much of the flesh had sloughed off, but some pulpy flesh remained, enough that, with effort, you could tell this was the corpse of Manny Gumms. The facial features were still mostly intact and that sinister sneer that Manny wore in life could still be discerned. It was that same sneer that he had on his face when Max had killed and buried him.

"Okay, Obediah. Now's your chance. Place the gold and let's cover him up to resume his rest."

"N-n-o M-m-max. R-r-remember that I must light the candles and say the chant o-o-or else this m-means n-n-n-nothing."

Max cursed silently to himself as he knew he was stuck for the duration and decided to sit down on an old crate and wait.

"W-w-what time you got, M-m-max sir?"

"11:50"

"Uhm hmm," was all that Obediah uttered as he quickly took candles out of his sack and lighted them. There were thirteen tall candles that he propped up around his brother's remains. The sneer that Manny wore in death was highlighted by the flickering light of the candles. Obediah produced a small red flannel bag that Max knew he kept his 'mojo', or voodoo charms in. Max knew that his 'mojo' bag would be filled with disgusting things like animal parts and other unsavory ingredients.

The large, black man reached down and placed the flannel bag on Manny's rotten skull. He then lit some incense and chanted. The chants were in dark and somber tones in a language that Max did not know. Like many men that stutter, Obediah did not stammer while chanting and singing.

At a certain point in the ceremony, Obediah got quiet. It was so quiet that Max thought he could almost hear his own heart beating. Obediah slowly turned to Max and asked for the time again.

"11:59. Are you done now?"

"No. You must place the heart with Manny. Here…", and with that Obediah tossed the gold heart to Max. Max thought about running right there and then as he looked at the gold in his hand. He felt how heavy of a chunk it was and thought it must be worth a lot. Although Max had been lost to reverie, he looked up and noticed that Obediah had him covered with a pistol.

"What is this, Obediah? I helped you find your brother! Why are you holding that gun?"

"You are the one who buried my brother in unhallowed grounds. You must place the heart before my brother awakes as a zombie. I have spoken the sacred chant, and now you must appease him with the placement of the heart." Distant bells could be heard from a nearby church. The bells had rung in eleven, and now they were tolling for the midnight hour.

Max's mind was racing now as he knew he had been discovered. He also realized that he had been taken in by Obediah's simple talk and stuttering, both of which were gone now. Max gasped, "How did you know it was me?"

"It does not matter. All is revealed to the inquisitive. Quickly, Max! Place the heart with Manny before he rises!" The urgency was escalating in Obediah's now perfect English as the church bells continued their ringing.

Max thought to himself that this was all crap as he walked over to Manny's grave. He wondered how Obediah found out about his connection to Manny's death, but he decided he would go along with the strange black man for now. As Max gazed upon Manny's corpse in the flickering light, he noticed that the sneer was tighter upon the face now.

The chest area seemed to be heaving up and down, a little, as if in respiration. He figured that his eyes were deceiving him in the candle light, but he saw Manny's skeletal arms lift up out of the grave and the bony fingers start contracting and releasing. Without another thought, Max dropped the gold heart into the open grave with Manny. Just as he did this a shot was fired and Max looked down at his chest in time to see blood spreading quickly on the front of his shirt from an exit wound. This was all he saw before he plunged forward. He did not feel the dead arms that embraced his body in the shallow grave.

All was quiet after the bells finished their somber tolling. Obediah looked down at the double grave. Manny's sneer had changed into a grisly smile and both bodies were now motionless in the candle light. Manny's damned soul had been appeased, and all it took was a chunk of lead painted gold and a single bullet. He thought it was funny just how easily some people could be fooled by their own greed. Obediah covered the grave back over with dirt and replaced the makeshift grave maker, then left the abandoned building. He had avenged his brother. His brother could now rest at peace.

Greg McWhorter is a teacher and pop-culture historian that resides in Southern California. Since the 1980s, he has worked for newspapers, radio, television, and film. He has been a guest speaker at several universities and at the San Diego Comic-Con. Today, McWhorter owns a highly acclaimed record label that specializes in vintage punk rock and hosts a music show for cable TV. Since 1985, McWhorter has been writing nonfiction music-related articles for print and recently turned to writing crime and horror fiction. He is a member of the Horror Writer's Association. You can follow him at: http://gregmcwhorter.blogspot.com

Amontillado Kisses

By Jason Andrew

On the last night of carnival, all inhibitions are shed. It is a magical time when our glorious city earns the secret title of the City of Masks. The revelry extends from the majestic canals to the bawdy taverns nestled between the rivers Po and the Piave, and finally ends in the exquisite villas of the nobility. Children throw confetti at each other with wild delight until they are sent to bed. Parades snake through the streets and canals, bringing wine and cheer to the revelers.

Doors are neither barred nor locked anywhere in Venice on this night. All faces are covered with masks and colorful paint to honor Janus, the two-faced god, guardian of the spaces in-between. By tradition, the wealthiest and ancient houses of the city host exquisite balls where any can attend, if they dare to experience pleasures both subtle and gross.

Come dawn's bright light, we remove our masks and return to our lives. Nothing that happened during the night is ever acknowledged. *A Carnevale Ogni Scherzo Vale.* Anything goes at carnival, as long as we pretend we cannot recognize our dearest friends in the throes of such passion. Some wear many different masks throughout the night, seeking to find the wives of their dearest friends for a secret tryst or two. It is not as easy as you might imagine. Few can distinguish between the wives and the whores.

Alas, such spurious sport delighted me not as I prefer the company of young men with a sly smile and a broad chest.

Such indulgences were frowned upon the rest of the year, for I am a family man, but on this glorious night I can sate that hunger I've suppressed the entire year.

It has long been fashionable to appear fully pious in public during the long drudgery of Lent. No Italian would dare to be seen violating the structures of sacrifice and thus we feast, knowing that a famine awaits us. I met my obligatory appearances with my wife, and then absconded to my private closet to don my disguise.

My valet chose a tight-fitting striped suit that accentuated my legs and buttocks, accompanied by a thin domino jester's mask complete with a conical cap and bells. Drinking with wild abandon, I escaped the civilized villas to the wild streets near the docks that were once familiar to me as a young man.

Dusk darkened the alleys behind a well-known bathhouse when I happened upon Montressor. I knew him instantly despite the white death's mask painted upon his face. He had grown a beard sprinkled with distinguished white hairs since last we spoke. Time had claimed his glorious curly mane of hair, leaving him with a monk's crown. His soft brown eyes were hard yet gleeful.

We did not part as brothers, yet still I yearned to kiss those soft lips as we did as boys. Montressor grasped my hand tightly and for a brief moment it was as though no time had passed since those endless summer nights of our callow youth. "Fortunato! How remarkably well you are looking this evening! I am quite lucky to have come upon you. I have purchased an entire pipe of what passes for Amontillado, though I have my doubts as to the exact vintage."

Sweet Amontillado marked our lips when last we kissed. Rarely did we drink anything else during our time as lovers. Was this an attempt at reconciliation? We had not spoken alone in almost ten years. "That is a rare discovery in the middle of Carnival! How could it be possible neither bandits nor whores did not abscond with it?"

Montressor smiled dubiously, then shook his head at the jest. "I have my doubts, I admit. I was foolish enough to pay full price without consulting you, but alas you were not to be found and I was fearful of losing a bargain."

Strange that Montressor would claim ignorance on this matter. His father imported Amontillado and other Fino wines from Spain and made quite the fortune in our youth. Why else would he call for my services in this matter, save to taste my lips? "Amontillado!"

"I have my doubts and I must satisfy them this night."

Carnival had undoubtedly drained the private stocks of the nobility and the wealthy on this last night. There would be nothing to drink but swill beer and cheap wines. Hidden caches would only be shared amongst close friends. Was it worth my one night of freedom to take the risk? I thought of those sweet kisses. "Amontillado!"

Montressor gestured toward the bathhouse and shrugged politely. "You are clearly engaged, my friend, as you should be on the last night of carnival. I am on my way to Luchesi. If anyone has a critical tongue, it is he."

Luchesi shared our mutual love of sweet wine and bearded faces. He was the youngest brother and relegated to the clergy. We had grown close since the break between myself and Montressor. Did he doubt the reconciliation? Was he jealous of my latest lover? I waved away any concerns Montressor might have. "Luchesi cannot tell Amontillado from sherry."

Amontillado is a variety of sherry and we both knew that. This sweet, but dry amber fortified-wine tasted faintly of almonds and honey. Montressor grinned slyly at the jape. "And yet some fools will have it that his tongue is a match for your own."

Luchesi was sweet as Amontillado, but somewhat lacking as a lover save for his enthusiasm. Was Montressor toying with me? "Such nonsense can not be allowed to stand, brother. Come, let us go!"

"But to where?" Montressor asked innocently.

"To your vaults, brother!" I bowed before him and smiled wryly. "The matter of the best tongue must be decided! I shall not withstand a stain upon my honor in this matter."

"I cannot impose upon your good nature." Montressor shook his head and tried to wave me away once more. "You have an engagement at the bathhouse and I would not wish you to miss your time. You have been ill of late and I would not wish you to miss your treatment. Luchesi is quite willing in this matter."

It was true that I had been ill for several months with pneumonia. The weakness had mostly faded save for the occasional cough. I clasped his shoulders as I did when we were young. "I have no engagement, sweet Montressor. I insist that I must taste this alleged Amontillado on my lips!"

"It is not the engagement, in truth, but concern for where I have stored the casks." There was great concern in Montressor's eyes. He was genuinely worried for me at that moment. "The vaults are insufferably damp. They are encrusted with nitre."

The doctor had bid me to stay out of the water and to ensure that I remain warm least I suffer a relapse. The chance for Amontillado kisses proved too tempting. "Nevertheless. Let us go. The cold is nothing for a short time if we are careful. Imagine the possibilities! Amontillado!"

I wrapped my arm around his and kissed him upon his cheek. We walked and laughed through the streets over the stone bridges and onto the hillside where only the wealthiest lived. We walked for an hour in the dark holding onto each other until we reached Montressor's villa. The rooms were dark and empty of attendants out for carnival save for a single maid.

"I am surprised that your family did not host a feast."

"I prepared something special for this night, dearest Fortunato." Montressor lit twin flambeaux and handed one to me. I followed him through several suites of rooms to the archway that led into the vaults. He opened the colossal door with a metal key and bowed. "The stairs wind steeply. Be careful, brother. We do not wish an accident on this night."

The air was damp. My cough grew as we descended down the stairs. Shadows flicked on the stone walls. We stopped at the base of the stairs and stood together on the damp ground of the catacombs of the Montressors.

"Where is the Amontillado?"

"A little farther, sweet Fortunato. I wanted to hide it from the servants. I worry for you. Observe the white webwork which gleams from these cavern walls."

I tried to contain the cough so as to not spoil the mood. "You did not jest about the nitre."

"How long have you had that cough?" He wrapped his arm around me and patted my back. "We should return. I can bring it up to you another night."

I felt that the fluid would never leave my lungs. Cough! Cough! I drank of the wine from the cup I had brought with me. "It is nothing."

"Let us return. Your health is precious. You are rich, respected, admired, and beloved. You have many sons and daughters. You are happy as once I was. You are a man to be missed. For me it is no matter. We will go back; you will be ill and I cannot be responsible. Besides, there is always Luchesi…"

"I am strong. I will not die from a cough."

"True. And I would very much like to taste the Amontillado with you, but let us take proper caution. A draught of this Medoc will defend us from the damps." Montressor handed me a dusty green bottle. I knocked off the neck of the bottle against the wall and we drank and toasted from our flasks. He kissed my lips. It was but a promise for a better warmer night. "Let us drink to your health and long life."

"I drink to your happiness, Montressor."

"Perhaps with your help, sweet Fortunato, I will find

that happiness this night." He again took my arm and we proceeded. "These vaults are extensive. I had not realized their length."

"The Montressors were a great family long ago."

"The Montressors are still a great family; a pillar of Venice with a mighty coat of arms."

The sadness drained from his eyes. "A huge human foot *d'or*, in a field azure; the foot crushes a serpent rampant whose fangs are imbedded in the heel."

I already knew the answer to my next question, but it was only polite to ask. "And the motto?"

"*Nemo me impune lacessit.*"

"Brilliant! Your enemies tremble at the thought of drawing your ire!" I knew this to be true. Montressor had humbled many in my fraternal order in the last year after he was rejected for membership. Some found his vengeful nature to be unpleasant, whereas I loved him for his passion. We laughed at the bells on my cap as they jingled, echoing around us. "Who would dare to challenge you?"

We had passed through walls of piled bones and abandoned wine casks to the inner hall of the catacombs. He held my arm close above the elbow, as though leading me to a secret picnic. The pale white webbing thickened and hung like moss upon the stone walls. Drops of water trickled down onto the bones. "We should return, brother. I worry for your cough."

I swallowed more Medoc, hoping to soothe my throat. My head and chest felt warm finally. I wiped sweat from my brow. "It is nothing." I drank the entire bottle and then threw it against the wall with a gesture forbidden to show outsiders. The glass shattered and sparked like fireworks. "Do you know this gesture, brother?"

Montressors smiled knowingly and then seemed to catch himself and blinked innocently. It was forbidden to show the gesture to outsiders, and I risked expulsion merely discussing it. "I am not of the brotherhood, but I am a Mason."

Was he jesting? Had there been a new initiation of which I was unaware? "You? Impossible! A Mason?"

"And yet I am." He fished under his robes and produced a trowel. "I am a true Mason."

"You jest well, friend!" Surely, if he knew, he had forgiven me long ago. "Let us proceed to the Amontillado."

"Indeed, let me lead you." He replaced the trowel beneath his cloak and offered his arm once more. We continued our route in search of the Amontillado. We passed through a range of low arches until we finally arrived at a deep crypt where the candles in our flambeaux flickered. "We draw near to the Amontillado."

The walls were lined with bones and antique armor in the fashion of the great catacombs of Paris. Three sides of this chambered were ornamented in this manner, but the fourth had been cleared away and revealed a smaller passage recently excavated by the evidence of dirt and brick nearby.

My head began to throb. The walls seemed to close in upon me. "Let me rest, old friend, just for a moment."

I sat against the wall and closed my eyes for a moment.

A ray of light from a single flickering torch cut through the darkness. I spat to clear my mouth as my tongue was thick with sleep. Had I been poisoned? My hands and arms felt heavy. How long had I sleep? I try to stand, but some force yanked me back to the ground with a rusty jingle far heavier than the bells upon my jester's cap. Bound in chains like a common prisoner! "Montressor! Montressor!"

A sharp scrape echoed from the granite walls. It was a not unfamiliar sound; a trowel slapping against brick and mortar. "Ha! ha! ha! A masterful jest. We will have many a rich laugh about this in the nights to come."

Montressor continued his work in silence. I pleaded with him until finally he stopped, and peered through the hole in the makeshift wall. "I never did provide you with the Amontillado."

My hands shook, but I tried to still them. "I would very much wish to taste that sweet wine with you." Could he be serious? Did he hate me that much? "It is late, and soon we shall have to remove our masks. Let us not spoil the entire night with this jest. Let us be gone from here to a place with a fire and blankets."

"Yes, let us be gone."

Could he mean to leave me here? "For the love of God, Montressor! You loved me once."

His voice was calm and dry as though any passion he felt for me had evaporated. "Yes, for the love of God!"

I sat quiet in the darkness. Surely this was a cruel joke; a punishment for rejecting him twice. He called through the brick and mortar. "Fortunato!" I did not answer. Tears were the only currency bastards such as this understand. I would deny him payment. "Fortunato!"

Montressor thrust his remaining torch through the small hole and let it drop to the ground with a thud. I tried not to weep as he continued his work. I bit back tears, and the only sound was the soft jingling of the bells. One by one, he laid down the bricks, occasionally stopping to hold his own torch to look upon me with great satisfaction. "I loved you."

"There is a price for breaking the heart of a Montressor."

The last brick was laid quickly. Slowly the torch died and there was only darkness. I can't remember if it was the cough or the lack of oxygen that finally killed me.

Was it my vices that kept me from heaven? I know not. My shade remained trapped with my bones. I tried to find my way out to haunt Montressor. He only visited my grave twice, but I could not find the rage to strike him.

Aged and crippled, to me he is still the young boy that delighted me with Amontillado kisses.

Perhaps this is but a test to see if I am worthy of Heaven. Perhaps, when he dies, I will finally meet Saint Peter. *A Carnevale Ogni Scherzo Vale.*

Jason Andrew lives in Seattle, Washington with his wife Lisa. He is an Associate member of the Science Fiction and Fantasy Writers of America, Active Member of the Horror Writer's Association, and member of the International Association of Media Tie-In Writers.

By day, he works as a mild-mannered technical writer. By night, he writes stories of the fantastic and occasionally fights crime. As a child, Jason spent his Saturdays watching the Creature Feature classics and furiously scribbling down stories. His first short story, written at age six, titled "The Wolfman Eats Perry Mason" was severely rejected. It also caused his grandmother to watch him very closely for a few years.

His short fiction has appeared in markets such as Shine: An Anthology of Optimistic SF *(Harper Collins),* Frontier Cthulhu: Ancient Horrors in the New World *(Chaosium), and* Coins of Chaos *(Edge Science Fiction and Fantasy Publishing). In 2011, his story "Moonlight in Scarlet" received an honorable mention in Ellen Datlow's List for Best Horror of the Year.*

In addition, Jason has written for a number of role-playing games such as Call of Cthulhu, Shadowrun, *and* Vampire: The Masquerade. *His most recent projects include* Hunters Hunted 2 (The Onyx Path), Anarchs Unbound (The Onyx Path), *and* Atomic Age Cthulhu: Terrifying Tales of the Mythos Menace *(Chaosium). Recently, he served as Developer for* Mind's Eye Theatre: Vampire The Masquerade *for By Night Studios.*

Life Sentence

By Cari Dubiel

The body is cold when I arrive.

Thomas Spencer lies on our bed like a sacrifice on a stone table, his eyes closed. Our hired girl hung her head when I asked her how they got that way. "It seemed disrespectful," she said, meeting my eyes only for a moment before casting her glance down again. "To leave him the way he was."

Few people know these days that to disturb a corpse is more disrespectful than to leave it. Lottie, certainly, is ignorant. I dismiss her apologies and examine his face. The cheeks, slack - the skin, as white as the marble angels presiding over our courtyard. At this precise moment, my own body turns to stone. Mirroring his, as it has done for so many years.

"Madam Spencer?" Lottie's hand shoots out to graze my arm. Without thinking, I bat her back like a fly. She shrinks away. I shake my head because I cannot speak.

In year nineteen of our marriage, we slept close, our bodies pressed together. There were times I could not stand his smell. My husband was a detective of the Metropolitan Police, and his work brought him to the foulest corners of east London. Lottie drew baths that I heated to scalding. Even that did not always help. The sweat, grime, dirt could wash away, but the blood never truly did.

One such night, we left the curtains open. Breeze passed through, as close to wind as it could be, and other smells with it: the filth of the streets. We lived in a posh neighborhood; while the police could not always provide high salaries, Thomas had worked hard for twenty years, and we'd inherited a decent sum at my father's death. Still, we could not escape the screams of women and urchins, the raving drunks. The breeze off the stinking Thames was more trouble than it was worth. That night, I got up to draw the window shut.

"Leave it," murmured Thomas. Already half asleep, he propped himself on an elbow, his eyelids drooping. "Come back to bed."

"I cannot stand the shouting." There was much I could not stand. The smack of my husband's lips as he ate, a hog snuffling in a trough. So fast, like a vulture destroying carrion. I was sensitive, as my mother had often observed. "I will sleep without the air."

"It will be too hot." He patted the bed beside him.

I stood in the window for a moment, looking out. The street was softly lit. Beyond the hedges of our courtyard, and the sharp eaves of our neighbors' homes, I could see the cobbled streets, the people in them who uttered the sounds that grieved me so. They are only people, I thought. Let them do what they will. I will tolerate it, to be close to my husband.

These are the compromises we make to nurture a successful marriage. My sister has asked me: how do we make a life where I could not bear children? She cannot conceive of it. It is true, I'd give so many things to be a mother: the house, the money, all of it really. But it is not my lot, and so I gave for my husband. And he gave for me.

Now, it appears, Thomas Spencer has given his life for me.

I am hungry, but I cannot eat. I sit in the drawing room, among these things that mean nothing. Lamps, curtains. A piano. I could play it, but music would cause my ears to bleed.

Sensitive. Lottie is in the kitchen, preparing a chicken, but the smell of that sickens me, too. I see the world in duller colors.

Detective Price and Detective Proudmoore have arrived from Holborn. Proudmoore swaggers in first, his substantial gut swinging. His blue coat strains across the stomach. Price is his contrast, a slip of a man, shorter than I. Even inside, he hides behind his cap, only removing it when I stare at him longer than I should. The buttons on his coat are cleaner than Proudmoore's.

"Violet. He was dead when you got here?"

I nod. "Lottie says he was ill all night. His bowels." I could picture it, every moment. The moans. The agony. The smell. I become keenly aware of Proudmoore's sweat, and I swallow.

"Where had you been?" Price bends over a notebook, scratching on the paper as I speak.

"Visiting a friend in Kensington. I wasn't far."

"This friend will vouch for you?" Proudmoore.

I have no reason to wonder why they are questioning me. So often a wife has reason to kill her husband. I nod.

Price scribbles, then looks up, tapping the pencil to his temple. "He showed no signs of illness?"

"You saw him more than I."

The men exchange glances.

"Why he would fall ill so suddenly?" Proudmoore again, hitching up his belt.

I adjust my skirt. "I have not been at home."

"Seems Lottie is in charge here. What do you do, Mrs. Spencer?" Proudmoore sneers, and with every step closer, a wave of stench rolls over me. Has he been sleeping with dogs? I may well vomit. I purse my lips. I have solved a hundred crimes in my husband's name. I have questioned midwives and maids, widows and whores. Women's work. The work only I can do. This man knows none of it. Investigating has been my life's work, but the only man who knew it no longer lives.

Lottie skulks behind the kitchen walls. I can see her scuttling past, a flash of movement. "Ask her," I tell them. "I won't be far, if you think of anything else."

Daisy finds me plucking at a cushion in the parlor. Same as I was; I haven't moved.

"Oh, my dear, sweet sister!" She rushes at me, aflow in skirts and laces. Her huge belly between us, she pushes her cheek at mine. Salty tears drip on my lips. "Whatever has happened?"

I see no need to explain. I shrug towards the kitchen. "A mishap of domesticity," I say.

Proudmoore and Price emerge. Lottie trails them. She is my prime suspect. Alone with Thomas in my absence - I do not know her motive, but her opportunity was prime. The motive will come, like soap rising to the surface of water.

"Case closed," Proudmoore says.

"Your dog's dead," Price adds.

"We don't have a dog," I tell them.

"A dog's dead, then," Proudmoore conjectures. "Little miss suspected last night's bread. She said Spencer remarked on its taste."

"We'd take the girl in, since she bought it," says Price. "But it's an honest mistake. The girl will pay for her sin in shame."

In truth, Lottie is red as Proudmoore's rosy cheeks. I am the only woman not crying.

"So there is the matter of the body." Price pulls the little notebook out again, presumably to write down the church details.

I put a hand out. "Burn it."

Daisy gasps. "Violet, you can't." Lottie looks ill.

"I won't say any more on the subject. If we cannot learn any more from my husband's body, I don't want it in the house."

No more is said.

"Very well, then. I'll send a carriage," Proudmoore says.

"Good luck to you." Price.

They leave.

Daisy, for her part, smells like lavender. The wrong flower. But then, I don't smell a thing like a Violet. She rubs her hand over the big belly. We'd thought the baby would be here by now. The signs were there. "What about a burial?" she asks.

I shake my head.

"Burn me when I die," Thomas said.

The night dragged on. The sounds and smells, and he still would not allow me to shut the window. I craved sleep, and yet it would not find me.

"Why?" I asked, pushing my face against the feather pillow.

"Worms," he said.

"No - why bring it up now?"

We'd hauled a harlot to gaol earlier in the day - Thomas had, at least, but I'd illuminated the crime. She'd killed a john, a Corinthian, not for abuse but out of spite. Because she could. She'd blamed it on another girl, but I'd tricked her into confessing intimate details. What he liked to do. My skin crawled, but I asked, and she answered. The other girl's answers didn't match the wife's, and the true killer was carted off.

I didn't want to talk of death anymore. People disappointed me. I wanted the safety of my husband's arms. I nestled back against him, to wall me against the tide of humanity, taking care not to breathe too deeply.

"One day I'll die," Thomas said. "And we won't have this anymore."

"Lottie!"

She hurries forward, wringing her hands. Daisy plants

her hands on her disappearing hips and huffs.

"Did you poison my husband's food?" I ask. May as well get to the point.

The serving girl's eyes grow round as a full moon. "I swear, I didn't know."

"The bread. Do you remember its color? Consistency?" I wait for the answer and worry. The dead dog may smell. The carriage from the crematorium should take that, too. "Well?"

"I don't... I don't recall."

"Why did you buy it?"

She shakes her head. "The merchant gave me a deal. Only two pence for the lot of it."

I want to shake her. She stands before me, huge eyes wide and stupid, mouth slack and gaping. Her curly hair is tied atop her head, falling pieces a ringed mess around her face. Behind me, Daisy wheezes.

A hundred more silent days ahead of me. I retreat again into memory, my only refuge now. Thomas Spencer exists only in my mind now. The body in the other room a cruel parody. What happens to love when it shrinks and dies? Which is the greater tragedy - love removed like a thorn plucked out, or love cut away gradually, shaved away, like a marble statue chipping?

Marble. My husband's white face.

"She wasn't happy," Thomas said, his voice fading into the sounds of the night. His lips moved against my shoulder.

"Not surprising," I said, turning over. Sleep was now the elusive prize I chased. His hands and fingers were hot against my body, the light shift all I wore. "You arrested her."

"You caught her," he said. I detected awe, ever so slight. "You solved the crime."

I scoffed. "Hardly justice. She should have been in gaol years ago. Murder is not the only crime."

Thomas ran his finger along my arm. I shivered in spite of myself. The clock on the first floor struck, heavy, resonating through the house. "That man's children will know his killer was punished."

"They'll also know he died with a prostitute." I squeezed my eyes shut. How I wished we would stop talking so I could slip away. So I could pretend I did not exist for another night. "Murder is not the only crime."

I willed myself to drift off, to ignore the sounds and smells. To relax against his broad chest. In moments, he was asleep. His snores filled the room. I was certain I'd hear the clock many more times that night.

Lottie is gone. Daisy sits on the edge of the chaise, leaned forward, face filled with concern. I have walled off everything she has said. I am still thinking of the silence, the absence ahead.

"You don't wish to detain the girl?" Sweat drips from Daisy's temples.

"I have no proof," I say. "The woman in the market could have been guilty. Without knowing it."

Daisy clucks. "It's a shame, these vendors, what they do."

"Still, I feel it was not entirely an accident." Burn me when I die. "A motive may turn up. I'm not finished with Lottie."

"Could it have been a business colleague?" Daisy sits up straighter. "An officer?"

I think back to Proudmoore. He is guilty of gluttony, at the least. Price and his pencil. "Possible."

Justice. I knew who killed that john. I knew who'd killed babies and grandmothers and husbands. The women in the weeds, in the dregs of society. Desperate women. Sad women. Women like me. I shake my head. "They will arrest me before they accuse one of their own."

"Then we will never know the truth." Daisy lays a hand on her belly. "If it's a boy, he'll be Thomas."

I don't want to see a baby, not even a nephew. Daisy

must leave.

The clatter of wheels, the click of hooves, and the carriage is pulling up. Grateful for the excuse, I rise to meet the men who will burn my husband. My sister does not move.

Dr. Hastings leans over the body in our bed. That's all Thomas is now. Cold and stiff. Turning blue. Stinking stronger by the minute.

"What did the detectives say?" I crane my neck to see where he is looking, but of course, my untrained eyes will not find anything.

He peers over thin-framed glasses, but doesn't reply. No confirmation or denial: I am still a suspect. A weak woman. I will be hauled away to a place that will smell worse than this house, these streets. I shiver at the thought.

Hastings throws up his hands. "I see no evidence of foul play."

"Why else would he drop dead, with no warning? A healthy man of forty?"

"Sometimes these things happen." He adjusts his spectacles. "You'll live your days. The police will pay a pension. Case closed." He snaps a finger for the men, to carry the body away.

It cannot be over this soon. I move between them, possessed by a sudden urge. I throw myself on his body, bury my head against his neck, and feel him unyielding. Stone. Not my husband - an object. But where his breath should be, a lingering smell. I can identify so many, my head pounds so often from the stenches about this town. The sickly sweet lavender perfume.

My halfhearted attempts at accusations. My discoveries, my missteps. All before this, blurring together into a sea of events. Piecing puzzles together. Fitting a key into a lock. Who was with him last night, while I was in Kensington?

I rush downstairs, into the parlor. Daisy's own hand is

on her back. She puffs out a breath, lips loose. "I think the baby's coming."

"Never mind the baby." Grunts from upstairs: the men are lifting Thomas's body. I will never see it again. "Did you--"

I stop.

The rage that fills me crashes like a wave. Murder is not the only crime.

I can keep pretending my husband was murdered. Throw Lottie on the sword, manufacture a motive, blame Price or Proudmoore. But I know it now, with instinctual surety. Bread made with acid. It must have burned going down.

I have solved so many crimes, and the most heinous was here the whole time. He wasn't alone when he died, of that unfortunate accident.

Daisy pleads with me, her back breaking, but I do not look at her.

That night in our bed, it must have been three o'clock in the morning and Thomas was awake again, talking again. His breath was sour and hot against my ear.

"Would you hate me?"

I wanted him to stop speaking. I had been so close to the void. All I could think of was sleep. "For what?"

"If I betrayed you."

"You wouldn't." An easy answer, but one that would get him to be quiet.

"I love you, Violet," he said, burying his head against me.

The wrong flower. The wrong sister.

I exit the train in Nottinghamshire and hire a carriage to the Galleries of Justice. I can afford the extra help. A woman would never move a trunk such as the size I've packed. The drivers can manage it. "You're sure this is the place?" the driver asks, and I nod.

I am dwarfed by the stone building. It seems to rise so high and go on and on. When I find the door to enter, there's a woman sitting at a rosewood desk. She too looks so small below the high ceiling, but unlike me, she is sure of herself. "You ain't supposed to be here," she crows, looking me up and down. "What's your business?"

"I'm looking for work," I tell her, standing up straight. "I've worked with the police in London for many years. I'm an expert investigator."

The woman scoffs. She's missing a tooth, but her hair is coiled in a tight bun, and her clothes are neat. "Right, and there are women investigators like there are flies in my ass. You expect to walk in here and get a job, when I begged for mine? Go back to London."

My legs shake, but I move forward, closer to her. Her scent is familiar, male. I recall the cloth of the coppers' uniforms, the shiny buttons on Proudmoore's belly. She's so close to a man that his scent has rubbed off. "I'm sure you were on your knees," I say. "I've earned my station."

"A woman's gotta do." But I've moved her in some way. She shrugs, and her hard exterior cracks. "You are good. Could you tell which officer he is?"

I shrug back and allow myself to smile.

She leans an elbow on the rolltop of the desk, scratching at her bun. "It'll be a hard sell, but you can work in the gaol until I get through to him. Come talk to me again, once you're settled. The name's Rosie."

"Violet."

Rosie grins. "We're sisters, then? Flower sisters." There's a lump in my stomach, but I nod. She slides a key ring across the polished surface. "I'll show you around."

I look back at my trunk, then hook the ring around a finger, jangle the keys. Gaoler. I don't know why I feel so free.

Cari Dubiel is a librarian and writer in Northeast Ohio. She serves as Library Liaison to the National board of Sisters in Crime. Her fiction and essays appear around the Web, and she is the co-host of The ABC Book Reviews *podcast. Find Cari at www.caridubiel.com and www.abcbookreview.com.*

The Scent of Anger

By T. Lee Harris

If she lived to be one thousand, she doubted she'd ever get used to this. K'Natu Golden Eye scanned the cloudless sky over the not-too distant city walls again. When she looked, there was nothing but barely visible wisps of white smoke, but when she looked... there was something else entirely. Something...

"Helllooooooooo!"

A hand waved in front of her eyes, blocking out smoke, city walls and interrupting the half-formed vision. Concentration snapped like an over-stretched cinch, psychically dumping her unceremoniously into reality just as the physically breaking strap would land her in the dust. She blinked and focused on her breakfast companion, Naashara.

Naashara's expression hovered between irritation and worry as she said, "I have been trying to show you this funny little bowl that Lord Kurash's messenger brought this morning, but you have been leagues away, my friend..." Her gaze slid toward the city. "Ah. It's that damnable fire, isn't it?"

The swordswoman sat back, arms folded across her chest and continued, "More like that damnable golden eye. Zakhiru told me he'd heard you pacing the halls all night. You knew there was something wrong before anyone even saw flames, didn't you?"

"Something awoke me from a sound sleep," the Seer said with a vague nod. "It was like a half-heard call that wakes you and you start awake, straining your ears to hear it repeated."

"Damned priests," Naashara spat with sudden anger. "They said that thing -- that eye -- was supposed to be a blessing, but there's been nothing but trouble since you got it."

Ki'Natu hid a smile, "Trouble? Like this horrible, airy house and courtyard? Maybe the awful, itchy elegant gown you're wearing? Or could it be the terrible time that little painted goat on Khurash's bowl has been giving you?"

"You know perfectly well what I mean." Naashara looked exasperated. "Along with all the fine things, there's always an element of danger. You were nearly killed sorting out Lord Khurash's problem. He needs to send you a lot more than an amusing bowl and a few pieces of gold."

"Shara, our lives have been filled with danger of one sort or another since the day we first signed on as mercenary soldiers. We may have had vastly different reasons for putting our marks on the enlistment roster, but we both knew we were agreeing to face death on a regular basis." Unconsciously, her fingers brushed the cheekbone just below the gleaming golden artificial eye that changed her life. From Soldier to Seer. It had been a surprisingly short journey. Realizing she's fallen silent again, she said, "Zak was right; it was a difficult night. I don't know how long I stood by the windows watching that fire rage. It wasn't the actual fire, though, it was that call. Something else pulled me to that window. Something that seemed to cry out from the very heart of the blaze."

Anxious to change the subject, she lifted the little bowl and turned it in her hands, smiling at the progression of images of the little goat eyeing a leaf high over its head. "It is very fine workmanship! The potter has managed to convey much with a few brushstrokes of glaze."

With a grin, Naashara reclaimed the object. "It is indeed a fine piece, but that isn't the truly wonderful thing about it. Watch!" Pushing back the remains of breakfast, she placed the bowl in the center of the table and gave it a spin. The movement of the bowl gave the illusion of life, making the little goat leap into the air to pull the leaf from the tree again and again. Ki'Natu watched it in delight, her laughter joining that of her old friend's -- until the faint call from the city intruded, pulling her gaze from the leaping goat back to the faint smudges rising over the merchant sector.

Naashara slammed her palm against the tabletop, guaranteeing her friend's undivided attention and making the little bowl wobble drunkenly. "'Natu!"

Ki'Natu Goldeneye pulled her gaze from the wisps of now-white smoke. "I'm sorry, Shara. It was that call again."

"Is it getting stronger?"

"No, it's just . . . persistent." Almost against her will, both eyes, flesh and golden, locked onto the point in the distance where fire had reddened the sky all night. She couldn't agree with her friend that accepting the golden eye and everything that came with it had made her life harder. Different? Definitely different. But that was Nashara. Even when they'd been mercenary warriors, the last commander was always better than the present one, the last mount the fastest, and...

There it went again. What was it?

Looking away from the half-sensed call, she found Naashara also staring at the faint columns of smoke in the distance.

"There must be something very wrong for it to bother you this much, but stare though I will, all I see is a smudgy sky." The smaller woman shifted slightly in her chair and said, "Well, we shall soon know the full story. Gammal had Sheddu saddled up and was out the gates at first light."

"I'm not surprised. From what Kurash's messenger said, a large section of the warehouse district was destroyed and the merchants are in a lather. Messages will be flying, so there's bound to be work for a rider -- even a disreputable boy on a foul-tempered demon of a camel."

Naashara absently twirled the little bowl. "With all that destruction, it's truly miraculous that only one life was lost."

The golden eye twinged. Ki'Natu concentrated, tried to raise a vision, but the feeling vanished like the fire's own smoke. Heavy black brows creased together in frustration. What sort of Seer couldn't even See for herself?

"Zakhiru is out poking around, too," Naashara observed.

"Then, something interesting is bound to happen," the Seer said breaking into a laugh. "Trouble finds that archer even more surely than his arrows find their mark. Zak might have to practice constantly with the bow, but trouble-making seems to be an inborn skill."

The smaller woman winced. "Practice. That's something we haven't done enough of lately. The only thing that kept you -- all of us -- alive in Kurash's debacle was our skill as warriors." She regarded the Seer who had fallen back to brooding on the city skyline. "Why not get our blades and have a session right now? It'll feel good to move and I need something to work the knots out of my muscles."

"And I need to take my mind off of that fire. Sounds good."

Tightening the last strap on her scaled cuirass, Ki'Natu lifted her *khopesh* from its stand, enjoying the familiar heft. She turned the blade, admiring the play of light along its curved bronze length, and smiled. Many people, including Naashara, sneered at the *khopesh* as the bastard child of a farm sickle. True, it probably did spring from such humble origins, but in the hands of one who knew how to wield it, few could stand before it. That usually included Naashara, who was astonished every single time. Smile widening to a grin, she strode for the courtyard.

Her companion was already there limbering up, her straight-bladed sword cutting graceful arcs in the air.

Ki'Natu paused to watch the fluid moves and, not for

the first time, wondered why she'd been chosen as Seer rather than her friend. Together they'd fought side by side, mercenaries in the same battle. Both were wounded in the final, victorious charge. Ki'Natu took a slash to the face and Naashara a spear in the side. Nevertheless, the healing-mages saw fit to replace her injured eye with a magical golden one and simply use healing spells on 'Shara. It was a bafflement. The other woman certainly looked more the part than she. 'Shara was elegantly small and lithe; Ki'Natu was taller than most men and solidly built. Add in her square jaw, dark complexion and rusty-black hair, she was definitely not the delicate, ethereal figure most people conjured up with the title 'Seer'.

Naashara noticed her standing to the side and snorted. "Took you long enough. I was about to declare victory by default."

"Yes?" Ki'Natu laughed and lifted her crooked blade so it glinted in the sun. "Are you sure you aren't just in a rush to not be defeated again by the 'farm implement'? Again?"

"Small chance of that!" the smaller woman sniffed. "Let's get to it. This time I'll knock that crooked waste of bronze into next week."

Grin broadening, Ki'Natu lifted her own shield and advanced.

Time lost meaning as they circled, slashed and parried. Seer was once again Warrior. Smoke forgotten, she reveled in the music of bronze on bronze and the intricate steps of the deadly dance. The sun edged toward its zenith and sweat rolled down their faces, making small spatters of mud in the dust. The dance continued until Naashara misstepped. Her shield dipped slightly. Ki'Natu leapt on the opening. In a flash, the *khopesh*'s rear hook grabbed the shield's edge, pulling it down. A twist of a wrist and the front hook tossed it aside. Teeth gritted, Naashara lunged, but Ki'Natu sidestepped the thrust, catching her opponent's blade in the curve of her own, and in one fluid move, disarmed and threw the smaller woman to the ground.

"You're dead again, my friend."

'Shara picked herself up and spat dirt. Wiping her mouth with the back of her hand, she laughed, "Some day you will have to teach me to use that thing. It looks so clumsy, but I never can beat it."

The Seer pulled off her helm, shaking her long, beaded braids free. "I've tried; you don't listen."

Naashara's reply was interrupted by non-stop profanity that approached at a steady pace. She cocked her head. "Is that Zak?"

"It certainly sounds like his brand of swearing."

A camel's bray punctuated the profanity, then Sheddu hove into view with Gammal and Zakhiru astride his back. As they cleared the gate, Zak slid off, spewing every curse he'd learned in every military he'd ever served in. Gammal, the alleged owner of the demon-camel was lost in soundless laughter. Sheddu, chewing calmly, watched the small, dark human bounce and gyrate. With a slight lift of his head, he spat once and resumed chewing.

"Uggggh! Look at this! This tunic was practically new. That devil has been biting and spitting at me all the way across the city!"

Naashara called, "Gam! Get that hell-beast back to the stable!"

Wheezing, Gammal saluted and wheeled the big animal toward the back of the house. The camel cast one final malevolent look over his shoulder and sauntered away.

Ki'Natu stopped laughing long enough to ask, "Zak, this always happens when you hitch a ride with Gam. Why do you do it?"

The little archer brushed futilely at his tunic. "Well, I had good reason, didn't I? That is unless you didn't want me to bring you news of a petitioner."

Ki'Natu was instantly serious. "Someone is coming to ask me to See for them? Who?"

"It's the wife of the merchant who died in the fire. Name's Tsuprinu. She wants you to look into her husband's death."

The golden eye zinged. She paused, then said, "But why should she need me? Surely she knows how he died."

Zak shrugged, "How should I know? You can ask her yourself. She should be here any moment."

"Whaaat? You let me stand here in these filthy things when a petitioner is almost at my gate?" She shoved the *khopesh* and shield at Naashara and ran for the Seer's pavilion in a flurry of muttered profanity rivalling Zak's.

Within the shadows of the pavilion, she peeled off her armor and fighting clothes. Dropping them into the camphor wood chest behind the Seer's dais, she fished out an elegant embroidered silken caftan. "Silliest damn fool nonsense," she groused, tugging the garment over her head. "I can never understand people. Being able to See doesn't matter. Looking like I can See is what seems to count most."

Cursing the encumbering fabric, she climbed onto the dais. "Bet I smell like a goat. A whole herd of goats." After a moment's thought, she tossed an extra handful of incense into the brazier, settled back into her chair, and arranged the garment to cover the very unseerlike military boots that still encased her feet. She'd just composed herself when she heard the clamor of a sizable entourage enter the yard.

By the time Zakhiru brought the lady into the pavilion, the air within was nicely fogged with spicy-scented incense. After leading the widow to the center of the floor, he took his preferred place on Ki'Natu's left, the side with the golden eye. The Seer was glad the shadowy pavilion hid her expression, because she couldn't completely stop the smile. Bless the pigheaded man. He could never quite understand that, though the eye was artificial, she wasn't exactly blind.

Tsuprinu stood straight and stately, outwardly calm, though the Seer's senses, magical and mundane, screamed she was on the verge of collapse. Her dress was rich, but subdued and a large, agate cylinder seal swung from her wide girdle. Ki'Natu liked her instinctively.

Moving into the flickering light of the brazier, the lady bowed and said, "I greet you, Goldeneye. I come before you seeking justice."

The golden eye hummed. Ki'Natu once again suppressed a smile, one of satisfaction, this time. She'd finally discover just what called to her. Sitting back, she motioned for the woman to continue.

Tsuprinu said, "I am sure you are aware my husband was killed last night in the fire that destroyed our family warehouses. The whole city is talking about it." She paused, then continued almost defiantly, "I believe neither were accidents. I believe my husband was murdered and our property set ablaze deliberately."

The Seer sat forward abruptly. "Tell me more."

Movement at the back of the pavilion distracted her briefly as Gammal and Naashara slid in. Good timing. The swordswoman had pulled on a fresh set of silks and the messenger, looking infinitely uncomfortable, wore what he considered his best robes. They were really going to have to buy him another set. She returned her attention to the elegant lady who now stood silent, eyes squeezed shut.

Lady Tsuprinu's voice shook as she finally murmured, "You believe me."

"Your words ring true, Lady. I, myself, felt there was something more wrong than a simple fire. Please, continue."

"Where to begin? I came prepared to argue my case and now... With Pagrazuz, I think. Yes, Pagrazuz, my husband's business partner.

"My husband, Sananur, was a military man. He fought for the king in many foreign lands and was richly rewarded for his service. When he left the army, he wanted to set up a trading business and make use of all the contacts he made during his travels. Unfortunately, even with all the king's honors, he did not have the money to fund such an ambitious venture. He turned to an older man who had been successful in other business dealings and was very rich. This was Pagrazuz.

"Sananur and Pagrazuz never got on well. Theirs was strictly a financial partnership and they had little in common personally. Recently the relationship worsened. They began fighting. It got so bad that, several days ago, I had to intervene, or I'm sure it would have come to blows."

"What were they fighting about?"

"I didn't hear much of it, but it seems that some items of merchandise were not what they should have been. Adulterated incense, gold and silver items that were not pure... it was very confusing and both of them were too angry to be coherent." Emotion choked her and it took a moment for her to finish, "Now my husband is dead and the warehouses with any evidence are burnt to the ground."

"What has Pagrazuz to say of this? Surely the city guard has spoken with him by now."

"That's just it, Goldeneye. When they went to his house, he was gone. So were his coin box and some clothing."

Ki'Natu stared at the floor. After a moment, she lifted her head, firelight glinting off the golden eye, and stated, "You did not get on well with your husband, either."

Tsuprinu drew a deep breath. "No. I did not -- but neither did I wish him dead. Ours was an arranged marriage. My parents saw the opportunity for a high bride-price and social advancement for the family. Sananur was not an easy man to get along with, a hard man with a volatile temper. However, while I did not love my husband, I honored him in all the proper ways, and he provided well for the children and myself."

The Seer nodded again. "I hear your words, Lady Tsuprinu. Go to your home now. I will look into this matter."

The lady's face flashed hope and gratitude as she bowed deeply, but Ki'Natu didn't see this or her exit. She had already bowed her head into the scented smoke and was riding the swirling waves into a land of visions.

When she came back to her surroundings, her companions were still in their accustomed places, watching her carefully.

Zakhiru spoke first, "You're going to help her, aren't you? I was watching your face as you heard the story. She spoke the truth?"

Ki'Natu paused. "Truth as far as she knows it."

Naashara straightened angrily, hand on sword hilt. "She lied?"

The Seer shook her head. "No. Not like that. There's something hidden, but it's not with her."

The archer frowned. "Where then?"

"I'm not sure, but I do know we have to go to the burnt place."

Gammal grinned. "Good! I'll ready the horses." And he was gone.

The merchant quarter was always busy, but today, it was a madhouse. There were people everywhere: merchants standing in clumps gossiping, beggars combing the wreckage for anything valuable, gawkers craning for a glimpse of something gruesome and city soldiers trying to keep everything under control. From horseback, it looked like a sea of heads. Under ordinary circumstances, it would have been impassable, but the Goldeneye's reputation worked wonders to melt the crowd before them and allow them to reach Sanaur's destroyed warehouse in good time. On the surface there wasn't much to see other than an expanse of blackened ground, rubble and, here and there, a charred support rising from the ashes like a skeletal finger. Over it all, tendrils of smoke still drifted skyward.

Ki'Natu halted her mount and swung down to the cobbles, ignoring the speculative murmur of the crowd behind her. Gathering her skirts, she stepped into the burned building and was suddenly overcome with a horrible sensation -- a wrenching nausea. It hit her like a solid thing, rolled over her and retreated. She whirled to follow its path so fast her beaded braids clattered and lashed her cheek. Scanning the crowd, she saw nothing but a beggar dodging through the milling humanity to disappear between two still-standing buildings. She saw only his back, but his ragged clothing and what skin she could see were blackened and smeared with soot.

She was still staring at the gap between the buildings when the captain of the guard approached. He bowed and said, "We are honored that Goldeneye has come. I am Captain Shumu. How may I be of service?"

The man's face was haggard. He and his armor were streaked with soot. From his look, he was one of the men who had fought the fire. It was a wonder he was still on his feet. She returned his bow, "I greet you, Captain. I have been asked by the widow of Sananur to look into last night's tragedy. Was it your command that found the remains?"

"Yes, Lady, and fought the fire that killed him."

She nodded, moved a little farther in, paused, and moved again. "I could see the flames from my house. It must have been a hard fight."

"It was, indeed, my lady. I hope we never see the like again." Ki'Natu recognized the signs. The man was exhausted, but needed to talk it out. She sympathized. She'd felt that way after many a battle, herself. She continued her halting tour of the smoking ruin as he spoke. "My squad was the first on the scene. It was raging by then and we figured it had been burning hot and fast inside the warehouse for a while before it burst forth. Most of the wares in there were volatile, and we had our work cut out for us. We've fought fires before, but this one was a vicious beast and refused to die easily. When this building collapsed, it took the others to either side with it. It all but exploded then."

"So it was quite a while before the victim was discovered?"

"Yes, it wasn't until we were clearing to be sure no fire lurked in the wreckage when we discovered the... remains."

"Given the fire and the collapse, the body must have been horribly damaged. I should think it wasn't easy to place a name on it." She paused, circled, then stepped over a charred beam to stand in a partially cleared area. "It was here, wasn't it? Where the bones were found?"

The captain's eyes widened. "Yes! It was. But this is. . . ." He bowed. "I have heard much of your powers, Seer Goldeneye, but the stories do you no justice."

She smiled slightly. If her methods seemed like pure magic, then so be it. True, she'd been searching for a feeling as she walked, but she had also been looking for places that were particularly cleared. Still . . . she concentrated. How strange. She would have expected fear, but all she felt in this place was anger. So much anger.

"How was the body identified as that of Sananur the merchant?"

The captain, stifled a yawn. He was starting to collapse, himself. He blinked and rubbed his eyes with his thumb and forefinger, the gesture smeared more soot than it removed. "Oh. Yes. He was identified mainly by this." Reaching into a pouch at his belt, he withdrew two pieces of blackened stone. He placed them in her hand, saying, "This is Sananur's seal cylinder – or what's left of it."

When the blackened pieces touched her outstretched palm, she stifled a gasp as a milder wave of her earlier sensation settled in. With a morbid curiosity, she examined the seal. It had once been a stunningly beautiful piece. Large and heavy, it was carved from local agate and bore the intaglio of a goddess in flowing robes flanked by two winged bulls. Its twin swung on a fine cord from the girdle of Lady Tsuprinu, unless she was mistaken. She rolled the broken seal in her hand. Yes. The ill feeling was definitely coming from it.

She gave the seal back to the officer who was swaying on his feet. "Thank you, Captain. You have been most helpful.

I hope you and your unit are relieved soon."

He grinned through the grime. "Thank you, Lady. So do we."

Before she got back to her companions, she could see something had happened. Their heads were bent together as Gammal talked excitedly. He saw her approach. "'Natu, I was talking to some people over there and one was a slave from the house of Pagrazuz! When she heard I was with you, she begged me to ask you to come to her Master's house and talk with the Overseer."

She raised an eyebrow. "That sounds urgent."

"I think she was scared of something."

Naashara interjected, "I saw the girl you were talking to. Terrified is more the word you want."

Ki'Natu swung back onto her horse and gathered the reins. "Then I'd suggest the house of Pagrazuz as our next stop."

The house of Sananur's partner was in an uproar. Some servants were doing chores with a feverish intensity; others had a dazed look and barely moved. Sobbing could be heard from deep inside the house as the four entered the courtyard.

A gray-haired man with a beard that fringed his sagging jaws stepped out of the house. When he saw the foursome, he almost fainted with relief. "May the goddess of justice be praised! The Goldeneye has actually come. I didn't believe Ammtu when she said she had seen you and requested an audience for us." He ran forward and bowed low. "I am Rabshag, the Overseer. I offer you the hospitality of this house."

Ki'Natu reined in her horse. "I greet you, Rabshag, the Overseer. My companion said Ammtu seemed frightened when he talked to her and it seems she isn't alone. Isn't this excessive for a master who has simply disappeared?"

"Not just disappeared, Lady, but is accused of murder." The old man sighed deeply. "I still don't understand how that could be. The Master isn't a man given to violence. Nevertheless, some of the servants are convinced that the slaves of a suspected murderer are put to death, too. I haven't been able to tell them anything to calm their fears."

"No, that won't happen." She raised her voice to be heard over the resulting babble. "I promise it." In a lower voice she told the Overseer, "Bear in mind, too, we still don't know what really happened. That is why I'm here, to seek out the truth."

"We will help in any way we can." Rabshag bowed low again.

A short time later, she stood in Pagrazuz' bedchamber. The Overseer hovered at the door as if reluctant to enter. The room looked like a whirlwind had hit it, with clothing hanging half out of chests and strewn across the floor. "It certainly seems someone was in a hurry."

"Yes, Lady. This is how we found it this morning when we discovered the Master was gone."

Stepping over to a tangle of fine wools, she ran her fingers along the embroidered border of a deep blue tunic. "The house has a large staff. With so many people in the household, it is amazing none of you heard your master leave."

"Most were asleep until the shouting about the fire woke us. This is usually a very quiet house and Master Pagrazuz rarely requires anything after he retires for the night."

She lifted an alabaster jug of ointment and rolled it in her fingers. "You said most were asleep?" She frowned at the little jar, set it down and picked up a comb. "Who was awake?"

"I was, Lady. I am a light sleeper and something woke me shortly before the shouting began. I'm not sure what it was, but I was making the rounds of the house, checking that all was secure when I heard the first alarm of fire."

She looked at him sharply, "You found nothing amiss?

There was nothing unusual?"

He looked thoughtful. "Now that I think of it, I did hear a noise from the Master's offices. I thought perhaps he had awakened, too, and went in to see if he required anything, but there was no one."

"That would be where the coin box was kept, no doubt." Rabshag confirmed this with a nod. She probed, "Was anything else disturbed or missing?"

"The coin box, some clothing and some jewelry. That's all we know -- it's hard to be certain in this mess."

She nodded, frowned at the comb and laid it gently on the table next to the jar. Turning to the Overseer, she asked, "Did you ever hear your Master arguing with Sananur?"

He looked pained. "All the time, I'm afraid. They didn't get along well at all. Pardon me for saying it, but Master Sananur was not a very pleasant person."

"So I understand. You said earlier that your master wasn't given to violence, yet he had terrible fights with his partner."

"That is true. Most of the time our master was a very pleasant man. Even when one of the servants erred, he was lenient -- too lenient to my way of thinking, but it wasn't my place to say. Actually, Master Sananur was the only person I'd seen who could incite Master Pagrazuz to anger. He seemed to enjoy doing it."

For a long time, the Seer stood by the table, fingertips barely touching the surface, seeming to look through the items arrayed there rather than at them. Suddenly, she smiled at the Overseer and said, "Thank you, Rabshag. You have been a great help."

Outside, her companions were already mounted and waiting. She stepped toward them and right into a surge of the rottenness she'd felt at the warehouse. It was in front of her this time. She ran to the gate and looked up and down the street, but there was no one. Only the sense of someone hurrying away and the noisome aura retreating.

Naashara was beside her in a flash, sword drawn. "What was it? Did you see someone?"

Ki'Natu shook her head. "Let's go home. There's nothing more to be learned here."

Light cloak clutched against the night chill, she sat in the darkness just inside the Seer's pavilion, waiting. Though the brazier was cold, the heavy scent of incense clung to the air and the fabric of the walls. She wondered idly if it had come from Sananur and Pagrazuz' stores. A small noise and the strengthening of the sensation she was coming to know told her he was just outside. It was the same emotion that battered her at the warehouse, that oozed from the ruined seal. It was the sense she'd searched for, but found curiously absent from anything belonging to Pagrazuz.

She stood and strode into the starlit courtyard, watched the dark figure scramble over the wall and drop into a crouch at the base. "Good evening, Sananur, the Not-So-Dead."

He startled, but recovered quickly, and stepped back against the wall. His skin was still blackened from the beggar disguise making him harder to see. She didn't need to see him. She knew where he was. The rottenness of his hate was like a lit lamp to the golden eye.

"Ah, Goldeneye, herself. I'm honored."

"Was it not me you came to see?"

His smile glinted in the dim light. It reminded her of a wolf she had seen once, snarling over a deer carcass.

She asked, "Did you really think that placing your seal on Pagrazuz' body would fool everyone?"

"It seems to have done just that, Lady."

"Not quite everyone or my services wouldn't have been engaged." She moved farther into the yard. "Pagrazuz caught you cheating, yes?"

"Cheating." Sananur laughed bitterly. "The old fool called it stealing. Thought he could talk 'sense' into me. Like I had no idea what I was doing. The wealth I've hidden will allow me to start over elsewhere and live like the king himself."

"How ironic that the same fire you set to cover your escape also prevented it. It must have been maddening to find yourself trapped within the city walls."

His smile vanished.

"I think there are many people who would like to talk with you about that fire -- and about that hidden wealth, too."

"That's too bad. I'd be a fool to turn myself over to the city guard, and I'm not a fool."

"Then we are at an impasse, Sananur, because I can't allow you to walk away. You've committed too many crimes, not the least of which is murder and my calling is to see justice done."

"Then I fear our interview is at an end."

"Not yet. The bones were too badly burnt to make much sense and all I could feel of his death was anger. I'm curious, just how did you kill your partner?"

"I thought you'd never ask." He drew a short sword from the tattered folds of his tunic and lunged.

Shrugging her cloak to the ground, the Seer countered with the blade she'd held concealed in the folds, letting the sword slide into the weapon's curve and skillfully shunting the blow aside.

He fell back a step, surprised. "A *khopesh*? How exotic." He lunged again. She let him come, dodged the charge and snared his leg with the front hook. He fell, and she brought the heavy pommel of the weapon down hard against the back of his head.

He was stunned, but still holding his weapon. He came up suddenly, sword point aimed for her gut. She'd been watching and had seen him tense. Sidestepping the thrust, she spun, bringing the curved bronze edge down with a sickeningly final crunch. The *khopesh* impacted at the same moment an arrow thudded into the man's chest from the side.

She stepped away from Sananur, the Very Dead, as Zak

emerged from the shadows, the horn tips of his bow shone dully in the starlight. He said, "You weren't the only one who couldn't sleep tonight."

"You heard him, then?"

"Not all, but enough to get the gist of the tale." Prodding the body with his toe, the archer shook his head. "Somehow, I don't think this is the kind of truth Tsuprinu was hoping for."

She wiped the *khopesh* with a rag from Sananur's disguise. "Perhaps not. We rarely get to choose our truths."

T. Lee Harris is a scribbler of the lowest order. Not only does she pen lies about people who don't exist, but she draws pictures of them as well. Harris has also been known to aid and abet others by putting their scribblings into book form and going so far as to devise covers for these publications. She claims she went to school to learn these things, but that shouldn't be held against anyone.

Harris is, in turn, aided and abetted by others in her assaults against literature. Among these accomplices are Per Bastet Publications, who have shamelessly published her untruths about an ancient Egyptian scribe and magic temple cat and spread her prevarications about a former football player and a 200 year-old vampire turned international law enforcement agents. Also implicated are Untreed Reads, who have promulgated her lies about a retired spy who keeps getting mixed up in other people's business, and the Southern Indiana Writers' Group -- possibly the worst offenders -- who have repeatedly permitted her to commit acts of literary vandalism with the Indian Creek Anthology *Series.*

Last Composition

By Giles Elderkin

"No time to waste, Theophilus," Mr. Fowler said at the lad's entrance into the public room of the Dansville Herald. "I printed a copy of a completed form of advertisements for the special edition. Plus, three pages of galley proofs are ready and more are coming."

Theo removed his gloves and clapped his hands together to generate warmth. He shrugged off the overlarge coat that had been his deceased father's and hung it on its assigned peg. The weak autumn sunshine had not warmed the newspaper office from an early cold spell that had frosted western New York. "What's the big news?"

The proprietor scanned the hand-printed article attached to a nail above the composing table. "Kill two birds with one stone," he said. Without glancing at the tray of type, he grabbed the letters one-by-one with his right hand, shifted them to his left, and placed them into the galley.

"I know, sir. 'Proofread and you'll get the story.' Sorry sir."

Fowler gave a curt nod and picked up another galley, adjusted the metal tray for the column width he wanted and placed a leading into the galley to give it a space at the top for the new column. He checked the page above the composing table, reached for the first letter—a capital from the right of the tray—and said in a soft voice. "You can't finish, Theophilus, until you start."

Theo startled into action. "Yes sir. Sorry sir." He slipped the printer's smock over his head and inhaled the slightly pungent smell of dried ink. His mother became apoplectic if he got printer's ink on anything more than his hands and would switch his rear end if he ruined another shirt or pair of pants with it. She worked on the laundry staff at Our Home on the Hillside — the water cure on the East Hill outside Dansville, New York — but even she could not perform miracles. He picked up the printed page lying atop the completed form containing three galleys of advertisements and turned his back to the window.

Theo found no errors in the advertisements. "I see you have several new advertisers," he said. "Congratulations."

"Long time in coming. The other papers, especially Jonathan Hooper, will not be happy to have lost their business. Getting the village bank account from Hooper influenced several other merchants to make the change as well. Serves him right, after all the scurrilous insults he has written about the Herald."

"Well done, sir." Theo put aside the advertisements and picked up the first galley, holding it so the light from the window clearly displayed the backwards letters. Now four months into his apprenticeship, it had become routine to read backwards, but he still needed to pay especial attention to minding his p's and q's. Those letters were easy to confuse and since Mr. Fowler would not have accidentally picked the wrong letter, Theo would be to blame for any such error because his job after the final printing was to strip the type from the galleys and place each letter in its proper place. That's when q's ended up with the p's.

Theo shook his head to clear his self-admonition so he could concentrate on the task. The first galley only held two lines of massive type. "Raid at Harper's Ferry" shouted the first line. "John Brown Holed Up" proclaimed the second.

"Oh my gosh and golly!" Theo carefully placed the proofed galley to one side. He picked up the second galley, which would be the top of the first column. He blazed through the summary of events, starting from the bottom left of the galley and working to the right and then up.

> *On Monday October 17 the noble citizens of Harper's Ferry, Commonwealth of Virginia awoke to find John Brown and his band of ruffians and run-away slaves had overwhelmed the guard at the federal arsenal in a heinous act of treason. Brown holds a number of hostages in the armory. Valiant citizens surround the armory and await troops under Col. Robert E. Lee's command. Eight of Brown's men are known dead.*

Theo placed this galley next to the first on the composing table. He picked up the next and continued to read. Near the end he found the first error and realized he had not actually been proofreading. After carefully perusing the earlier galleys, he waited until Mr. Fowler finished the type he was setting before handing him the galley with the error. "Mr. Fowler, you switched the "a" and "e" in beast. Which paper are you getting this story from?"

The newspaperman deftly rearranged the letters. "Morning Star, can't you tell by the tone? Mark my words, Theo, we'll have war yet if we are not careful."

"I knew it wasn't abolitionist," Theo said, and heard his voice squeak on the word abolitionist.

Someone stomped dust off their boots on the wooden sidewalk outside. Accompanied by the bell's tinkle and a stir of fresh air, Dr. Jackson entered the room.

"Ah, our opposing view arrives," Mr. Fowler said. "Take the new proofs I have finished and verify those while I interview the good doctor in the back office. Leave a note with any errors you find."

Theo was surprised "Father Jackson," as everyone at the water cure called him, was only an inch or two taller than his own 5'6". Theo had undergone a recent growth spurt and liked being taller, but hated that his pants legs were always too short. He would trade an inch or two of height for a voice that stayed low and didn't squeak whenever it would embarrass him the most. Theo was envious of Dr. Jackson's beard, which reached mid-chest, although when Theo got the chance, he planned to grow a mustache as well, just as his father had.

The men shook hands. Neither smiled and Theo could smell the tension over the scent of newspaper print. He was startled when Dr. Jackson stretched out a hand toward him.

"Theophilus Clarke?" Dr. Jackson said after the introductions. "Your mother does fine work for us. I am surprised that she allows you to consort with a known Democrat."

Unconsciously Theo straightened to his full height to match Dr. Jackson's strict posture. He knew after his father's death and the loss of their money in the Panic of 1857, his mother was too worried about keeping creditors at bay to be concerned about the politics of his employer. None of this did he feel free to say.

Mr. Fowler crossed his arms over his chest. "The boy can't vote for seven years. By then he'll be able to make up his own mind."

"Never too early to inculcate the young with proper values." Dr. Jackson removed his hat, revealing a large head sparsely covered with brown hair long enough in the back to flip at his white collar. He placed his hat on a peg next to Theo's coat. "Buck up, old man. Let me see what that scurrilous rag you're quoting says so I can frame a response." He chuckled and clapped Mr. Fowler on the shoulder. They shut the door to the back office behind them. Theo continued to search for errors in the proofs.

An hour later Dr. Jackson's voice thundered through the closed door. "It is a mortal sin, Mr. Fowler. Will you understand only after St. Peter refuses you entrance to heaven?"

The doctor slammed out of the back room. At the front

door he spun on his heel and slowly blinked. In a controlled tone he spoke across the front room to Mr. Fowler, who stood in the office doorway, "I shall return once I have regained my temper. Good day, sir." The doorbell tinkled at his departure.

Mr. Fowler's face was red and pinched. "Catching flies, Theophilus?"

Theo snapped his mouth shut. "He's forgotten his hat."

Fowler shrugged. "He'll be back. I had not realized he knew John Brown. They both had worked for Gerrit Smith whom I suspect had a hand in this. Jackson said he was unaware, but I wonder how far the doctor would go to ensure the abolitionists prevail."

Theo found his voice at last. "What caused the argument?"

Fowler dismissed the question with a wave, "No argument. I simply suggested that if we waited long enough slavery would end of its own accord. That's what happened in New York. I believe you heard his response." Fowler's eyes focused on Theo. "Almost done?"

"I've found only two more errors, and I have one galley remaining."

"Excellent. Finish up and then return at noon sharp. I shall be finished by then."

Theo checked his pocket watch. A quarter hour late. He hoped Mr. Fowler would not be mad. On his return he had stopped at the general store across the street from the newspaper office to consider the hard candies recently arrived from Rochester. Minutes had slipped away and now he had to face Mr. Fowler. Rubbing his father's engraved initials on the watch for good luck, he thrust it into his pocket.

The bell sounded angry as Theo rushed in. He shrugged off his coat and gloves. A pile of new galleys lay on the table in silent reproof of his tardiness. "Mr. Fowler, I have returned," Theo called toward the back room. He hung his coat on the peg and noticed Dr. Jackson's hat was now gone.

Theo picked up the top galley, sat down on the chair, and noticed type scattered on the floor. That was not like Mr. Fowler. "Mr. Fowler?" The hair on his neck prickled. He set the galley down and followed the path of the spilled type to a boot poking from behind the type cabinet. His throat threatened to squeeze off his air supply. "Mr. Fowler?" his voice squeaked.

He edged around the composing desk and gasped. Mr. Fowler lay on his back, a scalpel stuck in his chest. Theo wanted to turn away, to run, but like a bass to a worm, he was drawn to the sight of the scalpel. In one great purge, he emptied his stomach all over Mr. Fowler's boots.

Theo burst from the office. The next thing he knew, he was slumped in the proofing chair while a woman pressed a cold cloth against his forehead. Several voices in the room talked over each other.

"Miss Austin, has he come to yet?" a loud male asked.

"Just now. It is a shock for the young man, but I believe he soon should be able to answer your questions."

"Good. And you touched nothing?" the loud voice asked.

"One does not need to be a trained physician to know medical assistance could not help Mr. Fowler." She leaned down and looked into Theo's eyes. "How's your head, son?"

Theo recognized Dr. Austin, the woman physician at Our Home. She had piercing brown eyes, hair tumbling down in unruly curls, and—it continued to shock Theo whenever he saw them—she wore the American Costume: a short dress covering loose pants. She waved a bottle under his nose. His head snapped back at the smell. He tried to look beyond her to see Mr. Fowler, but a man with a metal star pinned to his coat blocked his view.

"You all right?" She spoke in a soft clear voice. "Does your head hurt?"

He touched the lump in the back. "Not much." The stench of death now reached his consciousness, causing him to realize that his mouth tasted of vomit. He started to gag and choked it down.

"What's your name, boy?" the sheriff asked.

"Theophilus Clarke, sir. Apprentice to Mr. Fowler. He's dead?" Of course he's dead, you idiot. That's why the funeral director and his two laborers are standing behind the sheriff. Theo whacked his forehead with his fist and paid for the blow with a flash of pain.

"His mother, Mrs. Clarke, is on our staff," Dr. Austin averred. "Have you sent word to her?"

The sheriff tightened his lips and pulled his eyebrows into a tight vee. If Theo's father had looked that way at his mother, she would have held her tongue and shrunk away from him. Dr. Austin stared right back.

The sheriff broke eye contact with her, pointed a finger at Theo, and bellowed, "Tell us what happened."

Theo's voice squeaked and worse, he stuttered his answer, a problem he had not had in years. Dr. Austin lightly touched his elbow and wiped the cool cloth across his forehead. He relaxed and finished telling them how he had found Mr. Fowler.

"Did you see him earlier today?" the sheriff asked.

Theo pointed to the now packed forms containing the first three pages of the newspaper. "He called me in early to proof those galleys for the special edition. I was supposed to be back at noon to finish." Tears streaked Theo's cheeks. He blushed at being so weak, more like a little girl than a man. He mumbled, "I was late."

"Did Fowler have any visitors today?" the sheriff asked.

Theo told how Dr. Jackson had stormed from his interview with Mr. Fowler. "He left his hat and now it's gone, so I assume he returned," Theo concluded.

"I shall find Father Jackson," Dr. Austin said.

"Just make sure you return with him, Miss Austin," the sheriff said. He faced the funeral director and added, "Go ahead and take the body." To Theo he said, "Once they're done, clean up the puke and ..."

The sheriff snarled at Dr. Jackson, who stood next to the composing desk holding a scalpel in his hand. "Well, is that your scalpel or not?"

"Again, one scalpel looks much like the next, and I have not used the scalpel from my kit since I arrived in town last year. That's not how I practice medicine. Come back with me and we can ascertain jointly whether my scalpel is where I last put it."

"The lad tells me you and Fowler had words today."

"Fowler tries...tried to straddle the swamp on every issue to be 'fair and balanced' as his masthead proclaims. He's a Democrat and in order to present an opposing view he interviews local Republicans. He wanted my perspective on the John Brown mess and was delighted to find out I had spent considerable time with the man some years ago. I filled in details of Brown's life. He—"

"Did you or did you not quarrel?" the sheriff asked.

"We did not." Dr. Jackson seemed to swell. His previously quiet voice now filled the room with the boom of the antislavery orator he had once been. "I lost my temper at his ungodly belief that slavery will go away if ignored and left to take a natural course. I asked if he would choose to be a slave until such time as all were free. If you can believe it, he said that was not the point." The doctor slapped his palm on the table, rattling the forms. "As if there were any other point."

In a conversational tone he continued, "I left in something of a huff and returned a short time later. The lad was gone. We finished our discussion, and I left him upright and whistling some Methodist hymn while putting our interview to type. I walked up the hill to our facility and spent time with our patients. That is where Dr. Austin found me."

The sheriff focused his hooded eyes on the woman who

silently stood by Theo, occasionally giving his shoulder a buck-me-up squeeze. "You found the boy?"

"I was headed to the general store to purchase a packet of buttons when Master Clarke exited this office. He was screaming and so distraught he missed the steps and fell off the stoop, knocking himself out. That was perhaps a quarter past midday?"

The sheriff scowled. "Do you know where your scalpel is, Miss Austin?"

For the first time the hint of a smile crossed her face. "Now you have finally found a use for a female doctor—as a murder suspect? My scalpel is in my surgery, which is on the way to Father Jackson's office. Shall we check for wayward scalpels?"

Dr. Austin nudged Theo toward the door. "Best get home. Your mother must wonder what has happened to you."

"I'm sure Mr. Fowler would wish for the newspaper to be printed," Theo said. "If you see my mother, please let her know I'm fine."

She appraised him with sharp eyes. "I'll see that she knows."

The sheriff followed the two doctors out into the fading light. At the door he said. "Theophilus, I think you should come along with us. Let your mother decide."

The lie came out smoothly: "Mr. Fowler paid me in advance. I feel I must stay."

The sheriff touched a finger to his hat. "The back door is locked. Make sure you lock the front while you're here. We don't yet know why Fowler was killed." He looked at the two doctors. "Or by whom."

Theo needed no further urging and latched the door behind the sheriff, feeling comfort in the solid click of the bolt sliding home. He proofed the remaining finished galleys and realized he felt great sympathy with the stern doctor's views on abolition. To Theo's way of reading the interview, it even appeared Mr. Fowler's questions tilted a little toward the doctor's point of view. To complete the paper, Theo needed to assemble the final page. He could start from scratch, or, since he needed to pick up the letters from the floor, he could 'kill two birds with one stone.'

Theo shuddered. The phrase had been one of Mr. Fowler's favorites and now he would say it no more. His tears reappeared and uncontrollable sobs racked his body.

He angrily brushed away the tears and carefully knelt to avoid the blood still in the cracks between the floorboards. The first part of the spilled galley had tumbled out more or less in order and was easy to reconstruct. The remaining letters were jumbled. He scooped them up and sorted them on the composing table. Like a jigsaw puzzle, after the first several letters it became easier because he had fewer remaining to choose from. With three lines in the galley, Theo discovered Mr. Fowler had not completely set that final galley. He must have been killed while filling it.

The remaining letters — a-a-e-h-h-j-n-n-o-o-o-p-r-t and an em space, did not spell the rest of the next line of text: 'the devil uses silence for his evil pur-'. After placing "t-h-e" and the em space in the proof, Theo again searched the floor for fallen type, but found nothing. He was about to pull the missing 'd' from the type case when scanning ahead he saw the letter 'j' did not appear anywhere in the last lines of the interview.

"What was Mr. Fowler thinking?" Theo asked the walls. "The...what?"

Theo separated the remaining vowels — a-a-o-o-o — from the consonants — h-j-n-n-p-r — and stared at the groupings, willing them to form a single word. He placed all the letters in the galley — they did not complete a line. He was so used to reading them in a galley, he simply rearranged letters to try to find a sensible word. "Honor" still left a-a-o-j-n-p. From those letters the word "japan" jumped out, leaving the letter "o." Japan should be capitalized and besides, the phrase didn't make sense.

With daylight quickly disappearing, he set aside the mysterious letters and completed the galley. While arranging the last galleys in the frame for the final page, he realized his mistake: he had tried to make the letters into one long word since there were no spaces included in the remaining type. What if there were two words with a space and "t-h-e" didn't spell "the" but were pieces of the puzzle?

Theo placed the form on the composing table, pulled type for t-h-e and an em space from the type tray, and tried again. Vowels: a-a-e-o-o-o; consonants: h-h-j-n-n-p-r-t. Now, if one of the words was "honor," the second word would consist of a-a-e-o-h-j-n-p-t. Again "japan" jumped out leaving the four letters of his name, Theo. Why wouldn't Mr. Fowler use capital letters? Maybe he didn't have time. That could also explain the missing em space and maybe a missing comma, although Mr. Fowler routinely skipped commas to save space.

Five minutes of fussing brought Theo no closer to a solution. What could "Theo honor Japan" possibly mean? There had to be a message; Mr. Fowler was too precise to grab any old letters.

"Two words," Theo said aloud. "What could two words say or was Mr. Fowler interrupted before he could finish his clue?" A name. Two words could be a name. The letter "j" is not often used. "Dr. Jackson. He did kill him! Theo grabbed the "j" and an "a" before he realized there was no "c" or "k."

Wait. Maybe the "theo" was right, leaving...Theo banged his head. Leaving all the same letters as he had tried the first time, except with one fewer "o."

A knock at the door startled Theo. His knees weakened and instinctively he ducked behind the table. The door handle rattled, once softly and again with anger, and yet the person did not call out. Had the killer come back? To do what? Should Theo run out the back door? After what seemed like a lifetime, but must have only been a minute, Theo heard footsteps clump down the wooden sidewalk.

Tall shadows painted the far end of the composing room in the glowing orange of coming sunset. Theo packed the forms and loaded the first page onto the printing press in the near darkness. He wanted to light a kerosene lamp, but remembered Mr. Fowler's prohibition because with newsprint stored inside, the risk of fire was high. Vigorous knocking on the front window interrupted Theo's inking the press. His hand jerked, drizzling ink on his pant leg.

"Master Clarke, your mother wants you to return home," Dr. Austin said. "I completed my duties and our house is only a few blocks away, so I offered to bring you her message. She is agitated, which is not good for her health."

Theo glanced at his stained pant leg and knew his mother would soon become even more agitated. The picture of the scalpel stuck in Mr. Fowler's chest entered Theo's mind. His mother was surely worried, and Dr. Austin seemed too nice to be a murderer, yet her appearance here seemed odd. The sheriff had not arrested her…Theo's mind froze in uncertainty. What would his father do if he were alive?

From the back room came the sound of breaking glass. With a whoosh, flame and heat flashed into the composing room nearly reaching the press.

Inside was sure death. Outside Dr. Austin waited. With another scalpel? Were the two doctors cooperating to burn him out? Theo's mind provided the jumbled phrase "from the fire to the frying pan." With trembling hands he unlocked the front door and rushed to the street, knocking Dr. Austin aside with a bent elbow. The draft from the opened door sucked the flames into the composing room.

"Fire!" Theo screamed at the top of his lungs. "Fire!"

Dreary rain clouds obscured the sunrise. Charred wood scented the air surrounding the sodden mess of the arson site. Theo, whose coat and gloves had burned in the fire, wore yesterday's ink-stained trousers and a hand-me-down coat brought by one of Dr. Jackson's sons.

The sheriff kicked at the rubble with the toe of his shoe. "I'm sorry, lad," the sheriff said. "We might never know. It's usually women or money that cause trouble. You sure you've never seen Miss Austin in there before? She's a strange one: no husband, dressing half between a man and a woman, and claiming to be a doctor—though people tell me she is. We'd be better off if women kept their place at home. We were lucky you got out safe and the wind was blowing in the right direction so the town didn't burn."

The sheriff continued talking, but Theo stopped listening once he decided the sheriff was talking to hear himself talk. He spotted the brass chime from the front door and gave it a shake. The harmonics rang and to his surprise, he knew the answer to the jumbled type.

Theo interrupted the sheriff's soliloquy and told him about the extra type and what it spelled.

The sheriff gave him a skeptical look. "What you say may be true, but you'll never find your proof." His wave included the building's acrid remains.

"I know where they are," Theo said. "The type case burned, but its type is over in the far corner. I had already laid the newspaper out in forms. The wooden forms may be gone, but the galleys and the type are metal and should be intact. The only loose type will be the jumbled letters." Before the sheriff could stop him, Theo ran into the debris, dropped onto his knees, and sifted through the wreckage.

Theo shadowed the sheriff as he walked into Mr. Hooper's newspaper office. Drs. Austin and Jackson were already present with a burly sheriff's deputy standing behind them. After exchanging salutations, the sheriff asked Mr. Hooper if he would run off the galleys from the Dansville Herald's last edition in order to see if they could shed light on the events of the previous day. "Let's start with the page he was working on when he died," the sheriff said.

"Rumor has it," Mr. Hooper said as he packed a form

with the galleys Theo handed over, "that you questioned the doctors at Our Home on the Hillside."

"I checked both their surgeries." The sheriff nodded at the pair. "Their scalpels were right where they were supposed to be. I hope what you print will provide a clue."

Hooper began to ink the press. "Maybe they had second ones. Doctors often do."

"How would you know?" the sheriff asked.

"Oh, my father was a surgeon in the War of 1812," Hooper said "Wanted me to be one too, but printing words got in my blood. Here, lad, you do this. My apprentice is not here."

Theo loaded the form and a piece of newsprint and cranked the press. His muscles relaxed with the work. Hooper, with a slight palsy in his hands, lifted out the finished page. Reading the interview with Dr. Jackson, Hooper's eyes scanned back and forth. Theo nervously tapped the heel of his left boot with his right toe, waiting for Hooper to read the last line, which Theo and the Sheriff had composed.

Hooper's face drained of color; the newsprint rattled in his hands. "That…that…that despicable backstabber. I'm glad I…"

Into the silence the sheriff said, "Killed him? That's what it says." He took the newssheet from Hooper and read. "jonathan hooper killed me with a scal—. It stops there, but we can guess he would have said 'scalpel.' Can't we?"

"This is preposterous." He pointed a palsied finger at the doctors. "It was Jackson. Those abolitionists will stop at nothing to get their way. Just look at this John Brown outrage—Did you know Jackson knew the man? Both of them crazy, you ask me. A doctor who treats the ill without medicines. He's just a—"

"Mr. Fowler secured from you the advertising from the bank and several other merchants' accounts," Theo said. "He was driving you out of business."

"Theophilus figured it all out." The sheriff held a

handful of loose type before Hooper. "Fowler held these letters when you killed him. He hid what he was doing from you in order to leave us his dying clue. Being another newspaperman, if you'd paid attention you could have spelled out the words as he grabbed type."

"And you burned the building so no one could buy the press," Theo said.

Hooper's fingers twitched at his side. He gave the sheriff a smile. "Everyone knows Dr. Jackson is a radical Republican. He couldn't put up with that Democratic tripe Fowler printed in the name of fair play. He's a doctor. He had scalpels." He raised his arm and pointed at Dr. Austin. "Or he got her to do it for him. No one would suspect a woman, but she hardly acts like one, and—"

"And as you mentioned," the sheriff spoke over him, "your father was also a doctor. Theo and I have just come from searching your house. Your father's scalpel is missing from his bag. I am arresting you for murder and arson."

"While he's in jail," Theo asked the sheriff. "Do you think I could use his press? I have a paper to get out."

Giles Elderkin is the pseudonym award-winning mystery author James M. Jackson uses for stories set in the distant past or the not so distant future. He has deep roots in upstate New York and New England, but now splits his time between the remote woods of Michigan's Upper Peninsula and the Lowcountry of Georgia. He is a member of the Short Fiction Mystery Society and the Guppy and Low Country Chapters of Sisters in Crime. You can find more information about him at:
http://gileselderkin.com or http://jamesmjackson.com

The Candy Cane Murders

By Roxanne Dent

London, 1878
Murder

It started snowing heavily on Christmas Eve. By four p.m., most businesses were closed and London streets deserted.

Sarah Wyndom, owner of "Discreet Private Inquiries," was looking forward to a quiet afternoon at home wrapping gifts. She tied an elaborate, red ribbon on a small box wrapped in silver paper. Inside was an elegant gold fob watch. It was meant to replace the one a criminal had destroyed when he stabbed Inspector Grove in the chest a year ago. Sarah hoped the Inspector wouldn't think it too extravagant. She could easily afford the gift but his pride might make him decline.

As she placed the box under the tree with the others, there was a knock on the door and her maid Mary burst in.

"Oh miss, I know you said not to disturb you, but there's been a murder next door at Dr. Royalston's."

"Good heavens, who was murdered?"

"Miss Diana Coombie-Walsh. She and her family were visiting the Royalstons. Inspector Grove just arrested one of the servants." Mary whispered, "I heard it was poison."

"How dreadful!"

"Miss Edith Royalston is in the office and insists on speaking with you."

"Bring a pot of strong tea. I will be down directly."

"Yes miss."

The office was located on the first floor of a modest, three story, brownstone building Sarah purchased from her inheritance ten years earlier. Before descending to the first floor, Sarah stood in front of a hall mirror and adjusted the combs in her auburn hair.

Her heart-shaped face showed few lines, even though she would be thirty-six next June. Her garnet earrings sparkled in the light. She had good bone structure, but her features were too bold for true beauty and she had long since made peace with that.

As soon as Sarah entered the office, sixteen year old Edith Royalston, unruly, brown hair escaping its pins, stopped pacing. She blurted out passionately, "Genevieve didn't do it. I want to hire you."

Sarah refrained from smiling as she sat behind her desk. She was fond of Edith, whose impulsiveness and outspokenness reminded her of her own nature at the same age.

"Have you tried the tea yet Edith? It's a very good Darjeeling."

Edith glared at her as she exclaimed, "You don't understand. There's been a terrible miscarriage of justice. Inspector Grove has arrested Genevieve, Mama's lady's maid, for poisoning Diana Coombie-Walsh."

Sarah sat behind the desk. "Yes, I heard but rushing to and fro won't help her."

Edith reluctantly plopped down onto the well-padded chair facing her.

"Inspector Grove is an excellent policeman. I'm sure he wouldn't have arrested Genevieve without reason."

"Of course he would," Edith protested, an angry, red flush staining her cheeks. "She's only a servant and a French one at that."

"Tell me calmly what happened."

Edith took a gulp of tea and shuddered. "It was awful. We were all gathered together, helping to decorate the tree. Genevieve brought in a tray with little glasses of chocolate liquor, a tiny candy cane in each one. It looked," she said wistfully, "so pretty."

"And who was present?"

"Besides myself, Mama, Papa, Lorena and Nicholas, Mr. and Mrs. Coombie-Walsh, their son Rolly who is going to marry Lorena next month, and his awful sister Diana."

"Why was Diana awful?" Sarah asked curiously.

"She once accused Kitty, one of our parlor maids, of stealing an expensive pin. She carried on so, Mama was forced to let her go without a reference. A week later we found the ugly thing, which had fallen under the couch. She didn't even apologize. She was horrid and laughs at all of Nicky's stupid jokes."

"Since your sister is marrying her brother, perhaps she was just trying to be friendly."

Edith snorted. "Diana was mad for Nicholas and wanted him to make her an offer."

"What were his feelings in the matter?"

"Papa wanted him to. I know it's vulgar to speak of money, but the Coombie-Walshes are as rich as Croesus."

Sarah bit her lip to keep from smiling. "Did anyone seem upset or nervous when the drinks were passed around?"

"Quite the opposite. Papa was in a good mood because Nicholas had graduated and was going to join him in his practice. Mama was so pleased Lorena and Rolly had finally set a date. Then Papa raised his glass in a toast."

"Did everyone drink?"

"We just sipped ours but Diana, who was mad for chocolate, drank hers down at once and then made a face and complained it had a peculiar taste. No one else thought so."

"Did she collapse right away?"

"No, but she did seem restless and nervous. When Mama approached her to ask a question, she let out a screech and nearly jumped out of her skin.

"How long was it before she showed symptoms of being poisoned?"

"Ten minutes. No more."

"What happened?"

"She went into spasms. It was ghastly. Her back arched. She gasped, clawing at her throat and made horrible noises and then fell over." Edith shuddered."

"What were everyone's reactions?"

"Papa examined her and announced Diana was dead. He and Nicky had to give Mrs. Coombie-Walsh a sedative. Her husband took her into another room to lie down."

"Was that when your father sent for the police?"

"He sent round for Dr. Morrison first. He's Papa's partner in surgery and lives only a few doors away."

Sarah understood. As a doctor, Edith's father must have recognized the symptoms and wanted confirmation of a poisoning.

"After Dr. Morrison examined Diana. he took Papa aside. Papa then called Benson to summon the police. That's when Papa realized I was still there and ordered me to go to my room. As the doors closed, I heard him mention poison."

"Where was Genevieve during Diana's attack? Had she already left the room?"

"No. Mama insisted she stay and join us in a toast."

"What made Inspector Grove arrest her?"

The poison was in the liquor and Genevieve prepared it. It was her idea," Edith admitted reluctantly. "She paid for it out of her own money. A Christmas Eve treat." Edith started to cry.

"Did Genevieve have any reason to poison Miss Coombie-Walsh?"

Edith sniffed and sat up straight. Her chin jutted out. "No."

Sarah felt certain Edith was holding something back. "What did Genevieve say in her own defense?"

"She insists she's innocent, but Inspector Grove arrested her anyway. And everyone is so relieved because," Edith colored up, "she's not one of us."

"Yes, I see how that would be more palatable," Sarah agreed dryly. "Was anyone else ill?"

"No. Perhaps the poison was in the bottle when Genevieve bought it and the rest of us didn't get sick because we only took a few sips."

That seemed unlikely. "Now, close your eyes, Edith, and think back. Where was everyone when Genevieve entered with the glasses?"

Edith obediently shut her eyes.

"Lorena and Rolly were standing together on one side of the tree. I was on the other side with Mama and Mrs. Coombie-Walsh hanging paper ornaments. Papa was at the marble table by the door removing the angel from the box and Diana was trying to drag Nicholas to the entrance, where a sprig of mistletoe was hanging."

"Did Genevieve go round to each person or did people hand out glasses to others?"

Edith frowned. "We were all ready for refreshment and crowded round Genevieve. I think we each took a glass off the tray, but Genevieve did hand out glasses, too," she reluctantly admitted.

"What happened when the police arrived?"

"They removed all the glasses and the rest of the bottle of liquor. Inspector Grove interviewed everyone except for Mrs. Coombie-Walsh, who was still lying down, and then they arrested Genevieve."

"I only know Genevieve by sight. Tell me about her."

Edith's eyes lit up. "Genevieve is kind, has a wonderful sense of style and works hard. She's saving her money so one day she can return to France and open her own dress shop."

"So she's ambitious as well as discreet and practical."

Mama relies on her. She never objects to doing something extra. Diana said she puts on airs, but she doesn't."

"If she heard such a criticism it must have angered her."

"Genevieve would never show it."

Sarah stood up. "I promise to speak to Inspector Grove and learn what sort of case they have against Genevieve. But I warn you Edith, if she's guilty, there is nothing I can do."

"She isn't. I promise you," Edith said jumping up.

And if she is innocent, Sarah thought sadly, someone else in that room is guilty but she kept such troubling thoughts to herself.

As Edith reached the door she turned back, a look of anxiety on her face.

"I suppose I should have mentioned this before. I've saved a little of my allowance, but I can't pay very much."

Sarah smiled. "We are friends, Edith. If I feel Genevieve is innocent, I will take the case for a shilling."

Edith ran over and hugged her. "Thank you Sarah. I knew I could count on you."

Inspector Grove

Inspector Grove wasn't due to arrive until Christmas morning to exchange gifts and partake of Christmas dinner with Sarah's other guests.

The prospect of quizzing him over the roast duck, or digging for information on a murder case brought a guilty blush to Sarah's cheeks. It was rare the Inspector had a day off, and she didn't want to spoil it for him by discussing murder. Her questions would have to wait until after the holiday.

A couple of hours later, as she finished wrapping the last of her gifts and put the finishing touches on the tree, Sarah glanced out the window. It had stopped snowing. Although the drifts were high in places, the snow had deteriorated to piles of grey slush and ice. A few carriages struggled down the street.

It was a miserable night and Genevieve would be spending it behind bars in a cold cell on Christmas Eve, friendless and alone with only a young girl who still believed in her innocence. Sarah wanted to meet this woman who inspired such passion in Edith, but to enter Brixton Prison she needed the help of Inspector Grove. She stood up and summoned Mary to get her a hansom.

Sarah sighed as she put on her new, fur lined boots. On the face of it, Genevieve sounded guilty. Speedy trials were the norm now and a person might go before a judge, jury and be hanged inside of a month. Time was of the essence. It was obvious Edith had a schoolgirl crush on the older woman and was acting from emotion. There was no need to hold out hope if there was none.

The drive to the police station took longer than anticipated due to the weather and the condition of the streets. Once, the driver had to get down and dig his way out of the ice. She worried that by the time she arrived, the Inspector would have already left the station. Fortunately, she spotted him as he was crossing the street. She leaned out of the window. "Inspector, would you join me?"

Surprised, he smiled. "Happily."

As he stepped in, she gave instructions to the driver to head toward Inspector Grove's address. It wasn't far from the prison.

He settled back on the worn cushions and remarked, "How lucky for me you happened to be passing just as I was leaving."

"Luck had nothing to do with it," Sarah replied honestly. I was hoping to see you before you went home."

"What makes me think it's not a desire for my company but about the murder of Miss Coombie-Walsh?" he said amused.

"It is," she admitted.

He laughed. To her delight, he took one of her gloved hands in his for a moment and squeezed it. "It is always a pleasure to see you, Sarah. You're never boring. The case seems pretty straight forward. What is it that disturbs you?"

Sarah was startled by the unexpected compliment, along with the intimacy of her hand being squeezed. The use of her given name had suddenly derailed her thoughts.

"The evidence against the maid is overwhelming, or I wouldn't have arrested her," he assured Sarah.

"I would expect nothing less."

"There's no secret about the evidence. Mrs. Royalston's lady's maid, Miss Genevieve Bouchon, purchased a bottle of peppermint chocolate liquor three days ago. After draping tiny candy canes in each glass, she brought the tray into the front parlor to present to the family. Dr. Royalston made a toast and –"

"Miss Diana Coombie-Walsh had a violent fit and died. From what Edith tells me, it sounds like strychnine poisoning."

"It is. Is Edith Royalston your client?"

"She is"

"And how much of her pin money did she pay you?" he asked, chuckling.

Sarah refused to be drawn. "Beyond the fact the maid purchased the liquor and served it, did you feel Genevieve was a murderer? I trust your instincts."

"I'm flattered. I was forced to arrest Miss Bouchon on the evidence and the fact she had a motive."

"What motive?" Sarah asked frowning.

"Apparently, there was an altercation a few days ago between Miss Coombie-Walsh and Miss Bouchon."

"I thought Edith was holding something back. What was it about?"

"Miss Coombie-Walsh accused her of flirting with Mr. Nicholas Royalston and words were exchanged."

Sarah sighed. "Do you think it's true?"

"The servants say Miss Coombie-Walsh was a troublemaker and fancied him herself, but that doesn't mean she lied."

"I disagree. The Royalstons didn't fire Genevieve," Sarah pointed out. "More to the point, what about the poison? Did you find any on Genevieve or in her room?"

"We did," he said grimly. "The kitchen had a box of it to get rid of vermin and we discovered a packet of the stuff in a hat box buried at the bottom of her closet."

For a few minutes as Sarah considered the evidence against Genevieve the only sound was the steady clop of horses' hooves striking the pavement, and the sound of servants shoveling snow and slush away from residences.

Inspector Grove cleared his throat. "In spite of the weight of the evidence against her, I'm inclined to believe her innocent."

"Really? You surprise me. Why?"

"She appeared stunned and her shock and disbelief put me in mind of," his eyes hardened, "the Jackson case."

Sarah knew the Inspector was haunted by the memory. The Jackson case occurred before they met, so she had never known Elenora Jackson or the members of the Jackson family who had gathered together for Sunday dinner one warm, summer night in July of 1858.

The evidence that the beautiful Mrs. Jackson had poisoned her much older husband of six months was overwhelming and the newly promoted Inspector Grove was forced to arrest her.

Members of the family who testified at her trial insisted she only married him for his money and was having an affair but the mysterious lover had never been located. Mrs. Jackson was found guilty and hanged.

A year later, Mr. Jackson's sister lay dying and confessed to a priest she poisoned her brother because he intended to leave his entire estate to his wife, and not her wastrel son. The doctor, who was standing outside, overheard and related the confession to Inspector Grove.

The intervening years had not diminished the guilt the

Inspector felt in arresting a person for a crime they didn't commit, and who was subsequently hanged.

"I appreciate your confiding in me, John," Sarah said feeling warmth spread throughout her body at the use of his first name. "Do you think you could arrange for me to visit Miss Bouchon tonight?"

"It's late."

"I've brought some lemon soap instead of the harsh lye they use in prisons, sandwiches, chocolate cake, and some fresh linen. She paused. "It's Christmas tomorrow."

Inspector Grove squeezed her hand again. "You are nothing if not kind."

Sarah gave the change of address to the driver and they continued on.

On the way, they avoided talking about the case. Instead, they chatted about the upcoming holiday, the weather and the latest books they'd read. Sarah began to hope Inspector Grove had put the tragedy of his wife's long death from opium addiction a year ago behind him at last. There had always been a strong attraction between them but it remained unspoken due in part to the tragedy and the difference in their social class. Sarah was born a lady. Inspector Grove's father was a tradesman and he a lowly policeman. Sarah didn't care, but knew it mattered to him.

As the carriage pulled up to the gates of Brixton Prison, Sarah added, "Since I'm not family, I doubt they'll let me in to see her without you but once I'm in, you can leave if you wish. You've had a long day. I know you must be exhausted and she may speak more easily without a policeman present."

"Now that the shock has worn off, I'm curious to see Miss Bouchon's reaction when you question her," he said, avoiding her hint to leave.

Brixton Prison

Many improvements had been made in prisons since

the early days when men, women and children were all held together in overcrowded, filthy cells. If they had no money to purchase food from their jailers, they had to beg from local people passing the prison.

When fights broke out, prisoners were shackled in irons and whipped. Demoralizing tasks such as "Turning the Crank" or "The Treadmill," were utilized as punishments to fill their days in the belief such endless, exhausting tasks would deter them from continuing a life of crime.

In these enlightened times, decent food was provided. "The Crank" and "The Treadmill" were abandoned, along with iron shackles and brutal beatings. But prisons were still dreary places that reeked of hopelessness and despair, despite their lime-washed walls.

The cab let them off in front of a cobbled courtyard. They entered an arched gateway which had a large door studded with nails.

Once inside, most of the guards were matrons who wore dove-colored woolen dresses with black cloth mantles and straw bonnets, trimmed with white or deep blue.

Inspector Grove requested a chair.

Sarah and Inspector Grove were led down a long, narrow corridor to a corrugated, iron door that opened into a small cell containing a hammock, triangular shelves, a small stool, a table, and a deal box for placing clothes and also resting the feet.

Blankets and rugs were folded up and stacked against one side of the stark, white wall. A single, small window was visible high up near the ceiling.

Genevieve, who had been sitting at the desk, stood up, her shoulders straight and her dark, almond shaped eyes defiant. A wooden chair was brought in.

Inspector Grove placed it in front of the desk. The guard departed, shutting and bolting the door.

Inspector Grove stepped forward.

"Good evening, Miss Bouchon. This is Miss Wyndom.

She is a private inquiry agent and has occasionally assisted me in my investigations. She expressed an interest into looking into your case."

"I've brought a few things I thought you might find useful," Sarah said placing the paper bag on the desk.

Genevieve glanced into it. "Thank you. That was kind," she said politely.

As Inspector Grove stood against the wall, Miss Bouchon studied Sarah curiously. "I had no idea English women were permitted to be investigators."

"I inherited some money a few years ago and decided not to do something ordinary."

A small smile appeared on Miss Bouchon's pale face. "Ah, have a seat." She sat down. Sarah sat across from her on the hard, wooden chair.

Miss Bouchon looked to be in her late twenties. She was not a golden haired beauty in the popular style, but she was striking with high cheekbones and glossy black hair, neatly pinned back into a soft knot at the nape of a long, graceful neck

Intelligence shone out of her dark eyes. Her figure, not more than five feet two, was slender and she wore a modest dress of soft navy blue wool and a black shawl. She sat with her hands folded in front of her, her back straight.

"I don't want to waste your time, Miss Wyndom. The evidence is against me," Genevieve admitted, unable to control a faint tremor in her voice.

"Inspector Grove has informed me of all the facts. Did you murder Miss Coombie-Walsh?"

"No."

"Do you have feelings for Mr. Nicholas Royalston as Miss Coombie-Walsh accused you?"

Miss Bouchon looked annoyed. "I do not even like him," she said dryly.

"Is he in love with you?"

"I doubt it."

"I understand Miss Coombie-Walsh was quite taken with him. Did he return her affections?"

"No."

"How can you be certain? Did he confide in you?'

"Mr. Nicholas Royalston is a young, wealthy man. I've never known them to be eager to settle down and Miss Coombie-Walsh was not his type."

"What is his type?"

"Beauty is important to him."

"The police found a packet of strychnine in your room in a hat box. How did it get there if you did not put it there?"

Genevieve paled. "I don't know."

"Are you suggesting someone put it there to frame you?"

"It is obvious, is it not? Everyone knew about the surprise I planned for Christmas Eve."

"The only people present beside the Coombie-Walshes were members of the Royalston family. "Why would any of them want to get rid of a woman whose brother was shortly to marry into their family?"

Genevieve shrugged. "Miss Coombie-Walsh was not a nice person."

"Describe her."

She hesitated.

"Let me remind you, you are facing a trial for murder and the victim is past caring what you say about her so I urge you to speak honestly. I need a clear picture of the dead girl."

"It won't affect my fate. I'm French. An English court will condemn me."

"If you are innocent, Miss Wyndom and I will do everything in our power to help you," Inspector Grove assured her.

Genevieve sighed. "When one dies, they become saints but Miss Coombie-Walsh was no saint. She would say things under her breath that made people laugh, but they were cruel. If you were foolish enough to confide in her, she would use what she knew to humiliate you. To be as you say, frank, she enjoyed causing mischief."

"She sounds like a most unpleasant person. Was there someone in particular you were thinking of who confided in Miss Coombie-Walsh and was betrayed?"

Genevieve gave a Gallic shrug. "She offended everyone. Why are you interested in helping me?"

"Edith Royalston hired me."

A genuine smile lit up her face. "The little sparrow."

"She is fond of you."

"And I return her affection." The smile left her face. "I did not like Miss Coombie-Walsh but I swear to you I did not kill her."

The matron unlocked the door, indicating the time was up and Sarah reluctantly stood as Inspector Grove joined her.

Genevieve also stood. She was resigned to her fate. "Tell Edith I am well."

Sarah and Inspector Grove did not speak until they returned to the handsome. It started to rain and they fell silent, each lost in their own thoughts.

As the carriage pulled up at Inspector Grove's home, Sarah reminded him, "Christmas Dinner is at one o'clock tomorrow. There will be six of us, all of whom you know."

"I look forward to it," the Inspector said warmly.

"I suggest you check the local pharmacies to see if anyone purchased strychnine recently."

"You mean in case it wasn't Genevieve who poisoned Miss Coombie-Walsh?"

"If it was one of the Royalstons or even one of Diana's own family, they wouldn't know where in the kitchen the poison was kept and wouldn't have the opportunity of getting it."

"An excellent suggestion."

Christmas Day dawned bright and cheerful. The rain washed away the snow and church bells rang throughout the morning while the Wyndom house was filled with the delightful smells of roast duck.

To Sarah's relief, Inspector Grove accepted the watch graciously and presented her with a book on famous trials and to her surprise, a tiny garnet pin that matched her earrings.

When it was time for the Inspector to leave, she walked him to the door. He took her hand in his and kissed it. "Thank you for inviting me, Sarah. This was the most enjoyable Christmas I've had in years."

Sara felt inordinately pleased. Tonight, the usual sadness that was ever present in his eyes had been replaced by laughter and pleasure. Once her last guest departed, Sarah's mind returned to the murder.

She decided to drop in on the Royalstons. It wasn't the most tactful thing to do when it was past visiting hours and a murder had been committed on the premises, but Sarah had a reputation for eccentricity.

Benson, the Royalstons' butler, led her into the front parlor where the family was gathered. While Diana Coombie-Walsh was not yet a member of the family, she had been murdered at the Royalstons' home. Instead of stark black, they were all dressed somberly in various shades of grey and navy. A tray of tea and barely touched desserts rested on a side table. Nicholas and Lorena, who looked even more beautiful in grey and white, sat next to each other. Their parents sat together on the couch while Edith sat on a chair at the end, almost as an afterthought Sarah thought sadly. The Coombie-Walshes were not in evidence.

Mrs. Royalston was the only one who showed any genuine grief. Her blue eyes were red rimmed and she clutched a white lace handkerchief.

"We weren't expecting visitors," Mr. Royalston said,

frowning.

"I realize how difficult this day must be for you," Sarah acknowledged. "I came to offer you my condolences."

"We're still recovering from the shock," Mrs. Royalston said in a wavering voice as she indicated Sarah should sit. "I find the whole thing unreal."

"I can't say I cared much for Genevieve," Lorena said coolly, "but I had no idea she was capable of murder."

"Stop saying that. Genevieve is innocent," Edith protested hotly.

"Your repeating it won't make the charges go away," Nicholas said, amused.

Mrs. Royalston rubbed her head. "Stop bickering. It's unseemly."

"How are the Coombie-Walshes holding up?" Sarah inquired.

"As well as may be expected,' Mr. Royalston muttered.

"The wedding will have to be put off, of course," Lorena said, "although I think it's medieval to forbid me to shop for wedding clothes."

Mrs. Royalston rounded on her. "How can you be so unfeeling, Lorena? Whatever Diana's faults, she didn't deserve to die like that. Think of poor Rolly and his family."

"Your mother is right," Mr. Royalston agreed. "Diana was poisoned in our house by one of our maids. To some extent, we bear responsibility for her death and if that is not enough to sober you, the manner of her death, which we all witnessed, was quite horrible."

"Too true," Nicky muttered.

"Was your maid insolent toward you or exhibit any signs of insanity before the murder?" Sarah asked.

"On the contrary, she was practical and helpful," Mrs. Royalston sighed. "I still cannot believe she did it."

"We all know she quarreled with Diana over Nicky," Lorena said waspishly.

"Diana made that up," Edith said, flushing. "She didn't

care a fig for Nicky."

"For God's sake, Lorena, Diana was the sister of the man you intend to marry. Show some respect, Dr. Royalston growled. "As for Genevieve, she may well use insanity as an excuse, but it won't save her,"

Sarah addressed Nicholas. "Did you perhaps in all innocence, show interest in Miss Bouchon which might have been misinterpreted?"

"Genevieve was a servant," Nicky said shortly. I have no interest in servants. Genevieve isn't even that attractive."

Edith glared at him.

"I saw no sign of her interest in Nicky," Mrs. Royalston said flushing, "or his in her."

Mr. Royalston's cold blue eyes turned to Sarah. "I hope you have really come to offer your condolences as you say and not to stir up rumors or snoop. I don't approve of women detectives."

Sarah felt a wave of irritation and controlled it. She knew Mr. Royalston disapproved of her profession. Most men did. "My apologies if I seem inquisitive. I was shocked to hear the news and simply wished to know if there was anything I could do," she said tactfully.

"Thank you," Mrs. Royalston said wearily, "but I can't think of anything."

"We all know she did it," Lorena repeated as Sarah stood up. "She's the only one who could have."

The Viewing

Bright and early the next day, Sarah consulted with her cook about the menu for the week before retiring to her office to work on billing, letter writing, and to compose her notes on the murder.

According to the papers, Diana's viewing was to take place that evening. Sarah knew the Coombie-Walshes only by sight. She planned on paying her respects, but it was hours away. It was then she thought of Bertie Goodman. Bertie loved gossip and his information generally proved reliable.

Bertie had a townhouse on Grosvenor Square and never rose before noon. At one o'clock, Sarah paid him a visit with her maid Mary and was escorted into the drawing room. The butler told her his master would be down directly and returned with a tray of coffee and tea, biscuits and a lovely raisin and nut cake, followed by Bertie himself.

"How absolutely delightful to see you, Sarah," Bertie said, smelling strongly of lavender water. Bertie's family and the Wyndoms had adjoining estates in Cornwall and were on a first name basis since childhood. "Has the rest of the clan forgiven you yet?" Bertie asked, referring to the break Sarah made with her aristocratic family when she became a private inquiry agent. A Wyndom didn't sully their reputation by working for a living, much less digging into murders.

"No and I'm not in the least pining to be forgiven."

"Good for you. Are you still friends with that darkly brooding, delicious policeman?" he teased as he gracefully sank into a chair opposite her and began to pour the tea.

Sarah tried not to blush but failed. "Inspector Grove was called in on a case I'm working on."

"The murder of Diana Coombie-Walsh. I thought as much. The murder is practically on your doorstep." He leaned forward blowing on his coffee. "What can you tell me? Was she truly poisoned by the French maid as the papers say?"

"She was definitely poisoned."

"Dear me, you aren't representing the maid? From all I hear, it's a hopeless case. The evidence is overwhelming and the fee must be nominal at best."

"I want to be certain of her guilt. Bertie, you know both the Coombie-Walshes and the Royalstons. I've seen you with Nicholas Royalston heading out to clubs. What can you tell me about them that I couldn't learn from a morning call?"

"A great deal," Bertie said chuckling, "but surely you don't suspect one of them?"

"At this point, I'm keeping an open mind."

"How intriguing. You know I can't refuse you anything. I do so admire your independence, determination and drive. It's so refreshing in our set."

"I don't have a set, Bertie. That's why I'm here."

"Right." He replaced his delicate Wedgwood cup on the table and sat up straight. "What do you want to know?"

"Tell me about Diana Coombie-Walsh."

"Not bad looking but willful and spoiled rotten. She could be spiteful and mean if she didn't get her way. My sister went to the same finishing school. Her only friends were those who feared her tongue."

"Was she in love with Nicholas Royalston?"

"Besotted."

"Was he going to make an offer for her?"

"Dear me, no."

"Even though she's an heiress and both families favored the union?"

"Money isn't everything, dear."

"True. I've only seen him with male friends."

"It's not what you're thinking, you wicked girl."

Sarah blushed. "Then what is it?"

"I recognize the signs. Nicky is violently in love."

"With whom?"

"That I don't know."

"You must have some idea."

"He keeps it well hidden although I've tried on a number of occasions to find out, without success, which makes me believe there's something scandalous about it. Perhaps he's infatuated with a gypsy or a Jew."

"What about his sister?"

He sniffed. "The divine Lorena. An acknowledged beauty."

"You don't like her?"

"She has Rolly wrapped around her little finger, but I'm not convinced she cares for the poor boy at all. A pity since he worships the ground she walks on."

"She seemed keen to marry him when I talked to her."

"Well, he is quite rich. But until a month ago, the chit wouldn't give him the time of day."

"Why did she change her mind?"

"A complete mystery, my dear. Suddenly last month, she capitulated. Personally, I think it was the realization of all that money."

"How do Nicholas and Lorena get along?"

"They're close. They dote on each other. I've dubbed them the tricksters. They're always up to some mischief together."

"Such as?"

"They went slumming together at a seedy club in the East End. It was Lorena's idea. If her parents found out, they'd ship her off to a convent in Europe."

"What does Nicholas think of Rolly?"

"At first he wasn't keen on the marriage. No one was good enough for his sister, but lately he's made peace with it and tolerates Rolly."

"What's Lorena's fiancé like?"

"Rolly's a sweet boy, but not terribly bright and no match for her. She'll run circles around him once they're wed."

"Lorena wouldn't be the first to give in to her parents' wishes."

Bertie snorted. "I doubt her parents' wishes had anything to do with it. Lorena isn't the dutiful sort. She's willful and wild. Always has been. Even Nicky can't control her when she's in one of her more reckless moods."

Sarah thanked him for the information and the refreshment and left. After talking to Bertie, she felt uneasy. Something he said held the answer, if she could only recognize it.

The viewing took place at eight o'clock at the Coombie-Walshes' brick townhouse. Sarah arrived at eight fifteen. There was already a crowd of the curious and family. Everyone looked shocked and somber, but there were few tears. Mrs. Coombie-Walsh looked haggard as she greeted Sarah at the door, thanking her for coming. Sarah sat in the back, watching the visitors come and go. The Royalstons didn't acknowledge Sarah, and sat with the grieving family. Sarah stayed as long as she could decently do so and finally left, feeling she had wasted an evening. On her return home, she was tired and went straight to bed. In the morning, her maid threw the curtains back, bursting to tell her the news.

"The Royalston family is under a curse, Miss."

"Because of the murder?"

"No, Miss. Last night, Mr. Royalston fell down the stairs and broke his neck."

"What? When?"

"In the wee hours of the morning."

Sarah jumped out of bed. She didn't believe in coincidences or curses, and feared there was a killer loose in the Royalston house. Scribbling a note to Inspector Grove, she gave it to Mary to deliver post haste. Fearing for Edith, she dressed quickly and pounded on the Royalstons' door.

"The family is not to be disturbed," Benson said firmly, and would have shut the door in her face if Edith hadn't rushed out of the study.

"You may let Miss Wyndom in, Benson."

"Yes, Miss," Benson sighed and left.

Edith's eyes were red and she looked worried. "Come in, Sarah. You heard about Father?"

"I did. I'm so sorry."

"The screaming of the maid this morning woke me up. Papa was lying at the bottom of the stairs. I couldn't believe it at first. He always seemed so alive. I can't imagine him dead."

Her voice shook.

"Here she is again. The private detective come to snoop," Lorena murmured as she emerged from the parlor with Nicky in tow.

"There's no need to be rude, Lorena," Edith snapped. Miss Wyndom is my friend."

"She shouldn't be here, intruding on us in our grief," Lorena said coldly.

"You're not even sorry Papa is dead," Edith objected. "You quarreled with him last night. I heard you. You called him a tyrant and wished he was dead. And he called you a terrible name."

"Shut up," Lorena snapped.

"Yes, do be still, pipsqueak," Nicky warned. "You're giving the detective all sorts of nasty ideas."

"People frequently fall out in families," Sarah murmured. She turned to Edith. "It must have been a shock. Would you like to join me for breakfast, Edith?"

"Or you could stay and join us," Nicky said smiling, although his smile didn't quite reach his chilly blue eyes. "Ask us any questions you wish. Have no fear of upsetting Mother. She's indisposed. We have nothing to hide. Right, Lorena?"

Lorena looked as if she were going to object but shrugged. "Why not?"

Sarah longed to reject the offer, but the opportunity of questioning the family was too good to pass up. "Thank you."

Due to the unusual circumstances, the servants had set out food on the banquet so the family could help themselves. There was coffee, tea, eggs, bacon, ham, and toast with three kinds of jam and butter. A place was quickly laid for Sarah and she sat down.

"It's true Lorena and I quarreled with Father last night, but that wasn't unusual," Nicky said, pouring coffee all around. "He could be difficult."

"He threatened to throw you out," Edith accused."

"It happened on a weekly basis," Nicky said, flushing.

"What was the quarrel about?" Sarah asked boldly, not really expecting an answer.

"He wanted me to start thinking seriously about marriage," Nicholas said. "I refused."

"And I came to Nicky's defense," Lorena added. "If he wasn't in love, he shouldn't marry anyone. Papa was livid."

Nicholas smiled. It was a secretive smile that Sarah found vaguely disturbing and difficult to interpret. She thought there was more to the quarrel than what they let on.

"How late was it?"

"I woke up at all the shouting," Edith chimed in. "The quarrel must have taken place upstairs on the landing, or I wouldn't have heard it. It was dark out and I immediately fell back to sleep."

"The pipsqueak is right," Nicky said smoothly. "Father stopped me in the hall as I was heading for bed. He was in one of his truculent moods."

"I heard the shouting too and joined the fracas," Lorena added. "He'd been drinking and was unsteady on his feet. Perhaps that's why he fell later on. After our quarrel, he must have returned to the study and poured himself another whiskey before retiring, and lost his footing on the stairs."

"No one heard him fall?" Sarah asked.

Everyone shook their heads.

Sarah turned to Nicky. "A friend led me to believe you were in love."

Nicky stiffened. "What gossip told you that?"

The door opened and a distressed Benson announced, "Inspector Grove."

The inspector entered, with two officers behind him. "I apologize for disturbing you at such an early hour Mr. Royalston, Miss Royalston, but I heard there was another death."

"An accident," Nicky said scowling.

"The servants found Mr. Royalston's dead body at the foot of the stairs," Sarah explained. "Apparently he fell in the middle of the night."

Inspector Grove glanced around the table. "Where is Mrs. Royalston?"

"Mother was extremely upset when she heard the news, as you may imagine," Lorena said. "We urged her to lie down and she took a sleeping draught. We gave the servants orders not to wake her."

"The inspector would be brief," Sarah said.

"Certainly not," Nicky exploded. "First Diana is poisoned in our house, and now Father dying unexpectedly has completely shattered her nerves. I won't allow it."

"I'm sure Inspector Grove will be careful not to tire her out," Sarah persisted.

The inspector took the hint. "I will be gentleness itself."

Lorena glanced at Nicky nervously.

"Come back tomorrow if you wish," Nicky added, "although I can't imagine why. Father's death was an accident and she was asleep when it happened."

Inspector Grove recognized the look of panic on Sarah's face. He rang for Benson. When the butler arrived, he said, "Take a cup of strong, black coffee up to Mrs. Royalston and wake her up. I need to speak to her."

Nicky stood. "What right do you have to give orders in my house?"

The inspector turned to a shattered Benson. "Be gentle, but make sure she is awake."

"Yes sir."

"I shall report you to your superiors," Nicky shouted, furious.

"You are welcome to do so, sir."

The tension in the room was palatable.

Benson immediately returned looking frightened. "I can't wake Mrs. Royalston, sir."

"Mother!" Edith burst into tears and tore out of the room. The Inspector let her go.

"Get Doctor Morrison," Inspector Grove instructed the

butler, "and tell him to bring equipment for pumping the stomach."

"No need. I'm as qualified as that quack Morrison," Nicky said, heading for the door.

"It would be best if you and your sister stay here, sir." The inspector's tone was icy and brooked no defiance. Nicky glared at him and the two policemen in the hall, his hands balled into fists. "You will regret this, Inspector."

"I am not easily intimated, Mr. Royalston."

Doctor Morrison entered a few minutes later carrying a black bag, conferred with Inspector Grove and rushed upstairs with the butler..

"I'd like to speak to you outside, Miss Wyndom," Inspector Grove said shortly. He glanced at Nicky. "You and Miss Royalston will remain here.

Sarah followed him out.

"What the hell is going on, Sarah? Was Mr. Royalston's death an accident or not?"

"There was a violent quarrel. Sometime in the middle of the night, Mr. Royalston fell down the stairs and broke his neck."

"You don't believe it was an accident."

"If so, it was a convenient one. I don't like coincidences, John, and there's been two deaths in this house in as many days. If Mrs. Royalston dies, it will be three."

"I don't like it. Her children will say she was so distraught she either took an overdose on purpose or by accident. Why would they kill their parents?"

"Let's hope Dr. Morrison revives Mrs. Royalston and she's willing to tell us what happened. I believe she may know."

Sarah suddenly recalled the secret smile Nicholas shared with his sister and Bertie's comment about them being thick as thieves and had a glimmer of what the ugly truth might be.

"What now?" Inspector Grove growled.

"It was Lorena or Nicholas, or both together, who killed Diana and possibly their father and I think I know why, but there's not a shred of proof."

"You can't keep us prisoners in our own home," Lorena said shrilly appearing in the hall, her eyes flashing. Nicky was beside her. "We want to see our mother."

"I'm afraid not," Sara said firmly. "Inspector Grove is posting men at her door. No one will be allowed in except Miss Edith and the doctor, myself and the Inspector."

"This is ridiculous," Nicky exclaimed, furious. "We wouldn't harm our mother."

"Except for Diana's poisoning which our maid was arrested for, there's been no other crime," Lorena said coldly. "My father's death was a tragic accident and if my mother dies, it will be from her own hand due to grief. We're leaving to report your outrageous behavior to the Commissioner. Unless you charge us for a crime, you can't stop us. Come Nicky."

Inspector Grove had nothing to charge them with. He stepped aside.

An hour later, Nicky and Lorena hadn't returned. An outraged Commissioner failed to make an appearance on their behalf demanding an accounting. The Royalstons had fled.

Dr. Morrison came downstairs. He looked weary. "I've done what I could. Mrs. Royalston is awake, but groggy and weak. She asked to speak to Miss Wyndom, but I would advise you not to linger. She's exhausted and suffers from extreme mental anguish."

"Inspector Grove will accompany me, but we won't overtax her," Sarah promised.

Mrs. Royalston's room was large and richly furnished. The mess had been cleaned up, but unpleasant smells lingered in the air despite an open window.

Propped up in bed in a pale pink dressing gown Mrs. Royalston looked ten years older. Edith, her eyes red from crying, sat on the bed holding her hand in a crushing embrace.

"Edith dear, would you leave us?"

"I want to stay with you," Edith pleaded."

"I'm going to be fine. Please go. I'll speak with you later."

Reluctantly, a teary Edith left the room.

Inspector Grove pulled up chairs for both himself and Sarah.

Mrs. Royalston's voice was faint. "Dr. Morrison said I nearly died."

"It's true," Sarah admitted.

She closed her eyes. "Where are they?"

Sarah and Inspector Grove exchanged looks. "Lorena and Nicholas left the house and haven't returned," Sarah said bluntly.

Mrs. Royalston slowly opened her eyes. "Lorena brought me tea last night after the...the dreadful quarrel and Godfrey's fall."

"Tell us what happened, for Edith's sake," Sarah urged.

Mrs. Royalston gripped the sheets. "Godfrey caught them in bed together. It was my fault. I always knew they were too close, even as children. I caught them kissing once. When Nicky went away to school I thought the unnatural attachment would end."

"It didn't though, did it?" Sarah said gently.

"The relationship became even stronger, more depraved when Nicky came home. I was afraid to tell my husband. The shame would kill him. When Lorena announced she was marrying Rolly, I hoped it was over, but then poor Diana was poisoned." She started to sob.

They waited until she stopped. "Lorena told me Diana saw them passionately kissing in the garden and threatened to tell everyone unless Nicky married her. On Christmas Eve, Nicky distracted her and Lorena put the poison in Diana's glass after she planted the evidence in Genevieve's room."

"Was your husband's death an accident?" Inspector Grove asked.

"When Godfrey discovered them in bed, Lorena laughed. She followed him out into the hall, mocking him. I came out of my bedroom. HGodfrey called Lorena the Whore of Babylon and threatened to throw Nicky out. She became enraged and shoved him. He lost his footing and fell. I still didn't realize the extent of her depravity until after the tea. I'm telling you this because I'm afraid for Edith. Lorena is quite mad."

"Why did you drink the tea?" Sarah asked.

"I still clung to the idea Godfrey's fall was an accident. I was so upset, I drank it down. I never thought she'd harm me. The last thing Lorena said as I was drifting off was I was going to go to sleep and not wake up. My own daughter." She shuddered and closed her eyes.

Inspector Grove paid an unexpected visit to Sarah two days later to report Genevieve was released, and Lorena and Nicky Royalston had been captured and sent to jail to await trial for murder.

"I feel sorry for Mrs. Royalston and Edith. They will have a difficult time living the scandal down," he said.

"Edith told me that after the trial they intend to go abroad for an extended stay."

He turned his hat nervously. "I was wondering, Sarah, if you would like to accompany me to a concert on Sunday."

"I would indeed, Sarah said pleased. "I'm very fond of concerts."

Roxanne Dent is a full time writer who lives in Haverhill, Massachusetts. She has sold nine novels, including her most recent, The Janus Demon, *an urban paranormal fantasy which is online in book and e-book form. Roxanne has also sold a number of short horror stories. Her latest, "Bug Boy," sold to Great Old Ones Publishing, came out in October 2014. She is currently working on Book II of* The Janus Demon, Beyond the Iberian Sea" *and a YA paranormal prequel. Roxanne also writes Regencies,* The Twelve

Days of Christmas, *and* The American Heiress, *and Sci-fi. In addition to fiction, Ms. Dent has co-written plays with her sister, Karen, produced at the Firehouse Theater in Newburyport MA. Her screenplay,* The Pied Piper *a thriller, won first prize in* Fade in Magazine. *Check out her blog tour on www.sistersdent.com.*

The Dread Secret of the Battle of Los Angeles

By Paul Wartenberg

The followed remains classified material pursuant to 18 USC. Any divulging of information directly conveyed from these sources will result in prosecution.

From the February 26 1942 transcripts of the preliminary inquiry into the February 24 37th Coast Artillery engagement:

GD = General Joseph Dammerschwarz, Commanding Officer Camp Hand

LCAT = Lt. Colonel Andrew Task, investigating officer March Airfield

SIP = Sgt. Ipkiss Putnam, gunner 37th Coast Artillery

LCAT: Sergeant. You're aware of the purpose of this interview.

SIP: Ah, yessir. About... uh, the shooting last night.

GD: You can relax, son, take a seat.

SIP: Ah, yessir sir. Ah... *(sits)*

LCAT: Now on the night of February 24, can you tell me where you were during your shift?

SIP: I... we were called in early, my shift usually starts around uh Twenty-Three Hundred but we got a call to come in and it was uh a thing about going through a practice air raid and so I got to base by Eight or uh Twenty-Hundred...

LCAT: Most of the other troops in your Artillery still got in at their scheduled shift, though.

GD: He's a Sergeant; we needed the non-coms in early to cut down on the chaos of a drill.

LCAT: Kind of defeats the purpose of an emergency drill, doesn't it?

GD: Does this star on my collar mean I gotta answer to you, boy?

(timed pause of ten seconds)

LCAT: Putnam, how did you get to be ranked Sergeant?

SIP: Well, ah, sir, I had been originally... I signed up early, before any draft, straight out of high school back in Illinois in '40 and so when Pearl Harbor happened, well they... I got bumped up to Specialist and then Sergeant right quick, practically one week after the other. It seems they needed us guys who had experience to get up the chain for all the new E-1s coming in.

LCAT: You were Private for a year?

SIP: Well I made Second Grade...

LCAT: Which is in sixth months in, an automatic promotion. You were still private for more than a year.

SIP: Thing is, sir, I had experience working an Artillery position, specifically the Ninetys, handling twelve pounds a round and getting it to target. I have experience, Colonel, and I was asked to get more men trained on it too before the Japs come back up on our coastline sir, just like they did at Ellwood.

LCAT: So your experience put you in charge of a battery position that night.

SIP: Every night yessir. (pause) Well, on the nights I'm scheduled to work.

LCAT: So what happened this night?

SIP: I get prepped for the incoming drill. We get the air sirens going fifteen minutes before the night shift comes on, as my Lieutenant notified me. I've secured my gun encampment and I get my four soldiers falling in inside of three minutes of the alert. I checked their gear, we checked the gun, wait for further orders.

GD: I'd like to note at this point we've had all positions manned within four minutes of the air raid siren.

LCAT: It's been noted. Were the searchlights on at that time?

SIP: Yes sir. Searchlights between our base and the other artillery positions surrounding Los Angeles. Had them crossing the skies for a good while too.

LCAT: So did you see anything then?

SIP: No. Just clouds, mostly. Didn't see anything, we just... heard.

GD: Heard what?

SIP: The alarms wouldn't stop. I mean, every fifteen minutes the air siren would go off again, another round, like the drill kept repeating itself. I called it in, the man at the HQ said the drill exercise had ended, but the alarm... sir. Every fifteen minutes my men re-manned the gun thinking this was it. We got to thinking it was real.

GD: Are you aware of the fact that of the guns we had manned at this airfield that you're the only one reporting the sirens still going off?

SIP: Sir, that's... General, I made three calls about it.

GD: We got the calls all right, son, but you were told the drill was over, your men should have stood down. You weren't hearing things right. What was wrong with you?

SIP: Sir, I... Colonel, what's going on?

LCAT: I'd like to remind the General that this is just a prelim, we're not charging anybody yet, and I'd ask if the General would allow me to control the question session if I can...

GD: You ain't controlling a thing in this room, Colonel. We're dealing with...

LCAT: We're dealing with a man in this here Army telling us he was hearing the air raid sirens continuing to blare well after your drill had ended. And I've seen the phone call reports, so he's not making up that part of the incident.

GD: I've seen those reports. It's a sign of a soldier overreacting to a situation...

LCAT: My understanding of this interview was to question the man, not judge him. I'm not going to have you...

GD: What the hell is a Colonel doing barking orders at a General?

LCAT: If you're having a problem with my interview, I can easily call my boss and have him conduct these interviews from now. And my boss has three stars on his neck to your paltry one. Care to pick up that phone, General?

(three-second pause)

LCAT: If you want to end this interview right here and now, I can pick up that phone and give my findings to Attersen, and let him know that the situation can all be blamed on a general with a short fuse. Or can I continue this inquiry, General?

(ten-second pause)

LCAT: Sergeant. It is your contention that you kept hearing air raid sirens all night long?

SIP: Ah, uh yes sir.

LCAT: Where was the siren coming from?

SIP: The direction of the siren? It was... we were pretty sure it was coming from the direction of the airfield behind us.

GD: I want it on the record, Colonel, that I can personally note that my airfield had stood down after the drill ended.

LCAT: Sergeant, did you make any effort to ascertain that the air raid sirens back at the airfield were indeed going off?

SIP: Colonel, we're supposed to stay at our posts until the drill is over. We're supposed to stay focused on manning the gun and keeping an eye out. I made the call to keep at alert and keep our eyes open.

LCAT: If there was a stand-down once the drill ended, didn't the searchlights get turned off?

SIP: Well, some of them had, but others stayed on. Especially over by the canyon.

LCAT: Which canyon was that?

SIP: I don't know the name of it, just some canyon about half the ways out, near the mountain range between us and the city.

GD: Impossible. We don't have any searchlights out that way.

LCAT: Aren't there spotters stationed at points along the mountain ridge? Couldn't they have lights stationed with them?

GD: We were getting complaints from the movie studios that the boys up there were shining the lights down on the swimming pool parties they keep hosting.

(indecipherable muttering from the Colonel)

SIP: If I could point out that those spotlights out that way was how we saw the aircraft in the first place.

LCAT: So you did see something?

SIP: Yessir, this winged silver airplane right there over the canyon, just as...

LCAT: Did you note the time that you spotted the craft overhead?

SIP: Well it wasn't over our heads, but it was over the mountains, just getting into the cloud cover and all and...

GD: Radar didn't pick up anything that night.

SIP: Maybe it was a plane that got past the radar...

GD: This is an investigation on the facts, not on maybes. There's no maybe, just the certainty that you opened fire on an empty sky for a full hour and you got half my other batteries opening fire at that same damn empty sky!

(pounding noise from the table)

GD: You know we had a weather balloon out that night from the Navy yard? Before the drill started? Even it didn't show up on the damn radar that night!

SIP: Sir, this wasn't a balloon! I know the difference! This thing had wings...

GD: Your first report in was that you didn't even know what it was when you opened fire!

SIP: I said it was an aircraft! Winged, possibly a cargo plane by the size of it...

GD: And no one else in the whole of Los Angeles saw it before you started the turkey shoot!

LCAT: We haven't spoken with the other artillery officers yet,

General, we ought to wait...

GD: You got it in your head that we weren't running drills, that the whole thing was real, and you got it in your head that we were getting Jap planes buzzing over a city of a million people who didn't hear or see a thing!

LCAT: Can we focus on the matter at hand, sir?

GD: You opened fire on a flock of bats, son. You didn't even hit the cloud cover with what you were shooting at!

LCAT: Sir, we did have casualties on the ground from where the shelling landed, it's one of the reasons General Attersen wants this investigated right now, and you need to speak to Attersen before you go off charging everybody before we even know what happened!

GD: You're saying it's a plane right now when I got my aide at the phone telling me you were calling in an oversized silver dollar floating in the sky!

SIP: I'm just saying. It was big and silver and you couldn't tell if it were a plane or one of them space rockets they show in them movies at the nickelodeon.

(five-second pause)

GD: Wait. Could you repeat what you just said, son?

SIP: Nickelodeon?

GD: DAMMIT, SON, THE FIRST PART OF WHAT YOU SAID.

LCAT: Actually I think you want the middle part of what... *(rest of recording unrecoverable due to GD flipping the table in response)*

Transcript of the following taken from the seized recordings off the Universal Pictures studio lot February 26 1942. Said recordings belong to unfinished serial titled Flash Gordon Against The Planet Killer.

(Film begins with clapboard)

SPEAKER (unidentified): Okay, Planet Killer, Scene Nine, Take Twelve, and... action!

ACTOR *(speaking to actress while men dressed in silver uniforms stalk them with lances and spears)*: Whatever Emperor Ming has told you, Bendu Warriors, we're here on a mission of mercy! Let us speak to the Bendu priests before it's too... what the... GET OUT OF THE WAY!

(Actor grabs Actress, dragging her by the arm off-camera. Chaos as off-screen screeching noise occurs as the extra actors step back, two of them tossing their spears in the direction of the noise)
(Transcript notes the appearance of an Army vehicle in the middle of the stage, forcing all of the background actors and a handful of prop handlers to run for their lives)

ACTRESS *(off-camera)*: Buster, what the hell is going on?
DIRECTOR *(appearing in front of the camera)*: What is this? Cut! I did not ask for a car for this scene! You're ruining the take!
GENERAL *(stepping out of the passenger side)*: To hell with your take! Are you the *(Hays Code censoring)* responsible for that setup in the canyon?
DIRECTOR: What are you talking about? Who are you, to be barging in here? You're not with this production, you should be over in Studio G on that war film they're making.
GENERAL: I ain't some damn actor you can order about, mister. You see these things? *(points to decorations across the chest and collar)* I am a real-life Army General and *(Hays Code censoring)* better respect my authority here!
DIRECTOR: Who... are... you?
GENERAL: I am General Dammerschwarz, and I am royally *(Hays Code censoring)* about you causing a disturbance with your damn movie props out in the damn canyon last night!
DIRECTOR: What disturbance? What are you talking about? Last night? We don't do any filming at night!
GENERAL: Is that your *(Hays Code censoring)* sitting out in that canyon a mile off from Camp Hand?
DIRECTOR: You mean the location shooting? We're getting set up for that next week!

GENERAL: But you're using these zeppelins as part of your filming, right?

(General waves his hand upward. Camera follows his direction towards a silver-painted cylindrical inflated aircraft, with long thin ragged wings jutting out from the sides)

GENERAL: You've got three of them sitting out there in the canyon and...

DIRECTOR: Three of them? I ordered seven to be made! Well, we got one here for the scene and there's one on backup, but... Wait. How is there three of them?

GENERAL: Because there's two mooring spots out in your staging area currently empty, that's why! Two of your (Hays Code censoring) balloons went up and (Hays Code censoring) confused my soldiers into opening fire on them for half the night!

ACTRESS: Oh (Hays Code censoring), so that's...

DIRECTOR: That's impossible, those airships weren't meant to be filled until the helium tanks were prepped...

ACTOR: Jenny? You okay?

(brief period as dialogues intersect)

GENERAL (points at the Actress): ENOUGH! You, ma'am, you said something along the lines of Oh (Hays Code censoring). I take it the situation sounds a little familiar to you.

ACTOR (cutting in front of the Actress): Hold on. It sounds like you're accusing her of something.

ACTRESS (pushes on the Actor's shoulder to move him aside): Oh, knock it off, Buster, might as well say something about it, and it was an...

GENERAL: So you admit you've got something to do with those balloons going up last night, girlie?

ACTRESS: I haven't been called a girlie since my tenth birthday, so shut it, soldier boy. You gonna call me something, use my name, it's Jenny.

GENERAL: Who?

ACTRESS: The next Dale Arden.

GENERAL: Who the (Hays Code censoring) is Dale Arden?

ACTRESS (rolls eyes in a professional, well-trained manner): Anyway. What happened was an accident.

GENERAL: Horse hockey! How was having those balloons flying across the night sky an accident?

ACTRESS: Can I explain first before you shout your own head off? We've got these three-seater sized zeppelins as props for this series...

DIRECTOR: Got them made real cheap, after all those airship crash and burns we hired a lot of unemployed zeppelin makers.

ACTRESS: Can I explain, Beebe? Thing is, General, what we're working on was going to include this battle sequence using live-action airships flying down this canyon instead of those model props because they wanted interaction with people on the ground along the canyon. So that's why there were those zeppelin craft waiting in the canyons for the helium and the pilots...

DIRECTOR: Nothing should have been inflated yet...

ACTRESS: Yeah, well, news about that. Ken mentioned his uncle had gotten an early delivery in and...

DIRECTOR: Ken? Who's Ken?

(off-camera noises. Camera swivels to spot a young man jumping behind a set of metal gear and film-making equipment)

DIRECTOR (camera comes back to him in mid-question): Him? What the heck was he talking about?

ACTRESS: He said he'd gotten some of the zeppelins up and working and... well, he invited me out there to show me how they flew.

ACTOR (almost whispering): You fell for that?

ACTRESS (whispering back): Well I got a thing for pilots and...

DIRECTOR: What did you do to my airships?

ACTRESS: Well I didn't do anything to them, Ken already had them inflated and...

(off-camera shouting of "Hey, you don't have to go into any details here.")

ACTRESS: ...And he gets the motors revved up on one of them

and tries to climb into the pilot's seat, trying to get me to sit with him.

ACTOR: Oh no, did you?

ACTRESS: Are you kidding? Have you seen the cabins on those things? Single seats in a row, and narrower than this dress I'm wearing. I wasn't about to share a seat with him. Didn't even have time to...

DIRECTOR: But those ships are built for three people to sit in them! And he had the engine running?

ACTRESS: That's the thing. I figured you needed more bodies for ballast, because that airship he sat in lifted right up and pulled the hooks off the mooring.

DIRECTOR: My airship! My artistically designed real-life rocketship babies...

ACTRESS: And so Ken goes jumping out of it before it gets too high, only he jumps onto one of the other airships and knocks it loose from the moorings as well. And into the night sky they went...

GENERAL: That explains the flying targets my troops saw. But what the (Hays Code censoring) was making the air sirens my men heard before they opened fire?

ACTRESS: Loverboy hiding over there was all in the mood for playing spaceman. He was dressed up in one of Buster's unitards and had a record player out in the canyon broadcasting the sound effects from one of his uncle's earlier productions.

(Off-camera noises of metal equipment collapsing as though someone was trying to dig into a hiding spot underneath it all)

ACTOR: So that explains where the red uniform got to...

ACTRESS: Along with the other problems, yeah. So I leave Ken there, scrambling, I didn't want to be there when Ken's uncle ever showed up or found out. When I was driving away from the canyon, I saw the skylights go crazy trying to line up on the one zeppelin with the engine running. I didn't see where the other one flew off to. When I got to the mountain road heading into Anaheim, I saw the sky light up with a bunch of explosions, figured there was a firefight or something, sped back home.

DIRECTOR: Now I know who you're talking about. One of the stupid prop people on will-call. What the hell was he doing messing with my babies?

ACTRESS: Does it matter? You can't touch him, he's the producer's nephew.

DIRECTOR: No he isn't. I said I just remembered who he is. He's the screenwriter's nephew.

ACTRESS (*grabbing a nearby battle-staff from a male extra*): YOU LYING (*Hays Code censoring*) YOU (*Hays Code censoring*) I CAN'T BELIEVE I (*Hays Code censoring*) AND (*record indicates the next two minutes filmed involve more curse words and violent use of a movie prop that the Hays Office would deem excessive*).

GENERAL (*attempts to calm down the Actress*): Stop, whoa, lady, don't swing that this way, whoa, WHOA, DROP THE SPEAR, WOMAN! ALL RIGHT, THAT'S (*Hays Code censoring*) IT!

(*General pulls out sidearm and fires into the studio ceiling in the direction of the airship*)

ACTOR: Are you crazy? There's crew up there! Stop shooting! Just stop...

(*Actor punches General across the chin, knocking him unconscious*)

ACTOR (*glancing at the camera*): I'm not going to get into trouble, am I?

(*The deflated skin of the punctured airship drops over the Actor and the prone General*)

Final memo included with the files:

With the investigation brought to the War Department and the President's office, it has been determined that the official result of the inquiry is that the night-time engagement of the coastal batteries were due to War Nerves and an unscheduled weather balloon release. All further inquiries are denied. General Dammerschwarz will be promoted and re-assigned. Colonel Task to be re-assigned to the War Department in Washington DC. All personnel involved to be transferred to separate battalions in preparation for other war-time deployments. Universal Pictures and the other film studios have been notified that this incident is to be downplayed and not discussed in public for now and the foreseeable future. Actor Buster Crabbe is to be commended for defusing the confrontation at the studio, and will receive a firm handshake from the President at a later date. The Los Angeles film industry has also been informed that if they pull a stunt like this again, the War Department will forcibly relocate the entire industry – every actor except for Crabbe, every producer, every director, even the screenwriters – to the middle of the New Mexico desert without their film equipment and left to rot.

And that, boys and girls, was why we didn't have any more Flash Gordon serials until the 1950s.

Paul Wartenberg, long-time resident of Florida, cannot confirm how he received these documents regarding the truth about the infamous February 1942 Battle of Los Angeles. He will confirm that he's published a short story anthology, Last Of the Grapefruit Wars, and has contributed to several mystery and horror anthologies such as Strangely Funny and Mardi Gras Murder. He now has to depart, not because the government is after him for revealing state secrets, but because his two cats Ocean and Mal are insisting on food and head rubs.

The Grave in the Grounds

By DJ Tyrer

It was a few years before Queen Victoria died that my father became a village doctor and moved us from bustling Birmingham to rural Norfolk, a flat and far too open place to live for someone used to the towering closeness of a bustling city. It took me a while to grow used to, even love, the countryside, its freedom and peace. It was a lonely county, wide-open spaces with too few people, an effect exacerbated by my having no friends. I'd had plenty back home, but the local boys called me a 'nob' and I found them unbearably boorish with terrible accents, and we had little common ground. Instead, I took to wandering the country lanes and across fields, pocket books of birds and plants my only companions.

The local boys, when they deigned to speak to me, would tell me tall tales intended, I was certain, to either scare or make a fool of me. One such was the story of a local 'big house', a Georgian mansion called Ambersham Grange, a few miles from the village. According to the boys, there was a grave in the grounds of the house, the grave of a young girl who'd died some years before and whose ghost haunted the estate. It was, I was sure, a ruse to cause me some sort of fright or embarrassment. Thinking, perhaps, they planned to play some trick on me there, I stayed away from the house for some time after it was mentioned, but, eventually, curiosity got the better of me and I had to go look, even suspecting, as I did, that they wanted me to get into trouble for trespassing on private property.

What harm could it do? I asked myself, little imagining what I'd discover there or what effect it would have upon my life.

So, I took the lanes I knew led to the house and, then, crossed fields to the rear of the grounds in search of an ingress. The estate was bounded by a tall flint-and-mortar wall topped with sharp jags of rock to deter intruders and although I found a wrought-iron gate in the wall, it was firmly locked.

Luckily, a pair of trees, one within the wall, the other without, embraced one another above those jags, allowing me to climb over into the grounds beyond.

The estate was lightly wooded in the main, with a lawn, ponds and flowerbeds closer to the house. In one section, where apple trees bore their nascent fruit, there was, as I'd been told, a grave. It was a simple thing, surprisingly so, not at all what I would have imagined in the grounds of such a grand house. The grave was nothing more than a slight rise of grassy ground with a plain, rounded gravestone which bore upon it only a name: Letitia Parride. There was no decoration nor any other writing; no date, nothing, just the name. It was a mystery. Who was she? Why was she buried here, amongst the apple trees?

As I stood there, I caught a glimpse of movement amongst the trees: it was the figure of a girl in a blue dress with blonde hair tied back with a blue ribbon. As she flitted amongst the trees, she had an ethereal quality to her and I knew she must be the ghost of Letitia. I confess that, despite there being nothing overtly scary about her – no grave shroud, no blood and gore, no absent parts – I began to feel fearful and, as she seemed to drift closer towards me through the trees, I lost my nerve and turned and ran as if Satan himself were at my heels.

I didn't head for the trees I'd used to enter the grounds,

just ran to the wall and clambered up the nearest tree. Climbing out as far as I could on a branch, I dropped to the ground and headed home, not caring that I'd turned my ankle and it hurt to walk. I was glad to be gone from there.

As happy was I was to return home, I found my thoughts returning to the girl and the grave. Curiosity was getting the better of me and, eventually, I just had to go back there and solve the mystery. My mother always said I was too curious for my own good; my father approved and said I'd the makings of a scientist. I suppose this was my first lesson that one can never deny one's true nature; I'd no choice but to return there.

A few days later, I climbed once more up the tree outside the wall and over to the other within and made my way to where the grave lay in the shade of apple trees. I remember it was a sunny day, which was probably why I felt little spooked when I saw the girl approaching through the trees. In the bright sunlight, she seemed flesh and blood to me, not at all ghostly.

"Hello," she called in a soft, uncertain voice as she drew nearer. "Who are you?"

"My name's Lewis. My father is Doctor Hornby, the doctor in the village."

"What are you doing here? Why are you standing by my sister's grave?"

"Your sister's grave? Letitia was your sister?" I gave a sigh of relief.

"Yes. Why?"

"I... Well, I thought it was your grave..."

"My grave!" she exclaimed as if I'd said something utterly mad - which, I suppose, I had.

"Um, yes. I, well, I thought you were a ghost."

"A ghost?"

Her blank expression almost twitched into a smile. "I don't think Letitia haunts this place; I haven't seen her, and if her ghost was here, I know she'd come to me. I'm sorry, I haven't introduced myself." She gave an unpractised curtsey and said, "My name is Sylvie."

"I'm sorry to trespass here," I told her, feeling embarrassed at my foolishness and rudeness.

Sylvie quirked a smile. "No, don't be. I've no friends; it's nice to have somebody to talk to. My aunt doesn't encourage visitors and nobody from the village comes here; I suppose they all imagine me to be a ghost."

"I'm so sorry," I said, and I was.

"Thank you." She smiled a little more widely.

I tried to imagine how lonely she must be. I supposed she must have been close to her sister.

"I love this place, don't you?" she asked. I nodded. "Letitia loved it, loved to climb the apple trees. That..." Sylvie stifled a sob. "That was how she died. She fell, I mean. She was buried here because she loved it so."

"I'm sorry." I didn't know what else to say. Tentatively, I reached out a hand and rested it on her shoulder. I was at that age when I was just becoming aware of girls as something distinct and both alluring and a little frightening. My father had sought to instill the virtues of a good gentleman in me and such said one should offer comfort to an upset woman, but not to be over-familiar with a woman one didn't know. I wasn't quite sure what I should do.

Sylvie smiled again and thanked me once more. She was my height and I guessed her to be my age or a little older. She was a little plain and reminded me of the village girls, the sort I could imagine clambering about in trees like her sister. There was a melancholy air about her, which I took to be due to our standing at her sister's graveside.

"Come," she said, "let me show you the grounds."

I'd seen some of them on my last visit, but it's a wholly different experience to wander through a place whilst on the lookout for ghosts and to be given a guided tour by someone who loves it.

"I think," Sylvie said, a little shyly, as we came to the end of the tour, "you and I shall be good friends, Lewis."

"I hope so," I told her, before leaving.

I didn't stay away long. My mother had me running errands the following day, I seem to remember, but the next I was back. I returned frequently after that: I was as desperate as Sylvie for a friend.

On my third or fourth visit, Sylvie looked at me with a mock-serious expression and produced a large iron key, saying, "This is for you."

"What is it?"

"A key, silly."

"No, I meant, what is the key for?"

"The back gate. When you come to visit me, you won't have to scramble through the trees to get in. Well, not unless you want to." She gave me a grin. I imagined her sister never used the gate. "Keep it safe. Being given a key to the gate is quite the privilege. Oh, and don't let my aunt know..."

"I won't," I said, and we continued our walk through the grounds. If I had one criticism of Sylvie, it was that she lacked the sense of adventure her sister had seemingly had. Sylvie didn't climb trees, saying it was unladylike, and never left the grounds due to the command of her aunt. So, we mostly walked and talked. But, she'd no objection to my climbing trees or similar activities, happily sitting and threading daisy-chains whilst watching me. It was far more fun than wandering aimlessly about on my own.

But, no matter how often we walked together and no matter how much we talked, I never quite felt I knew Sylvie. She was always reticent in her conversation and I never felt quite able to question her. When I mentioned her to my father, the mystery only seemed to deepen so that I imagined having discovered a ghost would've been a simpler proposition.

My father, in that slightly forced way fathers have when their sons reach a certain age, had asked where I'd been, attempting to take an interest in my life.

"I've been walking in the grounds of Ambersham Grange with Sylvie Parride, the girl who lives there."

"A girl at Ambersham Grange?" repeated my father as he sucked on his pipe. "I don't believe there is a girl there. There is old Mrs. Ockham and a boy, her nephew, I believe, and a couple of servants, but no girl."

"There is," I told him. "Her name is Sylvie and she lives there with her aunt."

"Are you sure she's not a village girl? I've never seen a girl there, nor heard one mentioned."

I shrugged and said no more. Had she not seemed so intimately familiar with the place and been wearing a more expensive, if slightly faded, cut of clothes, I might have entertained the notion that Sylvie was one of the village girls living out a fantasy within the wall of the Grange's estate. But, she wasn't, I was certain.

Then, I shivered a little, despite the heat, as I wondered if she could be a ghost, after all. Perhaps she was the ghost of Letitia's sister? Perhaps there was another grave in the grounds? But, no, I was certain she was flesh and blood, not ectoplasm.

So, if she was neither spirit nor imposter, I thought to myself, there was some mystery here. If her brother or cousin, as the boy must be, was allowed to be seen by rare visitors, but Sylvie was not, there had to be some secret as to her presence at the Grange. The aunt's reclusive desire to avoid receiving visitors, her refusal to allow her niece to leave the grounds, and seemingly hiding her away when anyone came, appeared to suggest either a need to protect her from someone or that she was being held captive as part of some plot. Both suggestions excited my imagination and, as might be expected, I entertained any number of wild and improbable scenarios concerning Sylvie's true identity.

When I next went there and let myself into the grounds through the wrought-iron gate, there was no sign of Sylvie as I wandered through the trees. We didn't always find one another straight away. I moved from the pleasant shelter of the trees into the garden proper, where the sun beat down mercilessly as I walked amongst topiary and beds of roses. As I neared the house – something Sylvie wasn't keen for me to do, lest her aunt see me and my presence irk her – I spotted figures walking along and I quickly ducked behind a bush that was shaped like a leaping lion.

As I watched from my hiding place, I saw an old woman in widow's black with a black parasol and a boy in a sailor suit who seemed just old enough that a sailor suit was childish upon him. I thought for a moment he must have seen me, but he gave no indication of having done. His expression was quite miserable. It was Mrs. Ockham, I assumed, and the boy my father had spoken of; of Sylvie there was no sign. I watched them ambulate around the corner of the house and out of sight, then I retreated from the garden to the apple trees in the vicinity of the grave. I was more curious than ever and resolved that, if Sylvie didn't soon appear, I'd sneak inside the Grange itself and learn what I could, no matter what the risk.

Perhaps fortuitously, for who knows what might have happened, Sylvie did appear ten or so minutes later. Today, she was wearing a lemon-yellow dress with a white pinafore over it and a white ribbon tying back her hair. Aloft, she held a yellow parasol, but her face was flushed from exertion and she had what my mother insisted was termed 'a glow'; clearly she'd come at speed. She seemed a little agitated, but calmed when she saw me.

"Ah, Lewis, I'm so glad to see you!"

"And, me you. I saw your aunt and a boy, up by the house."

"You did?" She sounded a little anxious.

"Oh, don't worry, they didn't see me. Who is he?"

"Who?"

"The boy."

"Oh, him; that's my brother."

"Does he have a name?" I chided.

"Bruno."

Had I been more aware of my namesake Mr. Carroll's other writings, I might have grown suspicious at this point, but I accepted the statement without any sense of equivocation. I was really only familiar with the adventures of Alice, to whom Sylvie bore a certain vague resemblance that day.

I proceeded to tell her I'd mentioned her to my father and that he'd been certain only her brother resided at the Grange.

Looking horrified, she exclaimed, "You shouldn't have told him of me!"

"Why ever not? Are you the victim of some scandal? Or, does your aunt hold you hostage as part of some vile plot?"

"Oh, yes," she grinned, her anger gone, "I am the secret daughter of a distant emperor, an imprisoned princess like out of a fairy tale!" She laughed and I had to doubt there was any great mystery after all.

Save that she hadn't answered my actual question.

She twirled and asked me what I thought of her dress, and I told her I thought it very becoming, then we proceeded with our usual rambling through the grounds.

But, as I left that evening for home, I knew there was still some mystery about her and, when my father told me a few days later that he was going to the Grange the next day for the old lady's monthly check-up, I asked him to take me with him, hopeful of some clue. He sent a note to ask if he might bring me and Mrs. Ockham wrote straight back condescending to receive me and inviting us both to stay for tea when the business was over.

When we arrived at the house, I was handed over to one of the maids, an old woman who must have been in the lady's employ all her life, who gave me a limited tour of the house's grander rooms and art and architecture. Then, my father having finished his medical examination of Mrs. Ockham, I joined them in the drawing room for a cup of tea and a slice of cake. The boy was also there.

"This," said the old lady through tight lips, "is my nephew, Bruno."

I said how pleased I was to meet him and received a grunt in reply. Even out of his sailor suit, and wearing a simple outfit of jacket and long trousers, similar to those I wore, Bruno seemed sullen. He refused to speak a word to me and his aunt was barely any more communicative, so that the brief tea passed in near-silence. Unable to elicit a response to the simplest matters, I dared not ask about Sylvie.

As we left the Grange, the horses' hooves and carriage wheels skittering gravel along the drive, I turned in my seat and said to my father, "They were a bit odd, weren't they?"

He gave a curt sort of nod and said, "The upper class are not as we are. It doesn't do to have too much to do with them, son."

I wasn't sure I wanted anything to do with vinegary Mrs Ockham or her sullen nephew, but I knew that Sylvie wasn't like them, whatever the mystery was that ensnared her and caused her to be hidden away.

That visit was towards the end of summer; the end, too, of my childhood freedom, for my father had arranged for me to attend a boarding school to gain the education necessary to get a good profession. I knew that if I were to solve the secret of Sylvie, I'd have to do so in short order or wait till Christmas before I could try again.

It felt strange, the next morning, as I looked up at the apples above the grave in the grounds of the Grange, whilst waiting for Sylvie, to realise they would ripen without me. In the short time I'd known Sylvie and Ambersham Grange, they'd come to dominate my life in a way that made being separated from them feel as if I faced death not a mere parting.

When she arrived, Sylvie was cross with me. "You had

tea with my aunt and Bruno, Why?"

I told her my father was her aunt's physician. "When he said he was coming here, it was too good an opportunity to ignore. I wanted to learn more about your family."

"You shouldn't have come." She looked as if she were about to burst into tears.

"Why ever not?"

"You just shouldn't. Why did you have to spoil everything?"

"Whatever are you talking about? They don't know I know about you. I didn't mention you. Nothing happened. It was quite possibly the most boring tea I've ever had, and," I added, hoping to raise a smile, "the cake wasn't that good. Distinctly mediocre."

Sylvie didn't smile. In fact, she was quite as sullen as her brother and it took some coaxing to draw her out of her ill mood and back towards something approximating her usual demeanour. I dared not attempt to discover just what it was I'd done wrong and let the day pass quietly.

The next visit I made to Ambersham Grange was the last I would be able to make before I was sent off to boarding school, and I decided I wanted us to do more than usual.

"Let's go into Norwich and visit the shops." It was a long walk, but not an impossible one. After all, that was what made it a day out.

"I can't..."

"Why not? Are you really a prisoner here?"

She shook her head. "I just can't..."

I explained that I would be away until Christmas and that I really wanted us to do something before I left.

"Do you have to go?" she asked. "I don't want you to go. I don't want to be alone again." Then she added, almost as an afterthought, "Fine, let us away to Norwich."

We left through the wrought-iron gate and strolled across fields and down rural roads until we reached the outskirts of town.

"I've..." Sylvie paused as if framing her thoughts. "I've never been to town before." Her statement seemed truthful; she seemed very ill at ease with the noise and bustle and clung to me and shrank away from the crowds. It wasn't quite the pleasant outing I'd envisioned and we cut it short.

"I'm sorry," she told me as we walked home.

"Oh, don't concern yourself. It's pleasant just to be with you. I'll miss you while I'm away."

"I wish you didn't have to go. I'll be so alone."

"I'll be back for Christmas. Save me an apple, eh?"

She laughed. "I will."

That term seemed to last an eternity, but I didn't forget Sylvie. I couldn't forget her. I never will. I wrote to her every week, but she never wrote back.

When I arrived home for Christmas, it seemed as if there were a conspiracy in place to stop me from seeing her, sending me on all sorts of errands and requiring my presence. I began to wonder if I would have the chance to see Sylvie before I was dispatched back to school in the New Year.

But, my opportunity came with just a couple of days to spare, and I trudged across fields knee deep in snow to the wrought-iron gate. Beneath the trees, the snow wasn't so deep, but the garden was just as bad as the fields except for the area immediately beside the house, which had been cleared. I doubted Sylvie would be out in the chill; I needed to attract her attention. I hoped I might see her looking out a window and be able to catch her eye, but had no such luck.

Then, I spotted Bruno walking aimlessly across the cleared area. He was alone. He didn't appear to be pleased to be out or interested in building a snowman. I supposed he must have been sent outside for some fresh air. With no sign of Sylvie, I realised he might be my only means of contacting her.

Carefully scanning the windows to make sure his aunt wasn't watching him, I approached the cleared area and softly called to him.

Bruno turned and saw me. His sullen expression turned to one of anger. "What are you doing here?"

"I'm sorry to intrude, but..."

"Go away!"

"Look, I just want to see Sylvie; is she there?"

He looked, for a moment, as if he wanted to punch me. Then, he looked up at the sky and bit his lip. He looked very much like his sister just then and I could see he cared for her. "You shouldn't be here," he told me, then, "I'll fetch her. Wait here."

My wait for Sylvie then felt as if it would take almost as long as the seemingly-unending term had.

"Good morning, Lewis," she said, a little awkwardly, when she finally did appear. "Bruno... Bruno said you were here. You shouldn't be here," she added. "What if my aunt saw you?"

"She didn't – I was careful to check she wasn't looking when I spoke to Bruno. I know I took a risk, but I just had to see you and he isn't that bad, I think."

She didn't reply.

"I wrote to you every week," I told her.

Sylvie's expression changed to one of horror. "You didn't! Oh, no! My aunt must've intercepted them. Oh, no! If she knows about you... You have to leave, right now!"

"Is it really that bad if she knows about me?"

"Yes!" she shrieked. "Go, now!"

"I don't understand!"

"You wouldn't if I told you. Please, go."

"If you really want me to..."

I turned and started to walk away, but she called me back.

"Here." She handed me an apple and I laughed.

"Thank you." I'd almost forgotten about the apple. "I won't write again; but I won't forget about you. I don't think I'll see you at Easter, but I will see you in the summer, I promise."

She leaned forward and kissed my cheek and we each said farewell, then I left.

The mystery of why her aunt was determined to hide Sylvie away from the world and prevent her from having any contact with anyone vexed me, but had to be put to the back of my mind as the train carried me away in a cloud of steam once more to boarding school. Despite all the pressures and distraction of school life, I yearned to be back there in the grounds of Ambersham Grange with her.

It was another blazing hot summer when I finally was able to return and let myself through the wrought-iron gate to ramble amongst the trees and stand beside the grave in the grounds that served as our meeting place.

After a short while, I spotted Sylvie coming towards me and, even hidden amongst the trees, I could tell something was wrong, even if I couldn't quite tell what. Then, as she reached me, I saw that, like myself, she'd grown in the time we'd been apart: despite being taller and broader, she still wore the same dress I'd first seen her in. I felt disgusted at her aunt for showing such a disregard for her, leaving her in ill-fitting and worn clothes.

"Greetings, Lewis." She spoke quietly and her voice sounded different to that I recalled. It was almost as if she were another person. "You've changed."

"So have you." Her face looked distraught at that. I hated to hurt her, but could hardly pretend otherwise.

Suddenly, she fell to the ground and began to sob, horrible raucous cries.

"Don't cry!" I dropped to my knees and hugged her, stroked her hair. "Please don't cry!"

"You don't understand," she sobbed into my shoulder.

"Well, I understand that you aunt must hate you, or she wouldn't treat you like this. But, I don't understand why and won't if you don't tell me."

"She's right to hate me. I hate me!"

"Sylvie! Don't say that!" I hugged her for a while, then said, "She seems to like Bruno. I just don't understand why she likes him and hates you."

"Oh, yes." She gave a sudden bitter laugh. "Perfect Bruno! Everyone loves Bruno! Well, I hate him, too!"

"I don't understand, Sylvie. Will you please explain?"

"Do you really not?"

"No, I really don't. Please tell me!"

She gave another bitter laugh. "Are you blind, Lewis? Can you really not see?"

I think, perhaps, in my heart I already knew. But, I didn't want to admit, wanted to think I was wrong.

"I am Bruno. Born in the wrong body like some horrible joke. Rather than the girl I should've been, I was born a boy."

"A Uranian," I said, recalling something I'd read in one of my father's journals. "A third sex."

She – I can never think of her as a *he* – shook her head. "Not a third sex, the wrong sex. I cannot bear to be a boy, but that is what nature has determined I am. It is what my aunt insists I must be; she loathes me being Sylvie."

She proceeded to tell me how she'd chosen her name from the title of Lewis Carroll story, Sylvie and Bruno.

"The clothes I wear are those of my sister, Letitia. She was my age now when she died. That's why I have no more clothes to wear that would fit me: I am become too big." She sighed. "It is age that is my greatest enemy, now."

"I don't understand," I said, then realised I did.

"It isn't just the clothes that no longer fit me. My body betrays me. Before, I could look like Sylvie. Now, I am becoming a man and that is a future I fear I cannot face."

I hugged her and told her a story vouchsafed by one of the older boys at school whose brother attended certain insalubrious clubs where men dressed as women.

Sylvie snorted and shook her head, understanding

what I hadn't then grasped in my naiveté. "I cannot see myself doing that. Maybe... No; I want to be me for myself, not others."

"You will always be Sylvie to me." I kissed her cheek.

"Thank you."

That summer passed all too swiftly and, despite my attempts to raise Sylvie's spirits, her mood grew darker as it passed. As the time neared for me to go, she grew distressed at the thought of me leaving.

"I don't believe I can face the future alone," she would say.

On the last day I could visit her, I entered the grounds as ever I did through the wrought-iron gate and walked through the trees to the grave of her sister. As I neared it, I saw movement up amongst the branches and, for a moment, thought Sylvie was climbing the trees as her sister had done so many years before. Then, I realised that was not the nature of the scene.

Sylvie had hanged herself from the apple tree that branched above her sister's grave. I was shocked and, yet, wasn't entirely surprised. The desperation to avoid the cruel trick maturation was playing upon her had grown as she had. That she chose where her sister had died and been buried made perfect sense.

I stood and said a silent farewell, then began to walk towards the Grange. I'd no desire to speak to Sylvie's aunt, but I felt it was my duty.

I rang the bell and a maid answered the door.

"Yes?"

"I need to speak to Mrs. Ockham."

"Who are you?"

"Lewis Hornby, the son of Doctor Hornby."

"And, why do you want to see her."

"It's about Sylvie." That obviously shocked her. "She has... had an accident. She's dead."

Whatever the household's feelings towards her, that elicited a response and I was shown through to the parlour where I gave the old lady a hurried account of my discovery.

"You are the one who wrote letters to my nephew."

"Your niece," I corrected and she stared daggers at me.

"He has brought shame on us."

"She has done no such thing. You've kept her away from the world, so none but I know about her."

"Suicide is an unforgivable sin!"

I snorted. "I can forgive her. I wish she hadn't done it, but I can understand why she did it, why she couldn't face the future. You made it worse for her," I added.

She surprised me, then, by bursting into tears. I realised that she had cared for her nephew, even if she hadn't understood his need to be her niece. I also realised that even if she'd been more understanding, it probably would've made little difference to Sylvie's fate.

I comforted her awkwardly and, when she seemed a little more composed, I told her, "You must bury her as Sylvie and not as Bruno. If she couldn't be herself in life, let her be herself in death."

"But, the scandal..."

"Do you not already have a grave in the grounds of the Grange?"

She nodded. "Bruno's... Sylvie's elder sister, Letitia."

"Well, bury Sylvie beside her. Nobody need know."

My father allowed me to remain a few days longer before returning to school so that I might attend the burial. He'd been very understanding when Mrs. Ockham called him to write the death certificate.

Mrs. Ockham had done what she'd never done for Sylvie in life: bought her a new dress. It was a lovely, lacy white gown that I was certain Sylvie would've approved of.

I helped the gardener dig the grave. I felt I owed it to Sylvie. I just wished I could have saved her from it.

Sylvie was brought out on a handcart by the gardener and taken to the grave that had been dug beside her sister's. It was a glorious summer's day and she looked beautiful. My father and I gently wrapped her in a sheet and lowered her into the ground.

There was no service, just a simple farewell, then the gardener began to shovel the earth back into the hole.

I've never forgotten Sylvie and would visit her grave every summer when I returned from school; every Summer a year older even as she remained unchanged in my memory.

Even now, married with children, I haven't forgotten her. To do so would be quite impossible, for I live at Ambersham Grange, now. I must admit I was quite taken by surprise when I learnt that Mrs. Ockham, having no other close family since Letitia and Sylvie had died, had willed the house to me in thanks for the love I'd shown her niece when she most needed it.

Today, whenever I so wish, I can stroll through the garden to the apple trees to visit the three simple graves that lie there marked by stones upon which there are no dates or words other than the names of those buried there: Mrs. Eustacia Ockham, Letitia Parride and Sylvie Parride.

My children have sworn to me that, there amongst the apple trees, they have seen the ghost of a girl dressed in the Victorian fashion. Although I doubt it is so, for I am certain she would've shown herself to me, I've told them there is no mystery: it's the ghost of Sylvie and she returns because this was the one place she was ever truly free.

DJ Tyrer is the person behind Atlantean Publishing and has been widely published in anthologies and magazines in the UK, USA and elsewhere, most recently in Steampunk Cthulhu *(Chaosium),* Tales of the Dark Arts *(Hazardous Press),* Cosmic Horror *(Dark Hall Press) and* Serial Killers Quattuor *(JWK Fiction), as well as in* Sorcery & Sanctity: A Homage to Arthur Machen *(Hieroglyphics Press),* All Hallow's Evil *and* Undead of

Winter *(both Mystery & Horror LLC) and* Fossil Lake *(Sabledrake Enterprises), and in addition, has a novella available on Kindle and in paperback from Amazon,* The Yellow House *(Dynatox Ministries).*

The Monkey's Ghost

By Rosalind Barden

It was our home back then, when I was a child in the Depression of the 1930s, the knob of a hill that rose impishly out of downtown Los Angeles' bustle. To live there was the height of fashion in the Gay Nineties of the previous century. The prominent families of the day decorated Bunker Hill's steep streets with colorful candy-like fantasies of Victorian homes.

The homes were still there, many broken up into apartments after the Hill fell out of fashion and the moneyed people left. But in some Victorian mansions, survivors of the original builders still lived, content with their childhood homes.

Me and my little sister, along with our best friend Carlos, lived in a "newer" brick apartment building. It gave us a wonderful vantage point to spy on the rest of the neighborhood, which was populated nowadays with a dizzying collection of people: silent film actors thrown out of work by the talkies, aging vaudevillian comics and dancers, mysterious old men who'd possibly done dangerous and exciting things in the Old West, young and poor artists and poets, and regular working people like our mother. Of all these, our fascination was most drawn to the fading Victorians, both the homes and the people in them.

Our curiosity was further fueled by two other residents in our apartment building, Oscar the Magnificent, a magician to the "rich, famous, and royal," and his assistant, Shalom, an ancient negro whom Oscar claimed was a "former slave seeped in the magic of the hoo-doo." Our mother dismissed Oscar as a "terrible old gossip" who was nothing more than a medicine show huckster run on hard times, and Shalom was an ex-river barge sailor of some sort, and no more an ex-slave than President Roosevelt. "Don't believe anything that silly man says," she cautioned.

Perhaps, but Oscar was our best source of information on Anything and Everything Strange in the Entire World. So, he was our obvious choice to quiz about the Monkey's Ghost. Oh, we'd heard about it from other kids, especially Carlos, since he was a few years older than us and more sophisticated in his knowledge of neighborhood legends. Supposedly, something terrible happened to an exotic monkey from a faraway land in the Victorian mansion right behind our very building! On certain nights, 'round midnight or so, you could see a strange light floating in the mansion's yard and maybe hear a monkey's scream. "There's kids," Carlos informed us, "who know other kids who saw the monkey's ghost and heard it too." Well, that was solid proof enough for us.

When Oscar and Shalom weren't at the beach doing magic tricks for tourist dollars, with Shalom spicing up the show with his strange "hoo-doo" dance where he'd shake his ankles tied with bells, or when Shalom wasn't doing secret fortune telling for neighborhood ladies--"Top secret, don't ya'll tell no one!" Oscar cautioned us over and over because fortune telling wasn't exactly legal and the police could shut them down--we liked to play in their little apartment.

It was a wonderland of strange props, such as a skull, jars of dead snakes floating in yellow liquid, and boxes of "trick" cards and other magic paraphernalia that we could look at but not touch. If Oscar was in a good mood, he might show us how to do a simple trick, though he only showed Carlos the card tricks because, "ladies should not touch the playing cards--not appropriate and I don't want your mamma getting upset now." Though, generally, he didn't show us the tricks because, "We don't work for free, understand? That's our profession."

That was fine with us because he was happy to fascinate us with his stories. As he regaled us from his deeply cushioned chair and foot rest with the horsehair stuffing popping out of both, Shalom always sat silently, cross-legged on a folded rug of the oriental style. Sometimes Shalom smoked an odd pipe with a long, curved stem. It all added to his air of mystery, and increased our interest in Oscar's tales of his and Shalom's travels through Europe and the Exotic East ("I doubt he could find either on a map," from our mother), the mysterious and dangerous origins of Shalom's dance, part of which he was only willing to whisper to Carlos and Carlos swore he could not tell us, being "ladies," ("Oh, for goodness sakes! No, you cannot go to the beach to see that old man dance!"), and his and Shalom's close friendships with nearly every rich, famous or royal person we'd heard of ("If he was friends with all those people, why is he living in our building? Honestly!"). But it all sounded plausible to us.

This being so, after conferring with one another, we asked Oscar one day what he knew about the monkey's ghost. His eyes exchanged looks with Shalom's, which we noted and it increased our excitement. Oscar let out a long sigh and said, "Well, okay, but it's a tale best left unsaid."

There was a beautiful and far too young only child of an extravagantly wealthy man, who built the very mansion, "just outside the window there" and Oscar pointed to the window heavy with musty velvet drapes. She had the misfortune of falling in love with a traveling scoundrel. She married him secretly, against her furious father's wishes. Her father was a hard man, but his daughter was the only light in his life. So, rather than throw her from his house, he reluctantly allowed her new husband to move in. The scoundrel spent the father's money freely, but not on his bride; only himself, with gold and diamond jewelry and a matched set of carriage horses that he'd tear around the neighborhood with. And the drink. And talk of women. (Here Oscar whispered details to Carlos, who again, refused to tell us later.) Fortunately, it wasn't long before he took off traveling on "business" to exotic lands: South America, Mexico, Florida. "That small round window, right up toward the top, is where she would languish all the days he was gone, running her hands over his silk shirts, touching his hats, sobbing." It broke her father's heart and one day, overcome with his daughter's sorrow, he collapsed, dead.

Now, truly, she was bereft. She sent a cable to wherever the scoundrel was off to, and within a month he was back, all smiles, like nothing was amiss. He gave her a pet monkey from the jungle wilds, perhaps to keep her company while he was gone. And he was gone again soon after. This time, he never came back. She's been a recluse in that big old house ever since, with only old Mrs. Gilbert living there to tend to her. And now and again Old Bob--"you know he used to be her father's stable boy back in the day"--Carlos nodded, yes he knew--"he helps about the yard and such, for no pay, because her fortunes are much declined."

"But what about the monkey!" we asked.

Oscar paused, and looked toward Shalom again, who said nothing and kept holding his pipe to his silent lips. It wasn't like Oscar to be looking toward Shalom, as though he needed permission to continue, so this struck us as strange. Oscar never was able to hold back, so he continued, lowering his voice, and leaning forward where we sat on the floor clustered about his chair. "They say that when he abandoned her for good, she got tired of sobbing all the day long in that attic room, so one night, she grabbed that monkey, and cast it out that little round window."

Our mouths were gaped open, which encouraged him. "But others say, she threw no monkey out the window. She cast it into that backyard incinerator, along with the trash, and watched it burn to death--alive!" We gasped, and Oscar leaned back with satisfaction, but his eyes were just as quickly drawn to a subtle shifting of Shalom's posture on his carpet.

Oscar seemed at that moment nervous. "Well, there's others say that's pure nonsense. That monkey died on its own, like creatures from the strange climates abroad tend to do. Their natures are sensitive. We had a colorful bird once, didn't we, Shalom? Beautiful. Gift from one of the crowned princesses of an Italian count, she was. Didn't live but a month or two. Seemed to acquire a respiratory affliction, didn't she, Shalom?"

Shalom said nothing, which seemed to satisfy Oscar, so he went on. "Of course, there's others say that was no monkey that went sailing out that round window. It was a baby!" Oh, my! Now he had us. This was news.

He beamed at the startled looks on our faces. "Yes. You see, what caused her father to die was seeing the baby. It came out dark." He leaned back to let this surprising gossip sink in. "Oh, yes, turns out the scoundrel had a far more, how can we say? 'varied' background than previously suspected. The father's heart could not bear the shock, so he up and died. Then when the husband comes back, he takes one look at it, and flings that inconvenient baby out the window. Uh, huh."

Then a pause to soak in our stunned silence, and, "'Course, others say that's absolute nonsense, though point out how helpful Old Bob is."

"How you mean?" from Carlos.

"Well, I think you are a sophisticated enough young man to understand these things. Some say, in her loneliness, with her husband being gone, she turned to someone else for comfort. No mistake."

Shalom rustled again on his carpet, so Oscar backtracked. "Though that could be gossip of the most malicious sort. You know how some people have absolutely nothing to do all day but talk idly."

Shalom in one fluid motion stood up, languidly for an old man. This was always our signal that it was time for us to go. "Ah, yes," Oscar said towards Shalom, "time for my medication."

We tore out of the stuffy little apartment and ran to the shed at the side of our building which served as our secret headquarters. We were talking all at once, so excited we were about this news. "Half this stuff, I never heard anyone talk about before!" Carlos exclaimed. We needed to know more, that was clear, but for some strange reason--which only added to the mystery--Shalom didn't want Oscar to say much.

We briefly pondered asking our mother, but she was so dismissive of anything Oscar said, we quickly abandoned that idea. Likewise, Carlos said he'd likely end up with a smack from his father if he started asking about mysterious babies being thrown out windows.

The course of action soon became clear. We'd consult the other person our mother labeled an old gossip we should avoid: Mrs. Tomes.

Mrs. Tomes was another old Victorian, but not a recluse like the monkey-throwing one. She kept her fine old mansion in good repair. It sat beside our building and catty-corner to the mysterious monkey mansion. She was highly respectable, though neighborhood kids knew she was one of Shalom's secret fortune telling customers, from regular sightings of her housekeeper Mrs. Mabaline letting Shalom in through the side door. This made old Mrs. Tomes interesting to us. She loved visitors, so we could always count on a proper sit down with cookies and cocoa, which Mrs. Mabaline brought in on fine china with a flower print, though Mrs. Mabaline gave us frowns like we weren't quite the company to warrant such service.

Mrs. Tomes spoke often about the monkey lady, whom she called Clara. They were of the same age and were introduced to society the same summer of the bright and gay Nineties. Beyond this, Mrs. Tomes gave no details other than to make a point that she had made a good match, with the sainted and all around wonderfully perfect Mr. Tomes, whose real estate development business had kept her "well and comfortable" all the long years since his passing, of which she still mourned, "in my heart, I mean, since neither black nor grey nor especially lavender favor my complexion."

This hardly made sense to us, but since she knew the monkey girl Clara, we had to pump her for more details.

It was as always, with Mrs. Mabaline coming in with a fresh made pot of cocoa and a peony print dish of cookies. "Orange rounds today, Miss Liz (the strange name she called Mrs. Tomes). Just out of the oven," and a smile to Mrs. Tomes and a pointed frown toward the likes of us as our hands grabbed for the cookies.

"Tell us about the monkey's ghost and the girl in that big house!" my little sister burst out, ignoring in her eagerness the subtle strategies we'd worked out ahead of time.

No matter, Mrs. Tomes was up and talking. She was a much more beautiful deb, of course, than Clara. Had more stylish dresses and overall more suitors, and of a better financial quality. Her marriage to Mr. Tomes was a society event. Everyone attended, even the governor.

"But what about the monkey?" It was important to keep Mrs. Tomes from veering toward her favorite topic, Mr. Tomes.

"Oh, that man brought back some kind of creature. It probably was diseased. It was a monkey from some kind of jungle. He traveled to strange places. Now, my Mr. Tomes..."

"Did she throw it out the window?" again my little sister blurting, with us nudging her to shut up.

Mrs. Tomes was not taken aback. "Why yes. She did. Our house boy at the time saw it and told Mr. Tomes. He said poor Clara was afflicted because of what that man had done to her. That man was spending all the money she inherited from her father. Flashed about with diamond jewelry, he did. Of course in the Nineties, many men wore diamonds, but fashions had since moved on. My Mr. Tomes never thought well of that man. Mr. Tomes never once wore a diamond, though he could have well afforded to. He was a business genius . . . ."

"The monkey!"

"Yes, she threw it out the window. I think it died. Probably was diseased anyway. Mr. Tomes..."

"But mightn't it be a baby, not a monkey, but a baby!" We'd given up nudging our little sister, seeing as the direct approach seemed to be working.

"Oh, there was talk that it was really a baby, but no. Mr. Tomes questioned that boy long and hard. It was the monkey. It was wearing that silly straw hat it wore. The hat came flying off as it fell. That's what the boy said. Oh, he went around telling everyone, everywhere. It was embarrassing, seeing as he worked for us. So, Mr. Tomes had to fire him. Mr. Tomes could not abide by gossips. Said, 'A gossip is the most destructive . . . .'"

"But what if it was a baby? What about old Bob!"

This was getting to be a lot of questions thrown at Mrs. Tomes, who was used to doing the talking. She paused, crinkling her brows, though she recovered her powers of speech soon enough. "Oh, I think she kept Old Bob's little nephew sometimes, like a play baby. That was common back then. To keep a servant's baby, almost like a pet. I imagine she was very lonely, and having to live on a shoestring after that man spent nearly all her money, then disappeared. I never asked, but I'm certain my dear kind Christian Mr. Tomes helped her out with the bills and such. I'm sure he arranged for Old Bob to help. Old Bob was always there doing work. He's always doing work around here too, for that matter!" She stopped, her eyebrows suddenly going up, as if realizing this might implicate her in a disreputable Old Bob liaison.

My sister, clearly the most talented cross examiner among us, took advantage of Mrs. Tomes' silence to drop, "Oscar says her husband was mixed."

Mrs. Tomes paused, speechless. Clearly, this was not talk she knew. She called for Mrs. Mabaline, perhaps hoping she'd have some insight, being on the light side of a little dark herself.

Mrs. Mabaline materialized in a quick flash and glowered at us. She must have been listening at the door.

"Mrs. Mabaline, did you ever see that man Miss Clara married?"

"Why, yes, I was in this house with you at the time. I tended to your dresses."

Mrs. Tomes crinkled her brows again, puzzled, her memory fuzzy on this detail. "Oh, yes, I suppose. Well, what about this talk about that man?"

Mrs. Mabaline paused, her stormy stare fixed on us. "Hard to tell. Many are but don't say so, and many are that don't know. Some presidents have been, that's a fact."

"President" was a dangerous magic word for Mrs. Tomes. She brightened and turned back to us, "Did I tell you my Mr. Tomes is a blood relation to three presidents?"

She most certainly had, many times. We still had a thousand questions, but with Mrs. Mabaline giving us demon eyes, we were out the door with a quick grab for more cookies.

Back to the shed. Clearly, our option was to investigate Old Bob. Old Bob was a neighborhood fixture. As Oscar said, he had tended horses for the monkey girl's father back when he was alive. As motor cars came into vogue, and monkey girl had to sell her father's and her husband's fine horses when she could no longer afford to feed them, Old Bob found employment in the new movie industry. He developed a special skill for training trick ponies. He still lived in the neighborhood, not far from us. He used to keep one show biz horse in the stable behind his little house. He'd raised it from a colt and taught it to nod, count by waving its hoof, neigh like it was laughing and even fall down like it'd been shot by a bad cowboy, which it did for lots of movies. Its name was Dodger, and when it was too old for movies, he charged a fee to have Dodger do tricks at birthday parties and pull kids on a sled up the steep streets, with Dodger all dressed up in a fancy harness full of brass balls and bells. Dodger had since died. Carlos said he saw Old Bob's nephew and his nephew's oldest son load up a large canvas-wrapped bundle into the back of the nephew's truck one night. Carlos knew it was Dodger, because he saw a hoof peek out from the canvas.

"They hauled the dead horse away at night, so the kids wouldn't see and be upset," according to Carlos, in this instance clearly not counting himself as a baby-kid that would go off crying. Carlos learned this detail from the nephew's youngest son, whom he was friendly with.

The youngest son, Marigold (named after a horse), lived in Old Bob's little house with his two older brothers, his bed-bound mother, and his father, Old Bob's nephew and one-time "play baby," according to Mrs. Tomes' account. The nephew ran a business with Old Bob, doing yard work, odd jobs, and hauling with the truck. Nowadays, it was mostly the nephew running the business with his two older sons, and Marigold helping sometimes when his mother allowed. Occasionally, Old Bob still got movie work helping to train horses for particularly complicated tricks. But more often than not, he was sitting on his wooden front porch, blandly rocking back and forth in his chair. Hard to imagine he could be part of a Gay Nineties scandal with a monkey, a diamond wearing scoundrel, and a rich heiress.

No doubt he, the nephew and the boys did regularly tend to the monkey lady's yard. We saw them often enough from our apartment building's back windows. Sometimes Old Bob went inside for an odd repair or two. Marigold also let drop that none of the others were allowed inside. "That old lady's secretive," Marigold told Carlos.

Besides them and the grocery delivery people, the only humans we saw coming or going from the mansion were ancient Mrs. Gilbert, who'd sometimes come storming out to yell at snooping neighborhood kids, including us, and her young niece. The niece came a couple of times a month from

254

Pasadena to help out in the house, but she didn't speak to any Bunker Hill kids. Carlos said she once told him, "Go away!" and "snobby-like too."

So, the niece was definitely out as an information source. But, Marigold was in.

The next afternoon, we made a point of wandering by the pharmacy, where Marigold was in the habit of lounging on the curb enjoying his daily candy purchase.

"Hey, Marigold," Carlos said casually. Marigold waved, his mouth full of something he was chewing. We all sat down on the curb with him.

It was a lot of small talk about candy, about how hot it was, a comic book Marigold read and was excited about. Carlos said he had the next installment and promised to share. Marigold's eyes lit up, excited by that promise.

"How's your uncle doing?" casually slipped in by Carlos, as we'd worked out ahead of time.

"Okay. His knees are bothering him more, I guess."

"We still see him in the yard of that lady. She's the one who threw the monkey out the window, huh?"

"Oh, yeah. I had to help last time. There were all these dead branches and things with stickers on them we had to cut out. I got scratches all over me. My mom got mad."

"Do you know where it's buried, the monkey?" And just at that moment, Carlos pulled the next installment of that comic book out of his back pocket and casually handed it to Marigold.

Marigold paused in his candy chewing, uncertain. "I'm not supposed to talk about that monkey." But his hand closed on the comic book, and he rolled it up to put in his back pocket.

After his eyes darted right and left, confirming that neither his uncle, his father, nor his brothers were afoot, he said, "There's this part of the back garden, by the trash incinerator, we're not allowed to go near. Only my uncle is allowed to burn the yard trash, no matter how much trimming we cut off or anything. Paint (his middle brother, also named after a horse) says that's where it is. But it's top top top secret, so you can't say anything."

We nodded, for sure, promising we would say nothing. Marigold, as if suddenly overcome with nerves, shot up, and after briefly thanking Carlos for the comic, took off at a run up the slope toward his house.

Carlos told us that he encountered Marigold later in the day, and hoped to get more information from him. Instead, Marigold looked like he'd been crying and said, "I'm not allowed to talk with you no more!" Furthermore, incredulous as it sounds, he shoved the comic book back into Carlos' hands. Carlos swore he could tell Marigold hadn't even read it by how new the pages still looked.

This was serious.

Our next option was clear. We would have to keep 'round the clock, or at least as long as we could stay up, watch on the backyard. We worked out the window assignments, one in Carlos' apartment, and two in ours, from which to keep watch. For close to a week, we camped out, until our mother became suspicious because we only wanted to have breakfast, lunch and dinner at the windows. "This isn't something to do with that ridiculous monkey story, is it? I have a mind to speak to that Oscar person."

Couldn't have that, and Carlos' father was threatening him with a whipping for suspicion of being a peeping tom. We had to pull back.

"I think," I said that fateful morning, "the time for talk has ended, and now we take action." This sounded good to everyone, so we got in a huddle and did our best thinking yet.

Old Bob had just this week past done the yard clearing, where Marigold got his arms all scratched up. So, they weren't due to come back until next month. The snobby niece had been by a few days ago, so she'd be safely in Pasadena for at least another week. The grocery delivery people had come and gone by late morning. When Marigold was still speaking to Carlos, he'd let slip that the monkey lady and old Mrs. Gilbert were always dead asleep in the afternoon for their "repose," some sort of Victorian ladies habit, apparently. So, they couldn't do yard trimming or make any noise from 1pm to 4pm.

That was our time slot. With shovels and a pitchfork borrowed from the shed, we carefully made our way into the mysterious backyard by way of a hole rotted at the bottom of the fence we'd discovered some weeks back when Mrs. Gilbert chased us away. That was at 10am though. Now we were at 1:30pm and totally safe.

The blackened brick incinerator was easy to spot in the back corner of the garden, where it met the back corner of Mrs. Tome's yard. We prowled the area, digging here and there, sticking the pitchfork through the weed thick ground that, sure as Marigold said, wasn't trimmed like the rest.

By the chime of the church tower, we knew it was 3:30, and our time was short. We were nearly ready to give up, when my little sister whispered, "What's this?"

Bones. Little bitty bones. A baby. Sure enough. Carlos now put some muscle into digging, and just as quickly, our excitement faded when a skull popped up. It was baby-sized all right, but the sharp, canine-like teeth clearly said monkey. No baby.

It must be close to 4, our danger line cut-off, but Carlos thought to give one more dig into the ground just in case something interesting popped up.

Something did. More bones, bigger bones, held together by tatters of cloth that had a curious burned look about them. On one burnt tatter was a gold and diamond cufflink. My little sister picked it up, then dropped it and screamed when she realized it belonged to no monkey.

Mistake. In an instant, Mrs. Gilbert was tearing out of the mansion's back door, fast for such an old gal, yelling much more than she'd even done before. We took off like lightning, forced to abandon our borrowed tools, and slipped under the hole in the fence before her reaching hands could grab us.

My sister was crying, I was crying, Carlos was trying to cover his crying with his shaking hands. We were hiding in the shed because we knew we were in trouble, some kind of serious big trouble.

After night fell, we knew we couldn't keep hiding, so as quietly as possible, made our way back to our apartments. Immediately, my sister and I heard yells from Carlos' father and "Ow!" from Carlos.

We were met with our mother's stern, angry face. She let us know that Mrs. Mabaline took the unheard of measure of coming to knock on our door to tell her that us kids had caused all manner of upset and distress to an elderly lady by messing around and tearing up her backyard. "I have never been so ashamed! How could you? What must everyone be saying?" and so on from our angry mother.

No mention of the bones, the cufflink, the burnt tatters. Clearly Mrs. Gilbert had told something to Mrs. Mabaline. We spoke of it later, were convinced Mrs. Mabaline knew more than she'd said that day at Mrs. Tomes', but what was told to our mother was an edited story. Of course, we kept quiet. We were in trouble enough as it was.

We were imprisoned in our room. No more running about the Hill, "causing trouble," no more candy. The cookies she'd just baked would never touch our lips, and so on. Prisoners until school started a few weeks away.

We didn't see Carlos much until school. He said his father was "really really mad," and put him to work in his house painting business. "I'm tired," Carlos said. "I have to paint after school now too." We asked if he'd seen any police or anyone investigating the garden and the bones from his back window. "Nope, and I don't even care anymore."

Later in the school year, we moved away from Bunker Hill, and settled into our new stepfather's bungalow east of downtown, on the other side of the river. We went to a different school, so never saw Carlos or any of the other kids, so didn't know if the police ever investigated the bones. Once, my sister and I asked to visit Oscar and Shalom and Mrs. Tomes too. "Absolutely not," our mother said firmly. "Those old gossips were a very bad influence on both of you." And that was that.

It wasn't until several decades later that I happened upon Carlos downtown, when I was working at a temp job there, and he was supervising a crew painting office interiors, because he had since taken over his father's business. We were heading into the same cafeteria for lunch, and happily agreed to sit down and catch up.

We mostly talked about old times, and the demise of our Bunker Hill, which was being slowly shoveled away to a much shorter and more manageable mound at that time, its streets unrecognizable or vanished altogether, its grand old homes nearly all gone in the name of progress. His family lived on the Hill until the decade turned to the 1950s. Like the Carlos of old, he still kept in touch with some of our former friends and neighbors. He had much news to report.

Mrs. Tomes and Mrs. Mabaline left early on, shortly before the war's outbreak. Mrs. Tomes sold her husband's family mansion that she'd lived in and loved for decades to a firm that demolished it for a parking lot. Surprisingly, she wasn't upset. She got top dollar for the sale, plus, as she was happy to tell, Mr. Tomes left her quite well off, so she could easily buy another fine home conveniently close to childhood friends in Pasadena. In light of the subsequent long slow death of Bunker Hill in the post-war years, her foresight was remarkable and made Carlos' father wonder if Mrs. Tomes hadn't been the business genius of the couple all along.

The strange old monkey lady sold after the war, partly because the city was beating the drums of mass demolition, and also, as rumor reported, she had completely run out of funds and had to take whatever she could for her home, even though it was pennies compared to what her fellow deb Mrs. Tomes pocketed. Carlos thought she and Mrs. Gilbert moved into a small house behind the niece's place, but didn't know what happened to them since.

As for Oscar and Shalom? There was a rumor Mrs. Tomes set them up comfortably with a stipend and a little beach bungalow, though no one knew precisely why or if this was even true.

Carlos' family only stayed a few months after the monkey lady left. His father saw no point hanging on to a doomed apartment they didn't even own.

"You know the back windows we always used to spy out of?" I most certainly did. "I guess I never did stop watching, and I finally saw some curious things right before we moved out."

The first curious event happened not long before Mrs. Gilbert and the reclusive monkey lady left. His eye caught a bobbing light. He was startled, and immediately remembered the stories of the monkey's ghost floating about the backyard. But soon he realized it was a person carrying a flashlight. It was a woman, from the soft keening cry she made, shuffling about near the incinerator. A second figure appeared, who could only be Mrs. Gilbert from her voice. After all that time, it was unmistakable, though quietly coaxing rather than the yelling we used to hear, and now she had a cane too. All at once, Carlos realized the figure with the flashlight must be the monkey lady.

Then, deep on the very night after Mrs. Gilbert and the monkey lady moved out, Carlos was woken by a quiet commotion in the soon to be demolished mansion's backyard. Old Bob's nephew and his oldest son were digging. After bundling up something in a canvas tarp, they headed past Carlos' line of sight, toward the front of the house. Carlos crept outside to get a better look. There Old Bob was, sitting in the nephew's truck because he didn't walk much anymore. He was motioning to them as though to say, "Hurry up!" Quickly, they loaded the canvas bundle in the back of the truck, exactly like they'd loaded Dodger all those years before.

Rosalind Barden's short fiction has appeared in print anthologies, including Mystery and Horror LLC's Strangely Funny and Mardi Gras Murder, and also Cern Zoo, part of the award-winning Nemonymous series, and in webzines, such as the UK's late, great Whispers Of Wickedness. She wrote and illustrated the children's book TV Monster. Her fiction has placed in numerous competitions, including the Shriekfest Film Festival. Her darkly humorous e-novel American Witch, now available online, follows the adventures of society's castoffs in a Hollywood stripped of glamour. She lives in Los Angeles, California. Discover more at RosalindBarden.com.

Death in the Library

By Joe Mogel

They scurried about, black and navy blue blurs. Their oak truncheons thumped the floor and walls of the high-ceilinged, mahogany-paneled front hall. Oil lamps and gas wall lights flickered, glinting off the silver badges and custodian helmet emblems of the London Metropolitan police. The rustlings of the thick, wool, high-collared coats they wore were muffled by the ornate moldings and grand, carpeted staircase set on the right hand side of the hall. Several popped in and out of the deep set thick doors that studded the hallway. Lamps inside rooms to the officers shadows on the Persian rug in the middle of the foyer. A clock's Windsor chimes rang eleven. Four doors, two on either side of the front half of the hall, were partially opened.

Three loud, metallic knocks shook the front door. All the officers froze. A large, broad sergeant with a massive mustache marched up to the door. His double chin jiggled under the strap of his helmet. He pointed to two officers, one of whom produced a net from under his tunic. The two took a corner each and spread out to either side of the foyer. They held the net up over their heads and walked within a couple feet of the Sergeant. Grunting with approval, he turned and opened the door.

"Please pardon the delay." The sergeant said in a deep east London accent, as he opened the door and stepped to the side. "But proper precautions had to be taken."

A man of medium height and build strode through the door shaking a fountain pen. He wore an open cutaway jacket, waistcoat, leather gloves and a pair of pressed trousers; all were black. The collar and cuffs of a white shirt peeked out. His thin-soled loafers had silver tips, as did the black umbrella he twirled. He had a bowler cap pulled down deep and tilted far enough forward that his eyes were completely shaded. His square, bearded jaw was firmly set with high cheekbones.

The new arrival stopped, the silver of his shoes and umbrella tapping the floor. The Sergeant shut the door, and the newcomer put his pen away. For a brief moment he sniffed at the air, rubbing the tip of his nose with his index finger.

"Begging your pardon, sir." The sergeant put a paw on the shoulder of the man in black. "But there's another bit of precaution we must attend to first." He guided the new arrival against the door, then waited for the officers holding the net. "All right lads, proceed."

The two offices holding the net walked forward, covering both the man in black and the Sergeant. Other officers came up and patted down the space between and around the men. When it was finished they took another way the sergeant cleared his throat.

"Can't be too careful with this, sir. What with a man who has a formula to turn himself invisible and all." The sergeant put his hands on his hips.

"Is that so?" The man in black replied in an ice cold baritone. "Is that why you did not have your men bring their net all the way to the wall before opening the door?"

The sergeant tried to answer. Only gibberish came out.

"Because Dr. Griffiths, our invisible man, could have been hiding in this corner." He flipped his umbrella over his shoulder, pointing the tip to the corner behind him. "Or that." He flipped the umbrella again, this time pointed tip over the sergeant's shoulders at the opposite corner.

The only reply was more gibbering. The other officers

nervously exchanged glances. Some visibly paled.

"It is a very good thing that I anticipated your incompetence." The man in black said, bringing his umbrella slowly back to his side. "By shaking my pen I sent out drops that would have marked him. Griffiths is too intelligent to risk being marked with ink. Most especially given the hornet's nest of officers that would await him just outside that door."

The sergeant harrumphed, his mustache twitching. "Well, sir... I... Um... I shall need to see your identification, sir."

The man in black's hand snapped up. Pinched between his index and middle fingers was a small, black leather folder. He rapped the end of his umbrella on the floor and extended his hand.

"My name is Engelbrecht Hathcock, special investigator, Scotland Yard."

The sergeant took the folder and looked over the card. He nodded after studying it, then handed it back to Hathcock, who took it back, folded it and pocketed it in one motion.

"Before you ask me," the investigator said, "The Yard has sent me because I am uniquely capable of dealing with the case at hand. However, for me to execute my task effectively I need information. Tell me everything, from the beginning."

The sergeant coughed, bringing his fist to his mouth. "Well sir." He composed himself, pulling both hands behind his back and rocking back on his heels. "Earlier this evening there was a thick fog, which allowed several townsfolk in the local village to spot Dr. Griffiths. They were able to drive him off, chasing him here, to Fuller Hall, which, by then, was well after ten o'clock."

The two men, investigator Hathcock leading, strolled over to the grand staircase. Hathcock poked at the first step with his umbrella, at one point dragging the tip across the step. The silver clicked against the narrow section of hardwood on either side of the stair's wide Berber carpet. He paused momentarily, then gripped the railing with his free hand and hopped up onto the step. Both railing and stair creaked loudly. He stepped down. Several loud clunks echoed from the second floor. Hathcock turns to the Sergeant, both hands resting on the handle of his umbrella.

"Where were the occupants when Dr. Griffiths entered the hall?"

"Well, sir," came the unsteady reply. "Madame Widdecombe has said she rushed the top of the stairs when she heard the door open. She says she called down to ask who was entering the house. When no one replied, she rang for her servants. After this they made a cursory search of the house, wherein they found a glass of whiskey spilled in the lounge."

"Spilled whiskey, you say?" was mumbled under his breath. Tapping the carpet with his umbrella, Hathcock asked, "Are the hallways of the second floor similarly carpeted?"

"Yes, sir."

"How old is Madame Widdecombe?"

"Sixty-seven years old, Sir."

"Does the house have a history of hauntings?"

"I beg your pardon, sir?" The sergeant grunted, retrieving a step.

"Please answer my question." Hathcock turned, beginning to pace about the hall.

"I don't see the relevancy…"

Hathcock slammed the end of his umbrella against the floor. "Answer my question. Now." He snarled, coldly.

The sergeant cleared his throat, brushed his mustache shakily and spoke. "According to local tales, if you believe such things, there is…"

"That's quite enough, sergeant."

"But, sir, you said…"

"I said…" Hathcock strode within inches of the sergeant. "That is quite enough." He raised a gloved hand to his chin. "Tell your men on the floor above to go outside. They'll be needed there in case Dr. Griffiths attempts to escape."

266

Hathcock strolled calmly past the clenched, twisting sergeant and past the left side of the stairs. Several smaller doors dotted this portion of the hall, a long table sat opposite, empty except for a silver tray.

"The servants, sergeant." Hathcock, his back to the Bobbies, pointed to the table. "You failed to mention them in detail when you spoke earlier."

"Well, sir," coughed the sergeant as he rushed to the back hall. "All any of them recall is hearing the front door open and their mistress calling out, then ringing for them."

Hathcock breezed past the sergeant, headed back to the front of the hall. He stopped dead center of the foyer. He pointed to the doors of the larger rooms with sweep of his umbrella.

"These doors." He knocked the end of his umbrella against the floor. "Which of these were open when the occupants investigated?"

The other bobbies had nucleated on the sides of the hall. The sergeant quickly shuffled up the front of the foyer. "All four were opened, sir," he puffed.

"Were they all opened to the same angle, or some more or less open?"

"The door to the drawing room was thrown open completely, sir." The sergeant crossed his hands behind his back once more. "The dining room door was only open a small amount. The doors to the library in the lounge were half open."

"And the windows? What precautions have you taken with them?"

The sergeant's brow wrinkled. He glanced back and forth to the confused bobbies at his flanks. "When we were informed that Dr. Griffiths had been located, I had my men prepare several nets coated in chalk dust. We put these nets over all the windows of the first floor." He straightened his chest and shoulders. "Given the height of the second story windows, sir, we conclude that Dr. Griffiths would break a limb if he tried to jump. So we saw no need for putting nets over the upper windows."

"And you know that Dr. Griffiths did not leave the house? How?"

The sergeant again glanced at his men, who were mouthing questions between each other. Rocking back on his heels, the sergeant said. "Well, sir, the grounds are bit muddy from the damp weather we've been having. Also, the groundskeeper spent the earlier part of the day straightening flowerbeds adjacent to the house; no footprints were found except for those leading to the front entrance."

Hathcock nodded. He began to pace again. "Good observation; very clever with the nets. You've almost redeemed yourself from your earlier incompetencies."

The investigator strolled past the baffled bobbies, heading toward the lounge. He stopped in the doorway and pushed the door open fully. Hathcock began tapping the silver tip of his shoe.

The lounge was a large room filled with leather-upholstered furniture. Wall sconce gas lamps punctuated the space between bay windows and a massive fieldstone fireplace. The embers of a fire glowed softly. A curio case along one wall had small trinkets from a dozen cultures. Six highball glasses and several carafes of various liquors were set on a corner table. A broken cut crystal highball glass was on the edge of the carpet beside the sofa. A light brown stain and the broken glass spread towards the windows.

Hathcock tapped the end of his umbrella on the floor and strode back through the knot of bobbies. He swirled his umbrella as he walked. He stopped at the entrance to the library. Again, he opened the door and tapped his foot. He then smacked the door latch with his umbrella. Hathcock turned to the sergeant.

"Is there a key to the lock on this door?"

The sergeant jawed the air for a moment. Then he barked at one of the bobbies, who took off up the stairs.

Clearing his throat, the sergeant replied. "Madame Widdecombe has keys to every one of the rooms the hall. One of my men will go and get it for you, sir."

Heavy footfalls and the officer causing them bounded down the stairs. Darting to the sergeant, he handed the key to his superior, who in turn handed it to Hathcock. With an oddly warm smile, the investigator took the key and slipped into the library.

"Do not disturb me," he said as he closed the door. The door locked with a muted click. The Sergeant turned to his men and shrugged.

Hathcock, his umbrella hooked over his forearm, tested the latch. Pulling the key out, he slipped it into his waistcoat pocket. He spun on his heel, facing the room. The bookshelves reached the twelve foot high ceiling. The top shelves were sparsely filled and full of knickknacks scattered across them. A rolling ladder, hooked to a brass rod that ran about the top of the shelves, was in the corner adjacent to the entrance. A broad, thick Persian rug covered most of the floor. A slab of marble extended out in front of the empty fireplace. A set of brass pokers stood on the hearth. A massive oak desk and chair were opposite the fireplace; a set of five half-filled cut crystal decanter highball glasses, matching the lounge set, sat next to it.

Hathcock took a step forward onto the rug. He hummed to himself. With a mumble of interest he strode to the desk and tapped his finger against the decanters.

"Would you care to join me for a drink?" The investigator turned to the bookshelves by the fireplace. "It certainly can't be comfortable perched on the shelf, Dr. Griffiths."

The hall clock chimed the quarter hour.

"My, who would have concluded that you would be shy?"

Hathcock rested the tip of his umbrella on the floor, both hands on the grip.

"Perhaps you simply don't want to jump from such a height." Hathcock walked to the rolling ladder. With a quick smack he sent the ladder toward the window side of the room. "Now you can climb down safely."

A loud harrumph echoed from the top shelf, followed by creaking as the ladder shuddered. "How did you deduce that I was here?" A gravelly voice queried as the ladder relaxed and two foot-shaped indentations appeared in the rug.

"Quite simple really," Hathcock raised his fist to his mouth, "when one considers the manner in which you left the doors. Attention is drawn to the doors that are more or less open, rather than those that are half open. Additionally, this room, at first glance, has fewer places to hide. The rug here would make it far easier for someone to spot you. Therefore, they would put in less effort in this room. You knew this and took advantage of it. I may add that rolling the ladder to the corner after climbing to the top shell was a very nice touch.

"There is also the matter of the highball glass. Despite matching the glasses in the lounge, the line of broken pieces extended toward the window bank. This indicates the glass was thrown into the room. Additionally, there are seven glasses, including the broken one, in the lounge and five in the library. It would be highly unlikely that this is the standard manner of the household. A decent attempt at redirecting attentions, yet futile."

"Impressive logic for a man who believes in ghosts."

"Asking about the ghosts was merely a ploy." Hathcock grinned slightly. "In a house of this age it stands to reason there would be some otherworldly stories. Naturally the inhabitants of a house like this would be keenly aware of footprints appearing out of nowhere on their hall rug. Had you actually gone upstairs, the inhabitants would have seen your footprints. However, to be completely certain, I needed to know that there were in fact ghost stories from this house. Knowing that there are stories and no one reported seeing a ghost, it was easy to conclude you had remained on the first floor."

The indentations in the rug shifted back astride. "You must think yourself a clever man."

"Coming from one who discovered a means of turning himself invisible, I take that as high praise."

The foot indentations advanced. "So you found me. Now what will you do to stop me from killing you?"

"Because you're not a fool, Dr. Griffiths." Hathcock clucked, tapping the tip of his umbrella against the silver cap of his shoe. "You must know the rug shows where you're standing. Any attack you make would be apparent to any with proper vision. In the event that you choose to use a weapon, you must know that there is no fire in this room's fireplace."

The indentations shifted slightly. "What difference is there if there is no fire?"

"The room is slightly cooler." Hathcock tilted his head to one side. "Surely you must realize that it is just cool enough for a touch of condensation to form on whatever you pick up. The clever man could deduce what you intend to do with your weapon from the pattern of condensation and the depressions in the rug."

There was a pause. When the highball glasses moved ever so slightly, a small ring of condensation formed around a fingertip-sized spot on the side.

"For a man unable to notice the footprints in the mud or the chalk-covered nets over the windows, you are most clever. Most clever indeed."

Hathcock grinned wryly, letting his head droop forward a bit. "We all have our burdens of life that make an impact on our perception. Incidentally, I did smell the chalk."

"Perception and chalk be damned!" Griffiths snarled. "I should throttle you!" Indentations advanced on Hathcock.

Brandishing his umbrella as if it were a sword, the investigator retreated a step. "Ill-advised, Dr. Griffiths," he retorted. "Any man who has grappled can tell you that when wrestling one relies on feeling his opponent's attacks, not seeing them. Striking would also not be advisable. I could tell from the change in your foot's pressure on the floor which strike you intend on throwing."

Griffiths snarled. "How can you claim that? You can't see me!"

Hathcock's lip curled. "Seeing isn't everything, Dr. Griffiths."

With a growl, indentations in the floor charged Hathcock. The investigator's umbrella snapped up, parrying first to his left, then right, lastly down, before the indentations moved back. Hathcock maintained a right-hand saber guard with his umbrella. He chuckled.

"Right haymaker, followed by a left jab and left kick. Really Dr. Griffiths, what was the point in testing me?"

The indentations charged again. Once more Hathcock parried, his umbrella bowing from the force of the hits it blocked. Hathcock then counterattacked, delivering several vicious strokes to his now grunting opponent. Leveling the point of his makeshift weapon at throat level, he advanced vigorously. The indentations retreated. Suddenly the umbrella was knocked off-line. Hathcock ducked as a whoosh launched his hat across the room. The investigator shot his left leg back as he thrust his weapon forward. A loud thump was accompanied by the expansion of the indentations to the size and shape of a man.

Hathcock straightened himself. His eyes were closed. With his left he smoothed his jacket.

"It has been a long time since I met a foe who forced me to use presata soto."

Indentations shifted, creating the impression of a man sitting on the floor. "So that's the game you're playing at," Griffiths grunted, indentation going from that of the seated man back to a pair of footprints. "You think that keeping your eyes closed and focusing on your other senses will give you an advantage?"

The footprints quickly crossed to the fireplace. A poker rattled, slid off the rack and levitated. The indentations and their new weapon advanced on Hathcock. The investigator began to smile.

"Now let us see if your little game will do you any good!" Griffiths crackled.

The poker swung; Hathcock whirled to a parry. Again, the poker whirred in attack. Again the investigator, eyes clamped shut, parried. Roaring, Griffiths launched attack after attack. Cold as ice, Hathcock blocked all. As the poker was being raised for another onslaught, the investigator lunged. The umbrella flexed as it hit its target. The poker clattered to the ground. The center of the umbrella depressed in the shape of a clenching hand. There was a click as Hathcock withdrew, followed by a flash of steel. The investigator lunged once more. Griffiths let out a short, pained yelp. Hathcock pulled his umbrella sword from his unseen quarry.

With a thunk, new indentations appeared in front of the foot shaped depressions. A dripping sound and panting was followed by another thunk in the formation of a hand shaped depression in the rug.

"This is impossible... You can't... You can't... You can't see me!"

"You, Dr. Griffiths, are more perceptive than you realize." Hathcock opened his eyes. The misshapen blobs of blue, lacking pupils, were barely visible under the thick, milky film over both eyes.

"You are... You are..."

"Blind? Yes, from birth." Hathcock stated, matter-of-factly. He walked to the desk, put his cane sword down and began pouring himself a Scotch whiskey. "The doctor who attended my mother when I was born believed that my eyes simply stopped developing whilst I was in the womb."

"How can you... How..."

"Can I move about as if I were fully sighted? Well, I

have developed two key skills. First, I use echoes to determine where objects are." He sipped his scotch. "My word, this is good," he mumbled to himself. "The difference in tone, pitch and time tells me every cranny and nook in the room, in addition all the objects, both large and small are made clear. My umbrella tip and the ends of my shoes assisting in this immeasurably." He tapped the tip of his shoe against the side of the desk. "Unlike your eyes, though, my ears tell me what is behind me as well as was in front of me." He swirled his glass. "But, alas, it tells me nothing of color. Hence my bichromal wardrobe.

"My second skill is the ability to feel vibrations in the floor with my feet." He raised a foot and gestured to it. "The thin soles facilitate this, despite wearing out swiftly."

"So you... You knew..."

"Where you were the moment I tapped my umbrella in the entrance to this room? Yes." Hathcock sipped his scotch and smiled warmly. "Who better to defeat the invisible man, than with someone who can see without eyes?"

"The mud... The windows..."

"Sadly, mud muddles the vibrations I can feel. And the wind interrupted much of the echoes I would have needed to identify the nets."

"But your... Your eyes were closed... Why..." There was a deep, melancholy sigh. "Closed your eyes... Make me think that you... You could see... To gain the upper hand... Had I known... I would have fought differently."

"Precisely." Hathcock quaffed the remainder of his scotch.

"Why don't you... Why aren't you calling your police officers... Have them arrest me?"

"We both know that my blade pierced your splenic artery and nicked your kidney." Hathcock put his glass down slowly. "You only have approximately five minutes before you lose consciousness. I imagined you wanted to go in peace."

"Thank you."

The indentation on the floor spread, taking on the form of a prone man.

"You're welcome." Hathcock said softly.

Joe Mogel, a born and raised New Englander, inherited his dry sense of humor from his equally dry family. Being home schooled, he had the time and opportunity to develop many hobbies, including painting, martial arts and writing. Going to college for engineering ("I'm not sure what I was thinking at the time. I like seeing the light of day on a regular basis," he says), he rediscovered his interest in writing. Now, having published ten stories though seven different publishing houses and having had his work included on several websites, Joe is considering turning to writing as a full time career.

He is currently working on a horror novella and several short stories.

Joe's Website is http://joemogelauthor.weebly.com/

About the Editor

Sarah E. Glenn, a product of the suburbs, has a B.S. in Journalism, which is redundant if you think about it. She loves writing mystery and horror stories, often with a sidecar of funny. Several have appeared in mystery and paranormal anthologies, including G.W. Thomas' *Ghostbreakers* series, *Futures Mysterious Anthology Magazine*, and *Fish Tales: The Guppy Anthology*. She belongs to Sisters in Crime, SinC Guppies, the Short Mystery Fiction Society, and the Historical Novel Society.

Sarah is the Editor-in-Chief and co-owner of Mystery and Horror, LLC, an independent micro-press publishing speculative fiction. She and her partner really appreciate your reading this book! If you would like to know more her and the press, she is active on social media.

Here are our social media coordinates:

Follow Mystery and Horror, LLC on Facebook:
https://www.facebook.com/MysteryAndHorrorLlc
Follow Mystery and Horror, LLC on Twitter:
HTTP://WWW.TWITTER.COM/@MAHLLC
Pinterest: http://www.pinterest.com/mandhbooks/
Favorite our Smashwords page:
https://www.smashwords.com/profile/view/mysteryandhorrorllc
Subscribe to our blog: http://www.mysteryandhorrorllc.com/blog
Connect on LinkedIn: https://www.linkedin.com/company/3635768
Visit our website: http://www.mysteryandhorrorllc.com

History and Horror, Oh My!

Twenty historical horror stories presented for your consideration. Learn the real reasons behind the trial of Socrates, the curse of Glamis Castle, and the writing of the Book of the Dead. Discover the horrors of the American Civil War and the English Civil War. Meet a vampire during the Dust Bowl and a Sasquatch traveling among the fur trappers of Canada. Featured authors include T. Fox Dunham, Kevin Wetmore, Gwendolyn Kiste, and Guy Burtenshaw.

www.ingramcontent.com/pod-product-compliance
Lightning Source LLC
Chambersburg PA
CBHW062139170626
46813CB00002B/748